RACHEL AND THE MIGHTY ARM THAT BUILT EGYPT

M.E. Ellison

This is a work of fiction. Names, characters, historical events, landmarks, or other places are either products of the author's imagination or used fictitiously.

ISBN: 9781981059409

For Ira
because I love you,
I owe you,
and you're my favorite.

CHAPTER 1

Mighty Ra raised his fearsome muscled arm, and the earth shook....

Rachel closed her book—*The Mighty Arm that Built Egypt*. This sort of reading was a guilty pleasure. Stories of Egyptian gods building a great society on Earth. Essentially Ancient Egypt fan fiction. As an Egyptologist, Rachel was definitely a fan, but she knew just how much fiction was involved in the fan retellings. Egypt was built by men who worshipped invisible gods. She knew that, but she was still drawn to books like *The Mighty Arm that Built Egypt*.

A voice over the airport intercom blared, "Dr. Rachel Conner, please report to gate 30. Dr. Rachel Conner, gate 30. Your plane is boarding."

While gulping down her coffee, Rachel slipped her book into her purse, grabbed her carry-on, and hurried off to gate 30—a plane that was taking her to Austin, Texas. An old mentor had asked her to be a special speaker at an Ancient Civilizations symposium. Rachel had been reluctant to agree to speak. All those people staring at her wasn't exactly Rachel's idea of fun. She loved being an expert in her field, but she didn't really like it when people expected her to act as a leader. She'd rather just stay in her office surrounded by her books, or take another trip to Egypt. But when her mentor—Dr. Selma

Goldblum—asked Rachel knew she couldn't say no. Dr. Goldblum was the one who had written all of Rachel's letters of recommendation that got her into graduate school, and then introduced her to a publisher which set her down the path to publish several important textbooks on the study of Ancient Egypt. Rachel basically owed her career to Dr. Goldblum.

"This is for Dr. Goldblum. This is for Dr. Goldblum," Rachel muttered to herself while stowing her carry-on in the overhead compartment.

She took her seat at the window. Before pushing her purse under the seat in front of her, she pulled out *The Mighty Arm that Built Egypt*. There was no reason Rachel couldn't enjoy the flight, even if she was nervous about the symposium.

> *Mighty Ra raised his fearsome muscled arm, and the earth shook. The people of Egypt cowered before his glistening bronze body....*

"Excuse me, I think you're in my seat."

Rachel looked up. An almost perfectly round face greeted her. The mouth at the bottom of the circle said again, "I think you're in my seat."

With only a slight hesitation, Rachel dug for her ticket in her purse, and showed the little old lady—the owner of the spherical face—"19C."

"Yes, dear," the tiny woman exhaled. "But you're sitting in 19 A. A is always the window seat. I'm 19A."

Rachel awkwardly moved from 19A to the aisle to allow the woman her rightful seat. Rachel took her seat. 19C. The aisle seat. Rachel hated the aisle seat. The aisle seat meant constantly being bumped. It also meant having strangers climb over you to use the restroom. Forced intimacy with strangers was probably the thing Rachel hated most about flying.

The occupant of 19A turned to Rachel. "I always get the window seat. I enjoy having the view. Airplane rides are the closest you or I will ever be to flying in spaceships like the aliens. I mean, unless you work for NASA. Do you work for NASA?" inquired the little old lady, the cloud of white hair around her perfectly round face bounced with excitement when she mentioned spaceships, aliens, and NASA.

"No, I don't work for NASA."

"That's too bad," the old woman frowned. "That's the only real way to spot aliens these days. The internet has really gone and scared them off. In my day you could count on a spaceship spotting every other day. Now they're hiding. They know we're looking."

The fasten seatbelts sign lit up above their heads.

"Looks like we're taking off!" she exclaimed, excitedly fastening her seatbelt. "My name is Hester Hilford Mays," she continued, extending a dainty wrinkled hand.

"Rah-Rachel Conner," Rachel stuttered, then shook Hester's hand. Rachel wasn't generally comfortable with overly friendly people, and Hester's talk of aliens registered pretty high on Rachel's personal crazy meter.

Hester's eyes got big—she looked like a child on Christmas as she nearly squealed, "Wait! Dr. Rachel Conner? Egyptologist, Dr. Rachel Conner?!"

Rachel's jaw dropped. Never had she been recognized in public by someone she didn't know. Egyptologists didn't usually have much of a fan following. She just nodded her head "yes" in answer.

Hester bounced up and down in her seat and continued to squeal. Rachel wondered how someone so old had the energy of a seven-year-old. She tried nonchalantly to look around the cabin to see if anyone was observing Hester's embarrassing display. No one seemed to notice. However, Rachel observed that every seat was taken except for the seat between Hester and her—19B.

The plane began taxiing down the runway. "That's really odd. This entire plane is full, but this seat here is free," Rachel said, motioning to 19B.

"Oh, it's not free. It's for my husband." Hester dismissed, and continued, "But don't change the subject! You're Dr. Rachel Conner!"

"Bu-bu-but, your husband—where is he?" stammered Rachel, looking around for a little old man to match Hester.

Exasperated that Rachel was still avoiding the topic she wanted to stay on, Hester said as though it were obvious, "He's dead. What I really want to know is— "

"Oh my goodness, I am so sorry!" Rachel professed, a little confused.

"Don't be! He's all right. He's always with me. That's why I bought him a seat."

Hester fondly patted the seat between them. Meanwhile, Rachel's crazy meter was going off again inside her head.

"Gerald goes with me everywhere. I can't get rid of him," she fussed as if saying an inside joke.

Rachel figured she was in this deep with the little old lady, what harm could digging deeper cause? "Your husband is a ghost?"

"Heavens, no!" laughed Hester, like Rachel had said the silliest thing imaginable. "He's a wraith. At first I thought Gerald might be a specter, because if I died, I think that's what

I'd be. But now I'm almost certain he's a wraith. Doesn't a wraith just sound smart and sophisticated? My Gerald has always been the smartest. He's gotta be a wraith. I called Madam Maria's psychic hotline, and she confirmed that Gerald was some kind of spirit, but she was hesitant to tell me what kind exactly. But, I think he's a wraith. I looked it up on the internet to be certain. It would be terrible for him to be walking around as a phantom, for example, and here I am calling him an apparition or something!" Hester laughed so hard she snorted. "I'm fairly certain he's a wraith."

Rachel eyed the empty seat between them and decided it was best to just agree with the old lady than argue. Rachel nodded.

"Oh! You let me get distracted by Gerald! You still haven't said if you are THE Dr. Rachel Conner," Hester impatiently intoned.

"Uh-uh-um," stammered Rachel. "I do hold a PhD in Egyptology, so that makes me Dr. Rachel Conner. Um, have we met before?"

"Goodness, no! But I have all of your textbooks!"

"Um, are you a student?" asked Rachel, rather confused. Hester was at least seventy years old. Sure, older students weren't unheard of, but they weren't usually Egyptology fanatics, and Rachel certainly had never encountered a personal fan.

Hester laughed. "Do I look like a student, dear? I'm eighty-three years old!" She laughed again. "Egyptology holds a special place in my heart. It has for a long, long time." Hester sighed, seeming to lose her train of thought. Her eyes traveled down at the empty seat next to her, then slowly up to Rachel. "It is truly a pleasure and an honor to meet you, Dr. Conner."

"Please, call me Rachel." Rachel always felt uncomfortable when people called her "Dr. Conner."

"Well, Rachel," Hester said, more like an old friend than a rather eccentric stranger, "I think I'm gonna get a little shut-eye since we're up in the air now."

Rachel had been so absorbed in their conversation, she hadn't noticed the plane had taken off and was in the air. Hester drew the window shade shut, and assured Rachel, "It doesn't look like the right weather to spot a spaceship anyway, might as well get some rest. I think I might sleep the entire flight if you don't mind. You and I will have plenty of time to chat later."

The tiny eccentric lady with the puffy white hair closed her eyes and quickly fell asleep. Opening her book, Rachel inwardly laughed at how odd Hester was. If Hester slept through the entire flight to Austin, they would end up without any more time to chat. Rachel knew she should be relieved, but she felt a touch of disappointment. "What could Hester talk about next?" she wondered. "She'd already covered aliens and ghosts (or wraiths, really)!" Hester was strange, but there was something fun and familiar about her. Rachel wouldn't mind having another conversation with the old Egyptology fan.

Rachel settled into her seat and looked down at her book.

The people of Egypt cowered before his glistening bronze body. Ra wasn't a man, he was a god. And like most gods, he was immense and he was terrifying....

♦ ♦ ♦

At the luggage carousel, Rachel stood with Hester. They both were looking for Hester's bag.

"It's lime green," chirped Hester. "Most people have black luggage. Better to get a bright color. Lord knowns you spend less time hunting for your luggage that way. It was Gerald's idea to go with lime green. Like ectoplasm. Or limes, of course. Oh! There's mine now!"

Hester bounced up and down while pointing to an old fashioned hard-shell suitcase spray-painted lime green. "Can you grab that for me, dear? It's hard for me to lift it off things, but once I've got a firm hold of it I'm fine."

Lifting the suitcase off the conveyor belt, Rachel noticed a bumper sticker stuck to the side—"Honk if You're Horus!" Rachel giggled. She enjoyed a good Egyptian god joke.

"Thank you, Rachel." Hester smiled, then glanced at her watch. "There's a car waiting for me, so I gotta go. See you later!"

The tiny octogenarian moved through the crowd in a flash. All Rachel could manage was a delayed wave before Hester's puff of white hair vanished into the sea of people exiting and entering the airport.

It took Rachel some time to find her own bag—a nondescript black rolling suitcase. It looked like over half the bags on the carousel. People kept elbowing in front of her to get their black bags that could have just as easily been hers.

"How can they tell which bag is theirs?" she wondered.

When there was only one bag left making the loop on the carousel, Rachel was sure it was hers. As she was placing her suitcase on the floor, she heard her name called. "Rachel! Rachel, my all-time favorite student!"

Dr. Selma Goldblum was standing ten feet from Rachel, her arms extended ready for a hug, a smile from ear to ear. Her mentor hadn't aged a day nor changed a bit since Rachel first met her fourteen years ago at freshmen orientation. Dr. Goldblum was dressed in her uniform of choice—billowy blouse, loose capri pants, and sandals bought purely for comfort, not fashion. She was tan and had streaks of gray running through her shoulder length black hair. It had been two years since Rachel had last seen her mentor—at an academic conference in Rachel's hometown, Chicago—but the moment they hugged it felt like no time had passed at all.

"Good flight?" inquired Dr. Goldblum.

Rachel opened her mouth to answer, but Dr. Goldblum was on to the next question already, "Did you pack anything nice to wear? I forgot to tell you there is an awards ceremony the first evening of the symposium."

Rachel wasn't sure if it was nerves or if she was already feeling the Texas heat, but she suddenly felt uncomfortably warm. She wasn't a fan of fancy dress-up events. Rachel was strictly a jeans and t-shirts girl. On laundry day a leggings or pajamas and t-shirts girl. She nervously took a hairband off her wrist, and swiftly twirled her hair into a messy bun, before answering, "Nope, this is as nice as it gets."

Dr. Goldblum rolled her eyes and led Rachel towards the airport exit to the parking garage. She teased Rachel, "Why are you my favorite student again?"

"Because I show up to symposiums when you ask me," replied Rachel with a sheepish smile.

"And because you really were the most dedicated undergrad student I ever encountered in any of my ancient civilizations classes." Dr. Goldblum reminisced and jokingly lectured, "Rachel Conner, come up for air! You cannot breathe a book, young lady! You cannot eat and sleep Egypt!"

Dr. Goldblum sighed. "Of course, I was wrong. You apparently can breathe books and eat and sleep Egypt. Look at you! I am so proud of you! Even if you didn't bring anything nice to wear to my symposium."

"Maybe I could just go back to my hotel room during the awards ceremony," Rachel suggested, hopeful to get out of going.

"No, no, no," said Dr. Goldblum. "You need to attend the award ceremony. Those of us working in ancient civilizations—be it professors like me, or big time writers like you—we are all a part of a community. It's about time you start acting like you're a member of the community. Leave your office every once in a while—and more than just to go to Egypt. Get your head out of a book. Come to a symposium. Go to an awards ceremony. And next time bring a dress."

Dr. Goldblum opened the trunk of her car. Rachel placed her luggage inside.

"I'll sit at the back of the room during the awards ceremony. No one will notice me. I will just blend into the wallpaper. I'm an expert at blending in," Rachel insisted. "No one will notice me there in my jeans and sneakers. Will that be good enough?"

"It will have to be," Dr. Goldblum relented, then returned to her lecturing tone, "Because you're going whether you like it or not, even if you embarrass me by wearing jeans and sneakers and your hair like *that*."

"I'm your favorite student."

"You're my favorite student."

CHAPTER 2

Rachel woke up early the next morning. When she was nervous, she always gave herself plenty of time to prepare. She was showered, ready, and down in the hotel continental breakfast lounge before the doughnuts were even set out.

At dinner the night before, Dr. Goldblum informed Rachel the awards ceremony was being held at her hotel—the Sunrise Inn and Suites. The hotel had been selected for the awards ceremony for its proximity to Dr. Goldblum's university campus and its pseudo-Egyptian décor. Above the cereal dispensers in the breakfast lounge was a mirrored portrait of Anubis in a massive gaudy gold frame. Rachel thought Anubis—the jackal-headed god of the dead and funerals—an odd choice for a breakfast area. Almost any other god would have been more fitting. "Well, except for Thoth, maybe," Rachel decided. "The god of knowledge would know better than to fill up on Sugar-Sweet-O's and Nutter Flakes."

When the doughnuts were set out, Rachel grabbed two—one chocolate and one maple—then headed to the university. With a doughnut in each hand, she was sure she was quite the sight walking across campus. When she reached the Ancient History and Classical Studies building, Rachel was grateful to find a man opening the door to leave just as she needed to open the door to go inside the building. The man smiled through his neatly trimmed beard and held the door open for Rachel without saying a word. Rachel was generally nervous with strangers, and men—especially good-looking men—but she managed to squeak out a "Thank you." The man politely nodded and continued on his way. Rachel speculated whether the handsome bearded man was a professor or a student. "He could be a graduate student," she guessed.

Rachel made her way down the hall, up a set of stairs, then down another hall to Dr. Goldblum's office. It was only 6:30 am, but Rachel knew Dr. Goldblum would be there. Like Rachel, Dr. Goldblum believed in being overly prepared. The symposium didn't begin until 9:00 am, but as Dr. Goldblum was fond of saying, "It's easier to put out a fire if you've already got the water hose ready."

Rachel tapped on Dr. Goldblum's closed office door with her foot while saying, "Knock, knock."

"It's open!" was the response from behind the door.

"My hands are full. Sorry. Could you open the door?" Rachel apologized to the closed door. As a student Rachel had always wanted Dr. Goldblum to think she was cool and smart, and not at all annoying or ridiculous. Rachel tended to feel ridiculous around people she respected, and she was constantly afraid of annoying them.

The door swung open. Dr. Goldblum was still seated at her desk. Her office was so small she could reach the door without getting up from her seat. Rachel surveyed the room. It hadn't changed since Rachel was a student. The same poster of the Acropolis. The same book shelves with the miniature busts of Socrates and Plato, a papier-mâché sphinx, and so many books there wasn't enough room, so they were stacked on the floor. This university was Rachel's alma mater, but she just thought of it as "Dr. Goldblum's university," because the only place that felt like home was that office and the classrooms where she had been Dr. Goldblum's student.

“You are a lifesaver,” Dr. Goldblum exclaimed. “I mean, I assume one of those doughnuts is for me.”

Rachel smiled, always happy to be appreciated. “You know I hate maple,” she answered, handing the maple doughnut to Dr. Goldblum. The professor took a bite and did a happy dance in her chair. Rachel tried to suppress a laugh, not quite succeeding.

“I appreciate that you came bearing gifts,” Dr. Goldblum said, indicating the now half-eaten doughnut, “but seriously, aren’t you a little early, kid?”

“I know. Bu-but I figured I’d find out from you which rooms I would be in today. Kind of get the lay of the symposium land. These things make me so much more anxious than conferences,” Rachel admitted.

The last symposium Rachel had attended was five years earlier, right after she had finished her PhD. Like this one, Rachel was expected to serve on panels to question and critique students who presented papers on their special research topics. She was also the keynote speaker. Her speech went well, but when serving on a panel she accidently made a student cry by asking a question the student couldn’t answer. Rachel felt terrible, and from that day swore she’d never serve on another symposium panel again. But, of course, she couldn’t disappoint Dr. Goldblum.

Rachel wished this were a conference. Conferences could be fun. Conferences weren’t just people presenting their papers or research. Sure there were wonderful lectures you could attend at conferences, but conferences also had showrooms with booths full of textbooks, and imitation ancient artifacts—tiny pyramids, fake scarab necklaces, Cleopatra costumes—and food. When Rachel attended she usually had her own booth where she sold her textbooks and talked with fellow

Egyptologists. It was in a booth like that that she had last seen Dr. Goldblum before this trip, two years ago. But, the best part about conferences was at a conference Rachel never made anyone cry.

"Looks like at 10:00 am you'll be in room 210, and at 1:00 pm in room 117," Dr. Goldblum announced. Rachel pulled her phone out of her purse to make a note of the room numbers and times.

"Thanks, Dr. Goldblum," Rachel said, slipping her phone back in her purse.

"Really, you can call me Selma now, *Dr.* Conner," Dr. Goldblum teased, emphasizing Rachel's title.

"Oh, okay, *Selma.*" It felt completely wrong and weird for Rachel to say, like calling her parents by their first names or calling the queen of England simply *Elizabeth.* "I think I'll go check out my rooms. Unless you need help with something. Can I help you with anything?"

"No. No fires yet." Holding up the last bite of her doughnut Dr. Goldblum continued, "And you've already helped me. Thanks, again, for the doughnut. Just try to be in the main lecture hall by 8:45 am, so you can get checked in—name tag, etc. You know the drill."

Rachel wandered the familiar halls. She first walked to room 210, since she was already upstairs. It was a path Rachel had walked many-a-time, and easy to find. She then traveled downstairs to find room 117. There was a comfortable desk chair at the front of the room, so Rachel took a seat. She had about two hours to kill before she needed to be in the main lecture hall. She might as well get comfortable. Digging in her purse past her wallet, keys, and emergency deodorant—"You never know when you'll be struck by panic sweats at a symposium," she reminded herself—she found the book she'd been reading at the airport and on the plane—*The Mighty Arm that Built Egypt.*

Towering over the crowd of people before him, Ra sneered, "Where is your tribute?! Where are your sacrifices?!"

The crowd trembled. One shriveled, tired farmer stepped forward. His voice croaked as he spoke up, "Your majesty, we've given you all we have. All our gold. All our crops. The sweat of our brow. We have nothing more to offer you."

Ra seemed to grow larger as the old man spoke. He was twice the size of any human. "YOUR gold! YOUR crops! IT IS ALL MINE," Ra bellowed, striking the man with a giant staff plated in gold and incrusted with rubies. The man's body traveled several feet before falling to the dust, never to rise again.

"This is what defiance gets you, slaves! This is what insolence gets you, people of Egypt!" the fearsome god warned.

Rachel became absorbed in her book. When she checked her phone to see how much time had passed, it was already 8:43 am.

She threw her book in her purse and hurried out of room 117 to the main lecture hall on the other side of the building. When she arrived, she was red-faced and out of breath, but she had made it by 8:45 am, as suggested by Dr. Goldblum. Rachel checked in, got her name tag, and took a seat on the aisle near the back of the room. The lecture hall was already over half full. Not a bad turn out for an ancient civilizations symposium.

Rachel didn't enjoy mingling with people she didn't know, and Dr. Goldblum was bound to be busy, so she pulled her book out again, thinking to herself, "Hopefully if I sit here with a book people will just ignore me." Between reading on the plane, and reading for two hours in room 117, Rachel was over half way through *The Mighty Arm that Built Egypt.*

> *The people of Egypt, though frightened, were not going to submit to their gods any longer. One Egyptian could do little against the size and strength of the gods, but as one force—as Egyptians joined together—they could achieve anything! They had built the mighty pyramids, had they not?! They would defeat Ra and the other gods with him.*

Rachel startled to attention when she heard the podium microphone at the front of the lecture hall making a terrible screech. "It's feeding back. The speakers are too close," she muttered, jumping up, eager to help Dr. Goldblum with this "fire."

At the podium, Dr. Goldblum looked annoyed while the speakers around her continued to squeal. Rachel swiftly repositioned the speakers further from the podium mic, and all was well.

Returning to her seat she caught a quick glimpse of a puff of white hair in the crowd, the face attached to the hair obscured by those seated in the row before it. Sitting down she pondered the likelihood of Hester Hilford Mays attending the symposium. "There are other people with white hair in Austin, Texas, I am sure," Rachel decided.

Dr. Goldblum welcomed the crowd and explained the format of the next three days—the symposium was a three day event, it was open to the public, except for the awards ceremony, which was invitation only. After this brief introduction, Dr. Goldblum described what the study of ancient civilizations meant to her and how proud she was of all the students participating in the symposium. After this speech, she invited Rachel up to the podium.

The night before, Dr. Goldblum had warned Rachel she would be asked to speak as part of the introduction to the symposium (in addition to the special lecture she was to give on the second day of the symposium), so the invitation was no surprise. While trying to drift off to sleep, Rachel made a mental outline of what she would say to the students and anyone else in the crowd in the morning. She had a PowerPoint presentation and thorough note cards outlining her lecture for the following day. Walking to the podium, Rachel wished she was just as prepared for this speech. "Why didn't I make notecards?" Rachel berated herself.

When Rachel reached the podium, she gripped it with both hands—something to hold onto and steady herself. She took a deep breath and addressed the crowd. "Hello, everyone. I am Dr. Rachel Conner. You don't know me, but you might own one of my textbooks if you've studied Egyptology. That's my specialty—Egyptology. I'm, uh, I'm an Egypt-Egyptologist," she stuttered.

Every face in the lecture hall stared back at Rachel. She could feel the nervous sweat forming all over her body. She took another calming deep breath, and continued, this time more composed, "Regardless of what we each specialize in or will eventually specialize in, we're all here for the same reason—we are all fascinated by ancient civilizations. The ancient Greeks and their philosophers. The Romans and their architecture, and the way they stole ideas from the Greeks..." Rachel paused to allow the crowd to laugh at the ancient history joke. Only a crowd of ancient civilizations academics would find that funny.

Rachel forgot her nerves and went on, "Mesopotamians, and the ancient Egyptians—all these civilizations fascinate us because they achieved wondrous things without the technologies we have today. How did they do it?" She paused, absorbed in her own thoughts for a moment. She continued, "A lot of people might try to make you think there is nothing left to learn about these ancient civilizations. Some people might try to say that researchers, scientists, and academics that came before you have already figured it all out. But that's not true. We're living in an exciting time because the new technologies that are being invented every day, provide new opportunities to dig deeper, decipher more tablets we couldn't before, see into burial chambers previously undiscovered. The further we go into the future, the clearer the past becomes. It is an amazing time to be studying ancient civilizations. There are still stones to be uncovered."

Looking out at the crowd Rachel paused again before saying, "Good luck to everyone presenting. I look forward to hearing about what each of you has uncovered or discovered."

Rachel returned to her seat accompanied by an unexpected standing ovation. Dr. Goldblum dismissed everyone to their assigned rooms, inviting those not presenting or on a panel to peruse the event program and to select rooms with topics they found most interesting. Half the attendees shuffled out of the lecture hall while the other half stayed to examine their programs or chat with those around them.

Rising from her seat, Rachel again caught a glimpse of white hair in the crowd, but it disappeared as quickly as it had appeared. Exiting the lecture hall Rachel almost ran right into the handsome bearded man who had held the door open for her earlier. Embarrassed, she stammered, "Ex-excuse me. S-s-s-sorry!"

Laughing, the bearded man responded, "It's totally fine, Dr. Conner. Pardon me," as he side-stepped around Rachel, then walked directly towards Dr. Goldblum at the front of the lecture hall. Rachel still wasn't sure if he was a professor or student. For a moment she experienced a shocked giddy sensation because he knew her name. Then she realized he had probably been in the lecture hall when Dr. Goldblum invited her to the podium to speak.

"I'll have to ask Dr. Goldblum about him later," Rachel thought to herself. "Or maybe I'll chicken out. Yeah, I'll probably just chicken out."

CHAPTER 3

Rachel made her way upstairs to room 210. She flipped on the light. She was the first one there. The theme assigned to this room was, "The Creation of Egypt." There would be three students presenting their research that fell under that theme.

The room was a typical classroom—whiteboards, desks for students, a podium. The door was at the back of the classroom. Once Rachel took a seat at the front—where she would be seated with the others members of the panel—her back would be to anyone who entered the room. That was okay with her. If she didn't make eye contact with anyone, and didn't start any awkward conversations, perhaps she might get a bit more reading done. Rachel wouldn't have admitted it to any of her Egyptology peers, but she was truly enjoying *The Mighty Arm that Built Egypt.*

Before she started reading, Rachel had to make sure she was ready for the presentations. She pulled out the notepad and pen she would use to take notes, then she pulled out her book and opened to the last page she had been reading.

> *....They had built the mighty pyramids, had they not?! They would defeat Ra and the other gods with him.*
>
> *But how would they do it? How would they defeat beings*

over twice their size and seemingly endowed with magical powers? The Egyptian people still referred to them as gods, but they were no longer certain these creatures were indeed gods. They were monsters, and they were not men. But what were they exactly, and how would they be defeated?

"Oh, that one's one of my favorites!" a familiar voice enthused right next to Rachel's elbow.

Rachel dropped her book, startled and slightly frightened. Looking to her left, Rachel observed the friendly round face belonging to Hester Hilford Mays. Hester motioned to the book and asserted, "It's a good one, isn't it?!"

"Yeah, I'm enjoying it," Rachel admitted, a little ashamed she shared literary tastes with the alien and ghost believing octogenarian. Picking up her book Rachel noticed she had lost her place. She would have to find it later. Rachel had a feeling Hester wouldn't allow her any more time to read before the presentations.

"Wait a second," Rachel thought. "What is Hester doing here?" Rachel asked Hester the question aloud.

"It's a free country, isn't it? Didn't that Dr. Goldblum say this was open to the public?" Hester answered, smiling defiantly.

Rachel laughed and replied, "It is a free country."

"Anyway, I picked the Egyptology presentations to watch because they're always the most interesting. This group should be a real blast with the theme 'The Creation of Egypt'. How many students do you think will mention aliens?" Hester asked, her eyes sparkling with excitement.

"Hopefully none. Since that's ridiculous and there is no quantifiable evidence that aliens exist or that they had anything to do with the creation of Egypt," countered Rachel, irritated that she was even having an 'aliens in ancient Egypt' discussion in a university classroom.

Hester's shoulders drooped and she replied, "There's no evidence they didn't either." She had a disappointed, hurt look on her face that made Rachel feel sorry. But still Rachel felt annoyed to be having such an absurd conversation, and a little annoyed that she felt sorry about hurting Hester's feelings.

Hester looked down at Rachel's book and sighed. "I am glad you like that book, at least. I think I'll find a seat. Come on, Gerald," Hester said. Rachel watched Hester move to the back of the classroom where she sat in one seat, and placed her purse on the table of the seat next to her's—"Gerald's seat," Rachel said to herself.

"What did you say? Are you talking to me?" asked a tall middle aged woman with wavy blonde hair, who had taken the seat next to Rachel when she wasn't paying attention. Rachel automatically recognized this woman as one of her past professors from her undergraduate days at this university—Dr. Kathy Holmes.

"No, sorry. I was just talking to myself, Dr. Holmes," Rachel replied, instantly feeling like an awkward, silly freshman again. Dr. Holmes had a way of making Rachel feel that way—insecure, like she wasn't good enough or smart enough. When Rachel had been a student, she never felt like Dr. Holmes liked her. She always felt like they were speaking two different languages. Dr. Holmes was glamourous, unlike

Rachel and most anyone else you might find in the Ancient History and Classical Studies department. Her hair was perfectly styled, her nails professionally done, and she was never without an expensive handbag or flashy new piece of jewelry. She did yoga, and she volunteered at the university rec center teaching Pilates. Rachel guessed that Dr. Holmes didn't eat carbs either, and suddenly felt embarrassed that all she'd had to eat that day was a chocolate doughnut. Her stomach growled as if to say, "Give me more doughnut."

"You were one of my students," stated Dr. Holmes. Even in the florescent lights of the classroom, her golden hair shone, making Rachel feel twice as dull and awkward.

"Yeah, I took your 'Introduction to the Egyptians' class," Rachel replied.

"Nice speech earlier," Dr. Holmes offered, and Rachel wondered if perhaps she had misjudged her former teacher. "I doubt any of these students have done adequate research," she continued rolling her eyes. "I really hate these things. Dr. Goldblum should have listened to me and only allowed PhD students to present. Anyone below that and I feel like I'm supposed to congratulate preschoolers on their finger paintings. Here's your participation award. And yours. And yours."

Dr. Holmes pantomimed handing awards to a half dozen imagined students in front of her, then chuckled. She had a snide sarcastic laugh. Rachel changed her mind. She hadn't misjudged Dr. Holmes. Dr. Holmes was mean and judgmental, and maybe a little shallow, too.

Rachel came to the students' defense, "I like to see the upperclassmen undergraduates, and the masters' students presenting. It's good for them, I think. It gives them practice presenting, and in a sense teaching. Two skills they will need to better develop if they go on for their PhDs or become professors."

Dr. Holmes smirked and her eyes narrowed. Her only answer was a derisive, "Hmmph," before looking down at her gold watch and declaring, "It's 10 am. Time for the first victim."

Dr. Holmes stood and dramatically cleared her throat, getting the attention of everyone in the room. "If you are one of our three presenters, please sit in the second row behind the panel." Three students stood, juggling binders and notecards, and apprehensively moved to the second row. Dr. Holmes looked at her watch, then studied the room before continuing, "We will begin as soon as the last member of our panel arrives."

The door creaked open a few inches, and someone peeked in, looking uncertain. "Come in, Mr. Hawthorne. This is the correct room. We were just waiting on you."

He was the same handsome bearded man that opened the door for Rachel. He was the same man she almost bulldozed on her way out of the lecture hall. He took a seat in the last row. "Mr. Hawthorne, we will need you to sit with the rest of the panel in the front row, if you don't mind," Dr. Holmes said, contemptuous and superior.

Mr. Hawthorne rose and marched from the last row of desks to the first row. He started to take Dr. Holmes' seat until she stopped him by saying, "No, that seat is mine."

A few people sniggered, and Mr. Hawthorne took the seat on Rachel's left. He was slightly pink with embarrassment, but still handsome. Rachel observed that though his hair was brown, parts of his beard looked red in the light. He turned to Rachel, and she noticed his eyes were a bright clear blue, like the oceans of faraway tropical places she'd only seen in pictures. Mr. Hawthorne extended his hand while quietly saying, "I'm Liam." He sighed and added, "That was embarrassing."

During this quick exchange Dr. Holmes went over the order of the presentations. "The first paper we will hear presented is from Jessica Schmidt, next will be Dominic Hernandez, then we will finish with Karen White. Please introduce yourself and give us the title of your paper before beginning. Jessica, are you ready?"

Jessica Schmidt gathered her notecards and on shaky legs walked up to the podium. Dr. Holmes took her seat.

"Here we go," Liam whispered to Rachel, smiling with evident excitement.

"This has to be a first," Rachel thought. "Someone is actually happy to be on a panel at a symposium?" Seeing Liam happy and excited to be there, even after Dr. Holmes had obviously tried to humiliate him, helped shift Rachel's mood. "If he can enjoy this, so can I," she concluded. Rachel relaxed. She wouldn't worry about making someone cry. She had only made that student cry before because she was trying too hard to ask hard academic questions. This time she would simply enjoy the presentations and try to be encouraging.

"My name is Jessica Schmidt, and today I am presenting my paper—'Egyptian Folklore and Its Creative Influence on Ancient Architecture and Art'."

CHAPTER 4

Both panels Rachel served on went well. Though most of the students were nervous, they all presented thoughtful research, and no one cried. The afternoon sped by and before she knew it, Rachel was back at her hotel getting ready for the awards ceremony that night.

She had packed one button-down shirt for the trip—a red and black buffalo plaid—that would be as dressed up as she could get for the evening. "At least it's not a t-shirt," Rachel shrugged. The reflection in her hotel room's mirror shrugged in unison.

Meeting Liam made Rachel wish she had packed more make-up—something more than her minimalist lip-gloss she always kept in her purse. She wondered if she'd see him tonight. He had been a panelist, so she guessed he'd be there. Rachel *hoped* he'd be there, even if she wouldn't have admitted it. But Dr. Goldblum said the awards ceremony was invitation only, so she couldn't be certain who would attend. Besides that, Rachel knew nothing about the award ceremony. She scolded herself, "You really need to start asking more questions when Dr. Goldblum asks you to do things.... Or tells you to do things."

Before leaving her room to take the elevator down to the ground floor, Rachel made sure *The Mighty Arm that Built Egypt* was in her purse. It would be good to have it on hand for emergencies—like avoiding talking to people like Dr. Holmes.

Thinking of Dr. Holmes made Rachel think of the first panel earlier, and of Liam. "Get a hold of yourself, Rachel," she warned herself. "You don't even know the guy. You just know he's got the clearest, brightest blue eyes you've ever seen, and that his laugh is perfect." With that thought she even disgusted herself. "I sound like a teenager," she said aloud just before the elevator doors opened to the lobby.

Those weren't the only things Rachel knew about Liam though. During the break between panels, before hurrying off to have lunch with Dr. Goldblum, Rachel had a quick conversation with Liam. From the conversation, Rachel learned that Liam was a PhD student at the university. He was there studying Ancient Civilizations. He wasn't specializing in one particular civilization like Rachel had. Liam said he enjoyed being a generalist because he couldn't pick a favorite—"They're all too interesting." Liam also explained to her his embarrassing situation with showing up late and peeking into the classroom. He said it was due to him not having an event program with panel room numbers. When explaining it to Rachel, Liam laughed at himself while admitting, "That was the sixth room I'd tried. Dr. Goldblum told me my first panel was with you, but I hadn't remembered to ask her for a room number."

Rachel grinned, remembering again the sound of Liam's laugh and his amazing smile. She crossed the lobby, passing its eight feet high faux Egyptian statue of Nefertiti. Everything in the lobby that wasn't fake stone or marble was gleaming gold plated. Rachel loved Egypt, but this hotel was overkill. Rachel picked up a hotel map from the front desk. Dr. Goldblum had told Rachel over lunch that the awards ceremony was being held at the hotel's newly renovated ballroom. Apparently it was a popular venue for wedding receptions. Rachel let her mind wander into dangerous territory. She pictured herself in a veil and flowing white dress—she was standing with Liam in front of their friends and family, saying "I do" surrounded by Egyptian god and goddess statues and tacky pharaoh portraits in gilt frames.

The hotel map led Rachel back past the elevators and down a wide corridor. She passed the indoor pool, the sauna, and the fitness center. She turned a corner, almost bumping into housekeeping, before reaching the ostentatious, ten foot tall, gold doors of the ballroom. A sign was on a stand before the doors—"University Ancient Civilizations Award Ceremony." Housekeeping had disappeared, so there was no one else in the hall besides Rachel. "Should I go in?" Rachel wondered. "I know I'm early."

Rachel nervously looked up and down the hall. It was only 6:30 pm, and the awards ceremony wasn't supposed start until 7:00 pm. "I can't just stand here in the hall. If I stand here too long, someone will eventually come down here and ask me if I'm lost." Rachel shuffled her feet and reflected, "That always seems to happen. I'll go in the ballroom and find a place to sit at the back of the room."

Rachel took a deep breath and opened one of the doors. The ballroom was larger than she had expected. Arranged around a large dance floor in the center of the room were several round banquet tables. The tables were covered in shiny gold table cloths. There were fake lotus flower centerpieces in the middle of every table. Rachel loved lotuses. She didn't even mind fake ones. Rachel had always told herself if she ever got a tattoo, it would be of a beautiful blue lotus.

She scanned the room—a large ballroom with gold accents and a stage hung with velvet curtains the color of ripe cranberries. Rachel was the first guest to arrive. The only people there were the caterers setting up food on tables at the back of the room on either side of the golden double doors. With the way the round banquet tables were set up in the middle of the room it would be difficult to stay inconspicuous. Rachel wasn't sure where she could hide. She walked up to one of the tables and gasped, "Oh, no!"

Little name cards placed above each place setting informed Rachel that it was assigned seating. That meant Rachel couldn't just pick the least conspicuous table—she would have to sit wherever her name place was located. For a brief second Rachel contemplated checking all the tables to see if Liam would be there, but then decided against it. "Be mature, Rachel," she thought. "You're Dr. Rachel Conner. Don't act like a big dumbo." Then she thought to herself what an idiot she was for mentally calling herself a dumbo.

Rachel eventually found her name place. It was at the last table she wanted to be seated—at the table directly in front of the stage. The center of attention. "You'd think I was the guest of honor or something! This is ridiculous! I don't want to sit here," annoyed and almost angry, she pulled out her chair and sat down. Her seat faced the stage. Most people would have acknowledged they had been given the best seat in the ballroom. Rachel was just aggravated.

She wondered how she had allowed Dr. Goldblum to talk her into this. Rachel hated award ceremonies. She wasn't dressed for this. And now she was sitting where everyone would stare at her, at the table in front of the stage. "The only thing missing is a spotlight," she sarcastically muttered under her breath.

No one would have heard her had she said it full voice though. The caterers were easily fifty feet away, and there was classical music playing through the speakers on either side of the stage. Rachel listened to the music and tried to regain her calm.

She enjoyed classical music, but wasn't good at identifying pieces or composers. Except Beethoven. When Rachel was in high school she went through a phase where she was certain had she been alive in late 18th century or early 19th century Vienna, Beethoven would have had no choice but to fall desperately in love with her. He would have written symphonies for her, too. It was her daydream. Other girls had boy band fantasies; Rachel had Beethoven. Her crush on Beethoven meant she could identify one of his pieces within the first few notes. Other composers all sounded the same to her—nice, beautiful, impressive—but not Beethoven.

Thinking about Beethoven restored Rachel's peace. She decided she would try to make the best of this arrangement. Rachel tried to ignore how close she was to the stage. She admired the fake blue lotuses on the table. She looked down at her place setting, then at the place setting to her right. Rachel gasped. The name place for the seat next to hers read, "Mr. Liam Hawthorne."

"Perhaps this isn't the worst table to be at," she giggled to herself.

Rachel opened her purse, took out her lip-gloss, and reapplied. "Better than nothing," she thought, placing the lip-gloss back into her purse and pulling out *The Mighty Arm that Built Egypt*.

She checked her phone to see how she was doing on time. It surprised Rachel to see it was just 6:34 pm. She looked around the room. There were a few people entering the ballroom, and a few others checking name places on tables, but no one she knew.

Rachel had lost her place in her book earlier when Hester startled her. She'd have to find it again. She remembered she had finished chapter seventeen earlier. "I think I was on chapter eighteen," whispered Rachel. "I'll just turn to the table of contents to find it."

Rachel opened her book. Flipping past the title page, she stopped to read the dedication. "To my Gerry, always by my side" it read. She turned the page again, located the table of contents, and discovered chapter eighteen began on page 220. Rachel flipped to page 220, then turned a few more pages until she found the last passage she had read:

> *....They had built the mighty pyramids, had they not?! They would defeat Ra and the other gods with him.*
>
> *But how would they do it? How would they defeat beings over twice their size and seemingly endowed with magical powers? The Egyptian people still referred to them as gods, but they were no longer certain these creatures were indeed gods. They were monsters, and they were not men. But what were they exactly, and how would they be defeated?*

Rachel rapidly became absorbed in reading. She guessed the Egyptian people would rise against their oppressors, their *gods*.

Rachel wondered what the gods were since the author was seriously hinting they were not what they appeared. "Maybe giants?" Rachel pondered, remembering an article she had read in a scientific journal that claimed anthropologists had found what appeared to be the remains of giant humans in Saudi Arabia. The article was later debunked, of course.

Seven brave Egyptian men volunteered to hide amongst the gods' living quarters—hide in pots and plants and under thrones—in an attempt to discover what the metaphorical soft underbelly was for these strange enormous beings.

Malachi, the bravest young man amongst them, proclaimed, "I will be like a shadow to the mighty Ra. I will find his weakness, and with this knowledge defeat them all!"

At nightfall the men melted into shadows. They held their breath while bounding over garden walls like pumas and scaling palace trellises like crafty monkeys. They divided, going their separate ways once they had reached the third palace balcony. They could no longer risk moving as a group.

They had to be stealthy, or they would most certainly die.

Malachi ghosted down a dimly lit corridor. The corridor would take Malachi to the bedchamber of Ra. It was a sultry summer night and sweat dripped down Malachi's face. He was anxious but sure. Malachi knew this was the hour Ra was always at evening feast with the other gods. He had time to find a good hiding place before Ra retired for the night.

Entering the bedchamber he was greeted by a bed larger than his own hut. There were also several large cushions scattered around the floor for the purpose of lounging. "They lounge all day while we work ourselves to death!" Malachi spit in anger.

Suddenly he heard heavy footsteps bounding down the corridor. Malachi hurriedly searched for a place to hide. The heavy steps had almost reached the bedchamber when Malachi squeezed himself behind a massive wardrobe. His heart

thudded. He held his breath,
and—

"You're about to get to the good part," said a small voice behind Rachel.

Rachel closed her book and turned in her chair to find Hester, dressed in a lime green polyester pantsuit from the 1970s, her puff of white hair somehow fluffier, more cloud-like. Though silly looking, Rachel kind of admired what Hester viewed as "getting dressed up." Then she noticed a pin on the lapel of Hester's jacket—"I Believe in Aliens." Rachel suppressed a sigh and greeted the alien and Egyptology enthusiast, "Hi, Hester."

"Hello, Rachel," Hester replied, much less excited, and far less friendly than she had been when they had met prior. Rachel observed that Hester seemed sad, deflated somehow. Her round face looked almost childlike—like a child who has been severely and unfairly disciplined—despite Hester's advanced age. Her large eyes were serious, maybe even hurt.

Rachel felt terrible. Clearly her comments about the ridiculousness of aliens in ancient Egypt had upset Hester. But she couldn't think of a way to make Hester feel better without compromising her own beliefs, which were firmly rooted in science. Then it occurred to Rachel that Hester was standing next to her at the awards ceremony that was invitation only. There is no way the university invited random Egyptology fans to the awards ceremony. Hester must have misunderstood when Dr. Goldblum mentioned it in her symposium welcome speech. Rachel didn't want to upset the old woman again, but she reasoned it would be better for Hester to find out she needed to leave now, than later when the ballroom was completely full of invited guests.

"Um, Hester, this event is invitation only," Rachel said, trying to be as sensitive and nice as possible.

Hester walked counterclockwise around Rachel's table until she found the seat that faced away from the stage, the one directly across from Rachel. "Here we go," Hester said, sitting. "Gerald, you sit over here on my left, dear."

Rachel was getting uncomfortable. She stuttered, "This e-e-e-event isn't open to the public."

"I know, dear. Why is that so important to you?" Hester asked.

She didn't know what to say. Could she tell this little old woman she didn't belong at this event? No, clearly she could not. She decided to just let whoever belonged in the seats Hester had claimed to straighten out the situation.

She answered Hester, "Oh, sorry, it's not important."

Rachel was relieved it would fall to someone else to kick the old woman out. Although Hester was a kook, Rachel found herself liking the silly old woman. She admired Hester's enthusiasm and spirit.

The speakers on either side of the stage softly played Beethoven's fifth symphony. Rachel smiled. Maybe she could have a good time at this thing. She set her book down on the table while pushing herself out of her chair. More people had arrived. She would do her best to mingle, or at least look for Dr. Goldblum... and possibly Liam.

CHAPTER 5

Rachel scanned the room for probably the tenth time looking for Liam. He wasn't there.

Rachel had been trying her best to mingle. She spoke with a few faculty members from the department of Ancient History and Classical Studies, and was introduced to the Dean of Humanities, Dr. Charles Woodford, and his wife Dr. Betsy Woodford. The only interesting bit of conversation that came from Rachel's mingling was when Dr. Betsy Woodford—a noted art historian—informed Rachel that not all the ancient Egyptian décor at the Sunrise Inn and Suites was imitation. Gesturing to the ceiling in the middle of the ballroom, Dr. Betsy Woodford said, "That stone disk is an authentic ancient Egyptian artifact. It is priceless! It's pre-Amenemhet—it easily dates back more than 4000 years. Frankly, it's inconceivable that this hotel had the collateral to cover a piece of that value, or that any museum would allow it to slip through its fingers."

Rachel had followed Dr. Woodfords gesture to the enormous disk and wondered how she hadn't noticed it when she first entered the ballroom. It was an impressive piece. "How is it affixed to the ceiling?" Rachel wondered.

The disk was carved out of ancient stone and its diameter was approximately eight feet. It had ancient Egyptian symbols, most Rachel recognized. Among them were "Ra"—the god, "Ka"—the spirit, "Shen"—eternity, and in the center a scarab which generally stood for transformation. It roughly translated to, "The god Ra or any spirit who passes is transformed to eternity." It didn't make a lot of sense to Rachel, but hieroglyphics were always guess work. You could never find an exact meaning, just an approximate one. Rachel snapped a picture with her phone. "Maybe I can get a more exact translation when I'm at home with my books," she theorized.

Rachel felt a tap on her shoulder and turned to find Liam. "Hey, Rachel, good to see you again," Liam said, smiling his perfect smile.

"Irresistible," Rachel thought, and forgot to answer back. She just dumbly smiled.

Liam laughed, a quick uncomfortable chuckle that brought Rachel back to reality.

"Oh, hey, Liam. Yeah, good to see you, too," she answered belatedly.

Rachel looked around and saw that most of the guests in attendance had already taken their seats. She hadn't noticed the group she had been talking with had wandered off while she stared at and photographed the disk. "I must have been staring a long time," she realized, amazed at her own ability to zone out.

Rachel put her phone in her purse as she said to Liam, "It's got to be almost time for the awards ceremony to start. We should take our seats."

"I have no idea where I'm sitting," Liam answered, chagrined. "I guess I should have gotten here a little earlier."

"You're next to me," Rachel responded confidently, trying not to look too excited.

Liam followed Rachel to their table in front of the stage. It was then that Rachel finally spotted Dr. Goldblum on the far side of the stage. She waved to her mentor, but Dr. Goldblum was busy talking to a man Rachel didn't know—probably part of the catering crew or hotel staff.

"It's okay she didn't see you. She's busy. You'll have time to talk with her later," Rachel reassured herself, then added, "And when you do get that chance you can tell her how unhappy you were to be seated front and center at the event. Also you can tell her 'thank you, thank you, thank you' for putting you next to Liam."

Rachel looked to her right and smiled at Liam. He smiled back. Rachel rarely liked beards, but Liam's beard was cute. It fit him. She liked how parts of it were red in the light, and how it seemed to make his blue eyes look even bluer.

Rachel's musing over the cuteness of Liam's beard and the blueness of his eyes were interrupted by Dr. Goldblum's voice. "Welcome colleagues, students, and honored guests. My name is Dr. Selma Goldblum, and it is my privilege to welcome you here this evening. The department of Ancient History and Classical Studies, along with the Dean of Humanities, Dr. Woodford, and the president of the university, Dr. Wu, would like to thank you for being here tonight," Dr. Goldblum's voice said loudly through the speakers. "The purpose of tonight is to honor a few remarkable people who have made a difference, or are making a difference in the study of ancient civilizations. Tonight we honor the past, the present, and the future of our field. But, before we begin handing out awards, the catering staff would like to invite you to start a line at the tables on either side of the ballroom. Food first, then the fanfare. Enjoy!"

Dr. Goldblum stepped away from the microphone and departed the stage. The award ceremony's invited guests began rising from their seats and forming lines for the buffet.

Liam got out of his seat. "I'm getting in line." He smiled at Rachel and asked, "You coming?"

"Sure," Rachel answered, following closely behind Liam to the line on the left side of the ballroom.

The buffet had prime rib, chicken, and vegetarian lasagna as entrée choices. "Did they have vegetarian lasagna in Ancient Greece?" Rachel jokingly asked Liam.

"No, I think it's a Mesopotamian dish," he teased back.

"If it was good enough for the Mesopotamians, it's good enough for me," Rachel said, taking a helping of lasagna.

Liam selected the prime rib, and they both got red potatoes and Caesar salads, because as Liam had put it, "What other salad is there for an ancient civilizations academic?"

They returned to their seats where members of the catering staff had placed glasses with a pitcher of water. There were also champagne flutes, but no champagne yet. Rachel assumed the champagne would be poured in honor of the award recipients.

Also waiting at their table was Hester. Rachel had forgotten about the old woman. When Rachel led Liam to their table minutes earlier, Hester wasn't there. But she was back now, with a plate full of food. Hester had also selected the lasagna.

Rachel worried to herself, "This could get awkward when the people who are *supposed* sit there try to take their seats." Rachel was starting to feel bad for the kooky old woman.

Both Dr. Charles Woodford and Dr. Betsy Woodford, along with Dr. Wu, the university president, walked up to Rachel's table. Rachel winced inwardly, certain these must be the people whose seats Hester had taken for herself and Gerald. Rachel couldn't watch the scene unfold, so she stared intently at her red potatoes, hoping that however it happened, they would be kind to Hester.

"Hey, that's my seat," an irritated Dr. Charles Woodford said.

Rachel's pulse quicken. Hester might be a crazy old woman, and she might be sitting in a seat that didn't belong to her, and she might have even crashed an event she didn't get invited to—but that's no excuse to talk that way to a nice old lady. Rachel looked up, ready to jump to Hester's defense.

She was shocked to find that Dr. Charles Woodford was not addressing Hester, but his wife, Dr. Betsy Woodford. Betsy replied, "Relax, darling. You can sit in my seat. I want to sit in this seat so I can talk art history with Dr. Conner, if we get a moment." Dr. Betsy Woodford flashed a friendly smile at the surprised Rachel. Rachel offered a feeble smile in return.

Betsy had taken the seat next to Rachel. Charles took the seat next to her, which was also next to Hester. Dr. Wu walked to the other side of the table and placed his overflowing plate between Liam and Gerald's empty place.

The table was now full, if Gerald's seat counted as being taken. Rachel was confused. Everyone at the table seemed completely fine with Hester sitting there.

Rachel ate her food in silence, pretending to pay attention to Dr. Betsy Woodford talk about the horrendous frescos in the courtyard of the hotel. "I get it—there were frescos even in the Old Kingdom of ancient Egypt, but it looks like a poor man's Tuscany out there! Absurd!" she exclaimed.

When eventually both Dr. Woodfords started a conversation together, Rachel felt relieved. She had just finished her meal, so she turned to talk with Liam.

Liam was looking down at the table. Rachel's eyes followed his gaze and realized Liam was looking at her copy of *The Mighty Arm that Built Egypt*. She forgot to put it away. It had been sitting on the table this entire time. Rachel was instantly mad at herself for not hiding that away in her purse before Liam got the chance to see her questionable reading choices.

"Oh, did you bring that for her to sign?" Liam asked. Though it sounded more like a statement than a question.

"For who to sign?" was Rachel's confused reply.

"The author of that book." He said, pointing to Rachel's book. "The famous sci-fi author—H.H. Mays. She's here tonight. Didn't you know?"

Rachel looked down at her book, dumbstruck. Her confusion was interrupted by Dr. Goldblum, again at the microphone. "Hopefully you've at least had the chance to mostly appease your appetites. If you haven't, just keep eating, we can give speeches while you chew."

The crowd laughed, and Dr. Goldblum continued. "This evening we are honoring three people. As I said earlier—each award recipient represents either the past, the present, or the future of the study of ancient civilizations. The first person we honor tonight represents the past. We wanted to present this award to someone who, while studying the past, made his own impact on it. The recipient of this award was an esteemed faculty member at our university—a member of our department for thirty years. Though he retired 16 years ago, he could always be depended upon to guest lecture, or offer advice to any professor in the department. His enthusiasm for research and new ideas was unparalleled. He was never afraid to test a new theory. Nothing was too farfetched until disproven. And this philosophy led to several breakthroughs in the field of Egyptology. Earlier this year, we were saddened to hear of his death. And we were later shocked to learn he had left our department 11 million dollars. This donation will provide the funds for countless scholarships, updates to lecture halls, and a new wing for the ancient history and classical studies building—which will begin construction in the fall. I'm sure most of you know whom I speak of. Of course it is none other than famed Egyptologist and beloved former faculty member, Dr. Gerald Mays."

Rachel's jaw dropped, and she reflexively looked to Gerald's empty seat. Connecting the dots, Rachel's stunned eyes fixed on Hester.

"On behalf of Dr. Mays," Dr. Goldblum's voice reverberated in the speakers, "his wife is here to accept his award. It is my pleasure to present to you, famed science fiction author, H.H. Mays."

The crowd erupted into applause as Hester pushed herself out of her chair. Dr. Charles Woodford rose and shook her hand before allowing her to pass. Hester swiftly climbed the stairs to the stage, her puff of white hair and lime green pantsuit brightly standing out against the deep cranberry of the velvet stage curtains.

Hester gave Dr. Goldblum an exuberant hug and accepted Gerald's award—a bronze medallion engraved with a scarab. Before leaving the stage, Dr. Goldblum helped Hester adjust the microphone to accommodate her small stature. Hester stepped up to the mic, grinning from ear to ear, and said, "Thank you! Oh, boy, this is a thrill!"

Hester glanced down at Rachel's table and spoke directly to Gerald's seat, adding, "Gerry, I am so glad other people know how great you are, too. And I couldn't be more proud of you."

The crowd clapped and cheered. Rachel's mouth was still agape with surprise. She clapped along with everyone else unconsciously. In her mind she kept thinking, "Hester wrote my book," before switching to, "Everyone here has no idea that Hester believes she's speaking to Gerald's ghost, or, um, *wraith* right now."

"This award means a lot," Hester told the crowd. "Gerald has always valued education and exploration above anything else. That was one of the things that made me fall in love with him. We shared a mutual thirst for knowledge and a drive to make sense of the universe. I know Gerald is receiving this award because to most of you Gerald represents the past—a foundation on which to build. But to me Gerry is... ever present."

Hester stopped to wipe her eyes on her lime green sleeve. "It's funny to be holding this scarab again," Hester said, indicating the bronze medallion. "Before Gerald's death he decided that all the Egyptian artifacts and tchotchkes he had collected over the years would be better suited in the hands of the university than taking up space in our home. He wanted to share his treasures with all of you. To be given one back feels like a real blessing. Thank you for honoring my husband."

The tiny science fiction writer stepped away from the microphone and walked back down the stage stairs while the crowd applauded. She took her seat and the awards ceremony continued.

Dr. Kathy Holmes claimed the stage to announce the next award recipient. Rachel had avoided Dr. Holmes while she mingled earlier, and again when Liam picked the buffet line on the left side of the room, while Dr. Holmes chose the line on the right side. Under the stage lights Dr. Holmes looked more like a movie star than an ancient history professor. She wore a tight black dress with red six-inch heels. Her golden blonde hair spilling over her shoulders could make a shampoo model jealous. Dr. Holmes adjusted the microphone before she began speaking.

"Thank you to the late Dr. Mays' wife," Dr. Holmes began. "For those of you who don't know me, I am Dr. Kathy Holmes.

I am a professor in the Ancient History and Classical Studies department. When I was approached about presenting an award at this ceremony, I was hesitant to agree. I believe we spend a lot of time in academia applauding mediocrity in the spirit of not hurting anyone's feelings. I've believed for some time that the effort we extend bolstering the self-esteems of mediocre students could be better spent offering more time to the truly exceptional students who pass through our halls and move into greatness. I agreed to present this award because the recipient of the award is an example of the exceptional student in which we should invest. Without further ado, representing excellence in the present, in the field of ancient civilizations, is Dr. Rachel Conner."

Rachel's throat constricted, causing her to choke on the water she'd just swallowed. Not only had she heard her name called as an award recipient, but it was by Dr. Holmes, who had just said nice things about her while also managing to insult most students.

Dr. Holmes continued, "Dr. Rachel Conner's research in the field of Egyptology has been featured in countless publications and her textbooks are now the standard in most ancient history departments. Dr. Conner truly represents excellence in the present study of ancient civilizations."

Everyone at Rachel's table stared at her. It took Liam nudging her and saying, "You should go up there," for it to compute that she needed to leave her seat and go up on stage.

With wobbly legs Rachel climbed the stairs and crossed the stage. Dr. Holmes smiled at Rachel while shaking her hand and offered her a bronze medallion identical the one Hester had received. In a daze, Rachel walked up to the microphone. She looked out on the crowd, but because of the stage lights couldn't quite make out the faces of anyone beyond her own table at the front. She saw the Dr. Woodfords smiling up at her, President Wu looking expectant, Liam grinning encouragingly, and Hester looking more like the Hester she'd met on the plane—cheerful, excited, possibly even bouncing in her seat a bit. Hester gave Rachel a thumbs up.

Rachel awoke from her stupor and nervously spoke. "Wow," she said into the microphone. "I, uh, had no idea this was going to happen. Obviously." She paused, motioning to what she was wearing.

The audience laughed, and Rachel's nerves subsided. "This is an amazing honor, to be recognized by my alma mater. And thank you Dr. Holmes for your kind words. And thank you to anyone who was part of selecting me for this award."

Rachel looked down at the medallion then continued. "When I was a student here, I felt out-of-place most of the time. I loved the information—the textbooks, the library, the professors—but I found the regular student interaction uncomfortable, and I just wasn't any good at it. With the recommendation of Dr. Goldblum, I went on to get my master's degree in Ancient History. Then I got my PhD in Egyptology. Along the way, people constantly asked me, 'What are you going to do with your degrees?' The assumption was always that I would become a university professor. But, um, that just didn't feel like the path for me. All I wanted to do was research and write. What I really wanted to do was write textbooks for students like myself—textbooks that would open the world of ancient Egypt for the next generation of Egyptologists. I know textbooks are usually written by college professors, but I didn't want to teach in a classroom. I knew I wouldn't be able to connect with the students. I wanted to teach through my writing. Um, anyway, all this to say—thank you for acknowledging my work and accepting me as your own even though I didn't become a professor."

The crowd clapped for Rachel as she returned to her seat. She simultaneously felt euphoric and embarrassed. Rachel didn't enjoy being stared at, but she relished having her work valued and appreciated. Rachel knew she owed this acknowledgement to Dr. Goldblum. She would have to get her mentor another maple doughnut, or maybe a dozen maple doughnuts.

Rachel looked down at the table in front of her and *The Mighty Arm that Built Egypt* caught her attention. She made a mental note to ask Hester to sign it. "Or would that be weird?" Rachel wondered.

Dr. Charles Woodford had taken the stage. Dr. Woodford spoke a little too loud into the microphone, "I guess it's my turn," he boomed before taking a half step back from the mic. "Thank you Dr. Conner for honoring us with your presence at our symposium. You are one of our success stories, for sure. The final award of the evening goes to one of our future success stories. We, the faculty and administrators, at this university believe the next recipient best embodies the future in the study of ancient civilizations. The award goes to a student who is currently working on his PhD. A student who constantly impresses everyone with his dedication and keen mind. I can also personally attest to his impressive patience with undergraduate students. I am pleased to announce that the recipient of the award for the future of the study of ancient civilizations is Mr. Liam Hawthorne."

Rachel turned to look at Liam. She could tell by his face and the zero hesitation he exhibited in getting out of his seat that this wasn't a surprise. "Dr. Woodford should have also said Liam has excellent deductive reasoning," Rachel reflected. "Of course Liam was getting the last award. I got one, and Gerald got one. All the award recipients are sitting at the same table. If you can count Gerald as sitting."

Liam took the stairs two at a time and greeted Dr. Woodford with an energetic handshake in the middle of the stage. Before leaving the stage, Dr. Woodford patted Liam on the back and handed him a bronze medallion with the same scarab engraving as the others.

Liam cleared his throat, then said into the microphone, "Thank you for this amazing award. I, I don't really know what to say. To be given an award the same night as Dr. Mays and Dr. Conner..." Liam made eye contact with Hester and then with Rachel. "...I'm speechless. I hope I will come to deserve this award the way you think I do. Thank you."

The crowd clapped as Liam exited the stage, and Dr. Goldblum returned to the microphone to invite everyone to grab dessert from the buffet tables. Rachel congratulated Liam on his award, but Liam seemed uncomfortable with the accolades. He suggested they go grab some dessert, so Rachel followed Liam again to the left side of the ballroom, though she was no longer worried about running into Dr. Holmes.

When Rachel and Liam returned to their table with their dessert—triple chocolate cake—they found their champagne flutes full of pink champagne. Hester was already seated again. She had two plates of chocolate cake.

After everyone had returned to their tables with dessert, Dr. Goldblum once more addressed the crowd. "Ladies and Gentlemen, thank you, again, for coming tonight. I want you to enjoy your cake, but I want to conclude this ceremony with a toast. Will everyone please raise their glasses to the award recipients? To the past, the present, and the future!"

Glasses clinked all around the ballroom. Hester smiled at Rachel across the table. Rachel smiled back and firmly decided she would ask Hester to sign her copy of *The Mighty Arm that Built Egypt*. "Even if the book is a silly book, and even if its author is a silly old woman with fluffy white hair who believes in aliens. It isn't every day you met the author of a book you're reading," Rachel thought to herself. A few minutes later she shared that opinion with Liam.

He laughed then said teasingly one-upping her, "Well, today I've met two authors of books I've read."

Rachel quickly looked around the room trying to find another famous author she might not have noticed. "What? Who else is here?" she asked, turning completely around in her chair to scan the room.

Liam laughed again, arching one eyebrow as if to say, "Really?"

Rachel repeated herself, "What other author is here?" As an avid reader, Rachel was curious if she had read any of the author's work.

"You," Liam replied with an exasperated laugh.

"Oooh," was all Rachel could manage. She sometimes forgot that to other people she was the author of the book they were reading. Writers still seemed like magical mythical creatures to Rachel. She didn't equate herself with other writers. To Rachel she was just a researcher who gathered information and synthesized it into an easier to grasp format. In truth, Rachel was not only a talented researcher, but a fantastic writer. She deserved the award she had received. She was doing outstanding work in her field. Rachel was an outstanding writer.

Liam was in the middle of telling Rachel about how he used one of her textbooks for a class he taught last semester when he was interrupted by Dr. Goldblum. "Excuse me, Liam, Rachel, could we get you to join Dr. Mays' wife over there for a picture? We'd like a picture to put on the department's website and for the university newspaper of the three of you with your awards."

Rachel hadn't noticed that Hester had gotten up from the table. She looked over her shoulder toward the direction Dr. Goldblum had pointed. Hester stood in the middle of the room, a photographer about ten feet away already poised to take the picture.

Rachel got out of her chair, put her purse over her shoulder, and placed *The Mighty Arm that Built Egypt* inside. "Don't forget to ask for Hester's autograph," she said to herself before following Liam to the center of the room.

The photographer asked Rachel and Liam to stand on either side of Hester. They obliged, and looked like obedient, loving grandchildren taking a photo with their tiny grandmother. All three held out their awards. The bronze dully shining. The scarabs identical. Rachel looked up and saw they were standing directly under the ancient Egyptian stone disk affixed to the ceiling. Rachel thought to herself, "I didn't notice earlier that it was glowing. It can't be authentic. Or if it is authentic, someone ruined it by adding LEDs."

The photographer said, "Smile big!"

The three award recipients smiled, then the camera flashed—too bright.

This is why Rachel hated flash photography—it usually left her seeing spots. But this was the worst she had ever experienced. The flash caused Rachel's vision to go black. She blinked several times. Still black. Finally she said, "Guys, I can't see anything."

"Me neither," Hester answered her, sounding small and a little frightened.

It was then that Rachel realized the room had gone silent. She couldn't hear the awards ceremony guests mingling, or classical music from the speakers on either side of the stage. Something wasn't right.

Right before Rachel's vision recovered, Liam grabbed her arm and shouted, "What the hell?!"

Rachel's vision cleared, and she saw what made Liam exclaim. The scene around them had completely changed. Rachel, Liam, and Hester were no longer in the ballroom at the Sunrise Inn and Suites. They had been transported some place else.

CHAPTER 6

"What's wrong? What happened?" Hester asked Rachel and Liam in a panic. The old woman looked around blindly, hands outstretched, still unable to see what the other two had seen.

Rachel gently put her arm around the tiny woman and said, "It appears as though we were temporarily blinded by a flash, and you seem to still be experiencing blindness."

"And that's not all," Liam jumped in, not able to master the calm Rachel had.

Rachel began to explain further, "We seem to have been— "

"Holy biscuits 'n' gravy!"

Hester's vision had cleared and she was looking around the space in front of them. Roughly cut stone walls surrounded Hester, Rachel, and Liam on all sides. They were in a cave, apparently man-made. Everything looked gray. What wasn't gray was shadow. The only light came from two torches burning on the wall ahead of them.

"Where are we?" Hester asked.

"We appear to be in a cave of some sort. The real question is—how did we get here?" Rachel replied.

All three faced the same direction—toward the wall with the torches. Liam stepped forward and took a torch from the wall. Turning back toward Rachel and Hester, he began, "I think we should take a better look around, then we can— "

Liam broke off mid-sentence. His gaze had stopped directly above Hester's head, but further back. His eyes were locked on something behind Hester, something that frightened him so badly he could not speak.

"Liam," Rachel said cautiously, "are you okay?"

Liam gulped and pointed. "There is something behind Hester."

Rachel and Hester both slowly turned to see what left Liam nearly speechless and shaking in his shoes.

"You can see me?" asked a surprised voice.

Hester gasped. She covered her mouth with her hands and stared at what stood before her.

"Gerry, I sure have missed you," she squeaked, tears running down her pale wrinkled cheeks.

Standing before Hester, Rachel, and Liam was the apparition of a tall old man. He was clean shaven and roughly the same size as Liam, maybe an inch shorter. Rachel noted that he didn't float in the air the way ghosts always did in movies. The ghost of Dr. Gerald Mays appeared to stand firmly on the ground like any self-respecting living person. The difference between Dr. Mays and a living person was that clearly Dr. Mays wasn't all there. He was transparent. He wasn't flesh and bone, he was spirit. He was also a beautiful blue-green.

"I've been with you this whole time, Hester," Gerald said.

"Oh, I know, Gerry. But before I couldn't hear you or see you. Though, I did imagine you said things to me sometimes," replied Hester.

"In the downstairs bathroom!" Gerald laughed. "It's got those great acoustics! I knew you heard me in there!"

Hester joined Gerald laughing and said, "I thought I was half crazy when I went in there, because I was sure I could hear you saying you loved me."

"Every night when you brushed your teeth," Hester's ghostly husband responded. "I love you, my dearest Hester."

"Oh, I love you, Gerald—so much!"

Hester walked forward to hug Gerald, but her arms passed right through him.

"Still no hugs, I'm afraid," Gerald said, looking down at Hester with a mixture of love and sadness.

Rachel spoke, trying to sound normal, "I'm sorry to interrupt, but... you're Dr. Gerald Mays? The deceased Dr. Gerald Mays?"

"Yes, but please call me Gerald." He replied, then smiled and said, "If we get along well, you can call me Gerry."

"Gerald, how are you here right now?" asked Rachel.

"I don't know, Rachel. Is it okay if I call you Rachel?" was Gerry's response.

"Of course," Rachel answered.

"I've been with Hester since my death. The real questions are why can you see me now? And where are we?" said the logical Dr. Mays.

"So you were with us at the awards ceremony," Liam stated more than asked.

"I was being honored, young man. I wouldn't have missed it," Gerald said proudly, before adding, "And I never leave Hester's side." Gerald and Hester exchanged a look full of the kind of love that can only be built over a sixty year marriage.

"The four of us were transported somewhere," Liam said.

"What? 'Transported'? We would remember if someone took us someplace," Rachel said, unconvinced. She laughed and mockingly added, "Unless you mean like 'Beam me up' transported."

The looks on the others' faces suggested exactly that—they believed they had been beamed somewhere else. Someplace that wasn't the Sunrise Inn and Suites, and might not even be Austin, Texas.

"Come on, you guys, you don't think we were magically taken someplace else, do you?" She asked. "There has got to be a logical explanation."

But inwardly Rachel felt the panic building. She couldn't think of a logical explanation. "Trap door," she suggested.

"We would have felt ourselves falling," Liam answered.

"A hypnotist was at the awards ceremony! We were hypnotized to go to sleep when we saw a camera flash!" Rachel offered. But she knew that wasn't logical either.

"There was no hypnotist there, and I can't be hypnotized," said Gerald. "We visited the state fair last month and saw a hypnotist. I tried to be hypnotized with the rest of the crowd, but it didn't work for me."

"Made me cluck like a chicken," Hester giggled. Gerald also laughed.

"Rachel, stop trying to be 'logical'," Liam insisted. "We're having a conversation with a ghost. This doesn't fit neatly into something you've researched, experienced, or read. The true logical thing to admit right now is that what we're dealing with is outside our understanding. We're not at the hotel anymore."

"*Are* you a ghost, Gerry?" Hester asked. "I had thought you were a wraith, you know."

"I don't know," Gerry shrugged his barely there blue-green shoulders. "I could be a phantom? I don't think I'm a poltergeist, though. Aren't they usually destructive? Noisy?"

"I'm sorry, I don't mean to be rude, but what sort of non-corporeal being Gerald is isn't really the point right now. We need to find out where we are," interrupted Rachel.

"We're not at the hotel, Rachel. Look around, this isn't the Sunrise Inn. This isn't Austin," said Liam. "Look at this!"

Liam had pulled his cellphone out of his pocket during Hester and Gerald's wraith verses phantom discussion. He now held it out for Rachel to see. The screen was completely black.

"What..." Rachel began before trailing off and fishing her own cellphone out of her purse. It was also dead.

"My phone had an almost fully charged battery at the awards ceremony," Liam said, putting his cellphone back in his pocket. "We've got to consider theories that defy logic."

"Fine. Okay, you're sure we've been beamed someplace," Rachel said sarcastically, pulling her hair band off her wrist and twisting her hair into a messy bun. She stalked to the wall before them and grabbed the other torch. "Then let's find the entrance to this cave. I bet you anything we're just inside the bat caves here in Austin."

"Though a nice hypothesis, Rachel, this cave is clearly man made," lectured Gerald in his best professor voice. "You can tell by the roughness of the walls. A natural cave would have clearer signs of erosion. Also, no bat guano." Gerald's see-through arm motioned to the clean cave floor.

Rachel sighed and walked towards one of the darkest corners of the cave. Rachel's inner monologue took over. "Our cake was laced with a hallucinogen. This isn't real. We weren't beamed anyplace and I'm certainly not being lectured by a ghost." She also decided that Liam was a lot cuter before he started jumping to crazy conspiracy theory conclusions. "I can't believe I was picturing marrying him earlier." Rachel blushed at the memory.

As she considered whether Liam's amazing eyes and cute beard could outweigh him potentially being the sort of person who might believe in aliens, the light from Rachel's torch revealed an arched tunnel entrance. Rachel advanced toward the tunnel opening and was struck by how tall and wide it was. Its ceilings were tall enough for a man more than twice Liam or Gerald's size to walk through, and their little group could easily walk shoulder to shoulder down the tunnel with room to swing their arms.

Soon they were doing just that—walking shoulder to shoulder down the tunnel. The four walked along in silence, all wondering if this tunnel would lead them closer to discovering where they were, or further away.

Light from Rachel and Liam's torches threw the group's shadows all around. The shadows jumped from wall to wall, not always obeying the typical laws of light and shadow. Rachel noticed the path before them seemed to flicker. The torchlight bounced off the roughly cut tunnel walls in ways that defied nature. Rachel saw these inconsistencies, but didn't say a word for fear of alarming the others or giving credence to any theories rooted in the paranormal or supernatural. "There has to be a logical explanation for this," she thought to herself as she watched her own shadow dance before the torch light.

The tunnel began to angle upward, making the trek far more difficult. The group was forced to take a break to allow Hester to rest. Liam asked Rachel to hold his torch a minute so he could take off his blazer. He folded it up, making a cushion for Hester to sit. The tiny woman sat and tried to make herself comfortable.

"We're not stopping because I'm old," Hester panted. "We're stopping because I have asthma and I left my inhaler in my handbag on my seat at that awards ceremony."

"Bunny, are you going to be okay? You know I worry about you with your breathing attacks." Gerald's brow furrowed. He tried to put a ghostly arm around his tiny wife, but his arm passed through her petite body.

"I'll be fine, Gerry. I just gotta not push myself too hard. I don't miss my inhaler yet, but I'm afraid if I push too hard I will," answered Hester, or as Gerald called her 'Bunny.'

After handing Liam back his torch, Rachel sat with her back against the tunnel wall, glad for the break. She had a gym membership but had come up with an excuse not to use it for the last three months straight. Her legs were aching from the uphill climb. A personal trainer had told her she needed to use the incline on the treadmill to get a better workout, but Rachel ignored the advice telling herself as a city dweller she didn't need to be good at hiking. "Apparently, I was wrong," she thought to herself, massaging her tired legs with her free hand.

Liam sat next to Rachel. He leaned in close to her ear and quietly asked, "Did you see the shadows? They're all over the place. It's totally crazy. It doesn't make any sense."

"Yeah, I know," Rachel replied.

"I know you don't want to think anything weird is going on," Liam said. He didn't finish his thought, but the implication was heavy.

From her blazer cushion a few feet away Hester asked, "What are you two kids whispering about?"

Gerald answered before Rachel or Liam could. "The shadows, right?" he guessed.

They stared at the transparent former professor, both wondering how he could have known.

"I don't understand," said Hester innocently.

Gerald explained, "The light doesn't create shadows the way it should here—wherever we are."

Hester nodded, trying to understand. Gerald knew his wife's facial expressions well enough to know she didn't.

Gerald addressed Liam, "Son, wave your torch around."

Liam moved his torch up and down, then from side to side. His own shadow jumped out in front of him, flickered to left then the right, onto the ceiling, and then disappeared.

"Whoa, that's some special effect!" Hester exclaimed. "You don't see that every day." She paused before adding, "What planet do you think we're on?"

Until this point no one had actually come out and suggested they were on another planet. Words like 'transported' and 'beamed up' were thrown around, but no one had explicitly said they might be on another planet. Finding the tunnel had given Rachel a temporary calm—she was so focused on discovering where the tunnel would lead that she had put out of her mind the four of them had somehow been transported out of the Sunrise Inn and Suites ballroom. Hester's question made Rachel feel like she was being roughly pushed back into a problem she didn't want and didn't know how to solve. Rachel sighed.

Rachel didn't attempt to mask the annoyance she felt. "Hester, I get it that you're a science fiction writer, and that you love aliens, but we have no reason to believe we're on another planet. The very idea is ridiculous," said Rachel.

"I don't think you're being fair, Rachel," Gerald replied. "We don't know where we are or how we got here. The light and shadow doesn't follow the laws of nature that we know. And, during my time deceased on Earth I have never been visible. It is not an outrageous hypothesis that we're on a different planet. We know that gravity works differently from planet to planet. It is not impractical to suggest that a different planet might have other different natural laws as well."

Rachel maintained eye contact with Gerald throughout his speech. She didn't break eye contact now that he was finished. She stared at him, her anger near the boiling point, her cheeks reddening as they always did when she was uncomfortable or angry. As an educated thirty-two-year-old woman, Rachel did not appreciate the way Gerald was speaking to her. She felt like he was being condescending. She was tired of being talked down to and she was tired of sitting still and getting nowhere. Rachel looked away from Gerald, turning her attention to Hester. "Are we ready to move forward? Hester, do you feel fine enough to continue?" Rachel asked through gritted teeth.

"Does a cow go 'moo, moo, moo'?" Hester replied. "Yeah, I'm all right. I'll probably have to stop again in a few minutes, though."

"Let's get going then," Rachel said, pushing herself up from the tunnel floor on achy legs.

Liam offered Hester his free arm. She grabbed ahold and he helped her rise to her feet. Hester tried to return Liam's blazer, but he asked her to hold on to it for the next time they took a break. Gerald looked on, happy to have someone helping his wife, sad he couldn't be the one to offer Hester an arm.

The tunnel began to lose its incline after the group had been walking for about ten minutes. The four now walked on flat ground. Rachel felt a breeze push the few loose strands of hair around her face. The torches wavered, flickering erratically.

"Feel that breeze?" Liam asked.

"Sure do!" exclaimed Hester. "If you don't mind, I think I'm going to put on your blazer... unless you need it."

"Go ahead, I like the breeze," Liam answered the old woman with a smile.

With every step the breeze increased in strength. It had graduated to a veritable wind. Then the flames of their torches blew out, and the group was left in darkness.

"Uh-oh," said Hester's small nervous voice.

"We've got to be near the mouth of this tunnel," said Gerald. "Since I can't run into anything or get hurt, I'll venture ahead to see what I can find. You three stay put."

They all agreed Gerald should be the one to explore the path ahead. Rachel and Liam threw down their now useless torches. While they waited no one said a word, until someone's tuneless humming broke the silence.

"Who's humming?" interrupted Hester.

Liam stopped humming to answer, "Me."

"Gerald does that. He hums to himself when he gets nervous or scared," said Hester. She laughed before adding, "When we were young he'd go on roller-coasters with me—'cause he knew I loved 'em—but he'd hum the whole ride!"

Rachel laughed, picturing the only version of Gerald she'd ever known—the old ghost version—humming to himself on a speeding roller-coaster, a roller-coaster he was only on to keep his adventurous pint-sized wife happy. "He's a know-it-all, but he loves his wife," Rachel thought to herself.

"I hadn't noticed I do it when I'm scared or nervous," Liam said. "I guess it's true, though. My ex-girlfriend used to give me a hard time because I always hummed when I drove on the freeway."

All three laughed. Rachel added another point to the cute column for Liam.

Gerald's voice interrupted their laughing. "Hester? Kids?"

Rachel didn't appreciate being called a 'kid,' so she didn't answer. Hester and Liam said in unison, "We're here."

Gerald's voice moved closer to them while saying, "There's light up ahead. I didn't explore any further after I found light. I turned around and came back here. I figure if the three of you can take hold of each other and walk slowly, it won't be long until we reach the lighted part of the tunnel again, and with that I imagine we will almost be to the mouth of the tunnel."

Rachel, Liam, and Hester agreed and blindly tried to find each other in the pitch-black tunnel.

"Oww!"

Rachel had accidently knocked Hester in the head.

"Ouch! That's my foot!"

Liam had stepped on Hester's foot.

"You kids stay still and let me grab you," said Hester. "If you keep trying to find me you're gonna kill me first."

Rachel noticed it didn't bother her one bit when Hester called her 'kid.' She felt Hester's small wrinkled hand on her forearm, then heard the tiny old woman order, "Now let's walk."

At a snail's pace the group walked forward in complete darkness. After a few minutes they could just barely distinguish each other's outlines. The blackness turned to gray, and Rachel wondered how it was she'd never noticed that in low lights color almost disappears. Hester's lime green pantsuit was a medium gray; Liam's brown hair almost looked black. Gerald stalked in front of the threesome, a light gray apparition instead of the bluish green he had appeared by torch light.

The group kept hold of each other but hastened their pace. Hester switched her grip from Rachel and Liam's forearms to their hands. If someone spotted them from far away, they might look like a family ready to enjoy an afternoon at the park—Liam and Rachel the parents, Hester the child in between.

Sunlight flooded the tunnel, and Rachel noticed that everything instantly shifted from gray to a rainbow of colors. She also noticed that the tunnel ceiling had drastically shortened. The group of four walked a half dozen more paces and stepped out of the tunnel, or to be more precise—they stepped out of the mouth of the cave.

CHAPTER 7

Rachel, Liam, Hester, and Gerald stood on the edge of a mountain. The mouth of the cave the foursome exited rested on a twenty foot shelf cut into the mountainside. Before them was an endless expanse of prairie—a sea of long green grass swaying in the wind.

"I told you we weren't in Austin," Hester said smugly to Rachel.

Rachel felt like the blood was draining from her body. She let go of the old woman's hand, and on uncertain legs walked to the ledge. She looked down and the green prairie seemed to rush up to her; though standing still she felt like she was falling. Rachel hurriedly stepped several feet back, tripping over her own feet. She began to lose balance, so instead of fall she lowered herself to the ground. Vertigo overwhelmed her senses. Everything was spinning. She wasn't in Austin. She wasn't anywhere she recognized. She was on the edge of a mountain.

"Are you okay, Rachel?" Liam asked.

"Yeah, I don't do well with heights," she breathed. "It looks like we're probably a couple hundred feet up."

Rachel pressed the palms of her hands against her eyes and willed herself not to vomit. Her mind didn't seem to know which panic was more important now—the fact that she really wasn't in Austin, or the fact that she was sitting hundreds of feet up on the edge of a mountain.

Rachel breathed deeply. No one spoke, but she could feel the others looking at her. She turned to encourage them to take a look from the edge if they weren't bothered by heights, but the words didn't leave her mouth. Liam, Hester, and Gerald were still standing a few feet in front of the entrance to the cave. Rachel's jaw dropped when she looked back and saw the cave's exterior. She expected to see a plain mountain reaching up above their heads, instead carved into the mountainside was a massive, menacing stone face. The tunnel—the entrance opening—was the mouth of the face. Terrible teeth rimmed the ten foot wide mouth, and black smoke-stained soulless eyes stared out to the horizon. Moss grew all over—on its bulbous nose, on its frowning brow ridge, on its sneering lips.

"Where are we?" Rachel's brain buzzed. The world swirled around her and everything went black.

♦ ♦ ♦

Several minutes later Rachel's eyes fluttered open. "See, she's okay," Hester proclaimed inches from Rachel's face.

Hester's almost perfectly round face stared down at Rachel. Looking up, Rachel perceived that the silly old woman looked like a tiny wrinkled angel. Hester's white fluffy hair infused with sunlight looked like a halo. "Did we all die?" Rachel pondered.

With a nudge to Rachel's shoulder, Hester commanded, "Rachel, say something."

Rachel became aware she was lying on the ground in the dirt. Something hard and lumpy was under her head.

"Leave her alone, Bunny," said Gerald. "She's in shock."

"I'm not bothering her. I'm making sure she's okay," insisted Hester.

"I'm okay. I guess I passed out," Rachel responded. Stretching her left arm up towards her head, her fingers reaching out to explore the lumpy pillow, while asking, "What's under my head?"

"It's your purse," Liam answered from somewhere to her right.

Rachel pictured the lumpy contents of her purse—wallet, keys, cellphone, lip-gloss, deodorant, brush, pen, *The Mighty Arm that Built Egypt*. It's no wonder it didn't make a comfortable pillow.

Rachel turned her head toward the direction Liam's voice had come. He was sitting cross-legged on the ground facing the cave opening, staring up at the immense face.

"It reminds me a little of the entrance of a cave I saw in Bali," Liam said to Gerald, gesturing to the carved image.

"The Elephant Cave," answered Gerald. "I know what you mean, but I think the workmanship is closer to that of a cave in Bomarzo. The face of the god Orcus. See, the face is wide like Orcus." He paused for a few seconds with a transparent hand on his clean-shaven transparent chin before adding, "This isn't quite Orcus, but it's close."

Rachel was rusty on any ancient civilizations that weren't ancient Egypt, but Liam and Gerald's conversation had grabbed her attention. "What is Bomarzo? Is that where we are?" asked Rachel as she eased herself into a sitting position. She considered the idea that Gerald had figured out where they were while she was passed out. He was an incredibly experienced and celebrated professor after all. "Even if he is a know-it-all," she thought.

"It's a small village in Italy. In it lies a garden built around five hundred years ago—I don't remember exactly. However old it is, it looks like it belongs to a much older time." Gerald said. "The garden is home to many stone sculptures, most rather menacing, like this one. It is sometimes called 'Monster's Grove.' Its biggest draw is a cave with the face of the god Orcus, a god often associated with the underworld."

Gerald was standing with his back to the prairie, his feet planted almost on the edge of the mountain, surveying the carving. He strode forward until he was standing directly in front of the mouth of the cave. He stared up, above the row of teeth and snarling stone lips. "Did you notice that?" Gerald asked Liam, pointing to a moss covered section below the bulging nose.

"Is that writing?" Liam asked, rising to his feet to join Gerald before the entrance of the cave.

Rachel slowly got up, as well, and she and Hester joined Gerald and Liam. The group tried to decipher the inscription.

"This is extraordinary," uttered Gerald. "At the Orcus cave there is also an inscription. It says... it says... I can't seem to remember. I should remember!" He slapped himself in the head as though he were trying to knock the information loose.

"Is that the cave you told me about where you could hear a whisper from the front of the cave as plain as regular talking while inside?" asked Hester, smiling up at the tall apparition of her husband.

Gerald beamed at his tiny wife, almost shouting with joy, "Yes, that's it! That's it! The Orcus cave inscription is something along the lines of 'All Words Fly.'"

Gerald and Hester exchanged jubilant smiles. Liam said, "We should try to move the moss to see if we can decipher the inscription—see if it's the same as the one in Bomarzo."

"Good idea," agreed Gerald.

"Rachel can get on my shoulders and I'll lift her up so she can pull down the moss," Liam suggested.

"Can't we find a long stick or something and knock it down?" asked Rachel. She had quit a dance class once after they did one day of partner lifts. After hearing her dance partner pant and wheeze under her weight, her self-esteem just couldn't handle another class. She pictured Liam lifting her, his face getting red and sweaty like her dance partner's. Rachel was a perfectly average-sized person, but that dance class experience had made her insecure. *What if she was too heavy and hurt him?*

"Look around, Rachel. There are no sticks," Liam answered while motioning to the stone that surrounded them.

"Why don't you lift Hester?" Rachel tried.

"Even on my shoulders Hester couldn't reach that high. She's too small. And do you really think I should put a woman Hester's age on my shoulders?" Liam asked before turning to Hester to add, "No offence."

"None taken," was Hester's smiling response.

Rachel sighed before relenting, "Okay, I'll do it."

Liam kneeled on both knees and Rachel reluctantly took her seat on his shoulders. Being in that position made her think of her grandparent's pool and playing chicken fight with her cousins as a kid. It had easily been over twenty years since she'd sat on another person's shoulders. At least she wasn't in a bathing suit this time. Liam carefully stood.

"Oh, wow. This feels really high up," came Rachel's voice from about nine feet off the ground.

"You okay?" Liam asked from between her thighs.

Rachel thought to herself, "No, I feel like I'm going to faint and this is so awkward," but she said, "Yeah, I'm fine. Let's just do this quickly."

Liam moved closer to the cave entrance. Rachel reached out and grabbed ahold of two of the top stone teeth to steady herself. She was eye level with the top most teeth. They felt warm from the sun, and smooth from years of exposure to the elements.

"Try reaching your arm up," Gerald suggested. "Can you reach the moss?"

Rachel stretched her right arm up and her fingers barely grazed the fuzzy moss covering the inscription. "I think I'm going to have to really stretch to get it," Rachel responded, sounding unsure.

"I can help," Liam said, moving to the balls of his feet, lifting Rachel up another couple inches. Rachel peeled the moss from the stone in chunks. The more she worked at it, the easier it seemed to come.

"Hey, do you mind?" laughed Liam.

Rachel looked down to find she'd been accidently dropping moss on Liam's head. She dusted him off and apologized before pulling off the last bit of moss that covered the inscription. Liam kneeled for Rachel to get off his shoulders, and the group of four stared up at the newly exposed stone.

The inscription read, "Το φως και η σκιά δεν έχουν νόμο."

"It's Greek to me," joked Hester.

The others chuckled, and Rachel asked dubiously, "Do any of you read Greek?"

"Yeah, a little," Liam and Gerald answered in unison, then laughed.

Still laughing, Gerald said, "Let's see if we guess the same."

"It says something about there being no law, I think," said Liam.

"Yes, yes, I agree," nodded Gerald. "And... about light and shadow."

"Light and shadow have no law," whispered Rachel.

"Yes, exactly. How did you know that?" asked Gerald.

"The inside of the cave," answered Rachel, "the shadows were bouncing everywhere regardless of where the light was coming. What you each said just made it click—'light and shadow have no law.' It's like that other cave you told us about—"

"All words fly," Gerald said, eagerly nodding with Rachel's explanation.

"Yes, it was a description of what happened in the cave—words from the front of the cave traveled to the back. Is it possible these two caves are related?" Rachel wondered.

"Anything is possible," replied Gerald.

"Would that mean we could be in Italy?" ventured Rachel, her spirits rising.

Gerald turned towards the green prairie, and the others did the same. The grass rolled like the waves of an ocean—green, peaceful, and almost hypnotic. Looking out, Rachel's heart sank. She knew this couldn't be Italy. Even in the country you would be able to spot telephone poles or cell phone towers in the distance. For miles and miles there was nothing but green before them.

Liam broke the silence and answered Rachel's question. "The landscape doesn't look right. I spent all last summer exploring Italy, and I can't think of a single place of which this reminds me."

Rachel sighed. "We don't know where we are," she said flatly.

"The sun is high in the sky and we've all got legs," Hester chirped. "Let's explore—"

"Wait a second," Rachel interrupted. "The sun—it's got to be mid to late afternoon. But it was night. The awards ceremony was at night. We have not been here that long."

"Rachel, for the last time, we're not in Austin," said an exasperated Liam. "It's time to accept that something supernatural has happened. You're too smart to keep insisting otherwise."

Rachel knew they were in the middle of an unexplainable situation, but her logical mind had to try to make sense of it. It was trying desperately to fit the information before her eyes into something she knew or understood. Liam's words stung. Rachel felt her eyes fill with tears and her face redden. She turned her back on the group and stiffly said, "Let's do what Hester said. Let's explore."

Quickly wiping her eyes, Rachel picked up her purse from the ground where she had left it when it was her pillow. She mentally went over its contents again and thought to herself, "I won't be needing that lip-gloss."

Gerald led the group to the left of the cave entrance. Hester and Liam followed close behind while Rachel kept her distance trying to avoid looking at Liam.

"The ledge appears to narrow then wrap around the mountain," called Gerald over his shoulder. "Everyone use caution. Stay as close to the mountain as you can." Rachel looked down at her feet, the path before her narrowing with every step she took after the group.

"Rachel," Liam called. "Stay close to the mountain. If you get dizzy again, it would be best if you were already leaning on the mountain. We don't want you to fall off."

"Fall off?" Rachel made the mistake of glancing down. Below, to the left of her feet, she saw jagged rocks. She gasped and promptly glued herself to the mountainside to her right. Rachel willed herself not to pass out though she could feel her vision tunneling. She pressed her cheek against the smooth mountain rock. The sensation somehow soothed her and her vision returned to normal.

Rachel followed Liam's advice. As she inched along, she leaned against the mountainside. Their path became even narrower and Rachel wondered if it was wise for them to try this path. Perhaps they'd be safer inside the caves if they could relight the torches. Suddenly it occurred to Rachel that they didn't know who had lit those torches. Rachel instantly cheered with the thought of there being *someone* there who had lit the torches—someone who could help them and tell them where they were.

From in front of her, Rachel heard Liam humming. "Apparently I'm not the only one nervous," she thought.

Rachel noticed the narrow path they slowly walked was gradually sloping downward. She kept her eyes on the path while groping the mountainside. She grew hopeful. They might find people to help them, and they were certainly making their way down the mountain. Rachel smiled to herself and inwardly laughed that she was obviously less freaked out than Liam.

"I'm getting tired," croaked Hester in a voice too small even for her diminutive frame.

Rachel quickly turned her head toward the old woman, but couldn't see anything past Liam.

"Bunny, are you okay?" came Gerald's concerned voice.

"I... I... I..."

Rachel watched Liam swiftly lunge forward on the narrow path. She gasped in horror and realization of what was happening. Hester slumped and Liam grabbed her just as she was about to fall off the ledge.

"Bunny, Bunny," Gerald repeated in a panic.

"Hester, can you hear me?" asked Liam, cradling the tiny woman against his chest.

"Hester, Bunny, please wake up," begged a distraught Gerald.

Rachel was speechless. She stared at the scene in shock. Had Liam not acted so fast, Hester would be dead on the jagged rocks below. Liam was a hero. It seemed every time Rachel was ready to stop liking Liam, he did or said something to endear himself to her again. Saving a sweet old woman from dying was definitely going to give him a point in the good guy column.

"I'm awake, I'm awake," the tiny old woman seemed to complain, before asking, "Where's my breakfast?"

Gerald and Liam laughed, before Gerald answered, "You don't get breakfast because you were a naughty girl and almost fell off the mountain."

Hester pouted which only made the two men laugh more. "Hester, I'm going keep you close like this for the rest of the hike down the mountain, okay?" said Liam.

"Just as long as I get my breakfast, I don't care how much you want to hug me," she answered with some sass.

"She's likely dehydrated," Gerald suggested. "That's probably why she passed out. It's making her delusional. That's why she thinks it's breakfast time."

With the mention of the word "dehydrated" Rachel became aware of how thirsty she was. Her mouth felt dry and sticky.

She hoped that along with help they would find water at the bottom of this mountain.

The group continued their trek down the mountain. After some time, their path widened, and they were no longer at risk of falling off the edge. Just to be cautious, Rachel maintained her position glued against the mountainside for the entire journey. Rachel didn't look up from the path before her until she reached flat ground at the bottom of the mountain. When she let go of the mountain and lifted her eyes she was met by an unexpected landscape. Instead of the green prairie she had seen from the ledge in front of the cave, she was greeted by trees. Apparently, as they descended the mountain, they had also been going around it. The opposite side of the mountain had a completely different terrain. Before the group stood a large forest filled with tall ancient trees. On her lips lingered the same question that had dogged Rachel from the moment her vision became clear in the cave—

"Do I get breakfast now?" Hester asked hopefully.

"Where are we?" whispered Rachel.

CHAPTER 8

"She's definitely delirious," said Gerald to Liam and Rachel. "She's always a silly little thing, but I think she's dehydrated and maybe a little over tired from all this excitement."

"Let's put her under one of these trees and search for water," Liam suggested.

With an arm still wrapped around Hester, Liam guided the old woman to an inviting shady spot beneath a large oak tree. She rested her head against the trunk of the tree and smiled at everyone.

"I've got a secret," Hester giggled to herself.

The others exchanged looks and Gerald gently asked, "What's your secret, Bunny?

Hester frowned. "I don't remember."

She closed her eyes and fell asleep. Gerald turned to Rachel and Liam and said, "Two of us should look for water, and one should stay with Hester."

Rachel said a little too eager, "I want to look for water!" She also wanted to look for people—for help. She didn't want to be sitting still watching a sleeping old woman when she could be searching for the answer to where they were.

"I want to look, too," said Liam.

"All right. I will sit with Hester," Gerald said as he seated himself next to his sleeping wife.

As to not get lost and separated from Gerald and Hester, Rachel and Liam walked along the tree line that bordered the mountain. When they were descending the mountain, they had been traveling clockwise. They knew if they headed counterclockwise they would end up in the green prairie, so they continued their clockwise walk.

Rachel felt awkward in the silence of their walk, but didn't feel like she had anything to say to Liam. One moment he seemed like a great guy, the next he was inferring crazy conspiracy theories were possible or talking down to her. "Of course, the moment after that he might save the life of a sweet old lady. But still," Rachel thought to herself.

Liam broke the silence. "I hope we find water."

"Me, too," Rachel agreed.

"I didn't want to make a big deal about it when Hester is obviously worse off than we are, but with the hike in the cave, the hike down the mountain, and all the time in the sun..." Liam trailed off.

"We really need water," Rachel finished his sentence.

Liam nodded at Rachel, and they continued to walk in silence. It was warm, but the shade from the trees and a slight wind that caused the leaves to rustle kept them cool. Rachel was eager to find help and water, but she hadn't the foggiest idea of how they were going to find either aside from dumb luck. Her mother had tried to encourage her to go camping and learn survival skills as a teenager, but it had never interested her or seemed relevant to her life. "I guess I can add that to the 'things I was wrong about' category," Rachel thought to herself.

She cleared her throat and admitted to Liam, "I have no experience with camping, outdoorsy stuff, or adventure stuff. I haven't the slightest idea of how we're going to find water."

"Really?" he asked, sounding surprised. "Aside from your extreme fear of heights, you seem pretty natural out here. In the cave especially—you grabbed that torch and started exploring like it was nothing."

Rachel laughed while shaking her head. "Yeah, I've always thought if I were an animal I'd be a house cat, if that gives you any idea of how outdoorsy I am."

Liam chuckled. It made Rachel feel better to hear. When she met Liam, aside from thinking he was incredibly cute, she thought he seemed like a nice and cool guy. A big part of her wanted him to like her even if it wasn't romantically. Though, she wouldn't rule out romance.

"I work at a camping store," Liam confessed.

Rachel stopped to exclaim, "What?! That's great! We could use your knowledge, for sure."

Liam put his hand in his pocket and pulled out a tiny yellow box. "I'm embarrassed to admit that I forgot I had these in my pocket all along."

Liam shook the yellow box in his hand. Rachel heard a dull clinking.

"Waterproof matches," he said. "When we were stuck with our torches extinguished it never occurred to me that I had matches. I was too busy freaking out to remember that I was literally carrying the solution to our problem in my pocket."

"The torches would have gone out again anyway from the wind in the tunnel," Rachel reassured him. "And we made it out of the cave fine. Those matches could come in handy later if we need to build a fire."

Liam shrugged, then shared, "I enjoy camping and survival stuff. I spend every summer backpacking different places. Between that and working at the camping store it's hard not to be in the mindset of always being prepared."

"That's smart," offered Rachel.

"I usually carry a number of survival tools on me, but I only put the basics in my pockets when I left for the awards ceremony. I didn't think I was at risk of needing water purifying tablets, for example," he said.

"You usually carry water purifying tablets?" asked Rachel.

"Yes, I do," answered Liam. He smiled and laughed at himself. "I generally think you can't be too prepared. Unfortunately for the awards ceremony, besides my phone and my wallet, the only things I put in my pockets were my waterproof matches, some paracord, and my multi-tool."

Rachel motioned to her purse and said, "I've got a hair brush and a book written by Hester."

"Good to know we're prepared for a bad hair day or an autograph signing by H.H. Mays," he said. His smile was genuine and his laugh infectious. She couldn't help but join him.

They started walking again, and Rachel asked, "Mr. Outdoors, do you know how to find water?"

"We'll probably have to go more into this forest. But, I still think it's worth checking the perimeter first, since it's the easiest way for us to not get lost. If we don't find anything, we can just follow the tree line back to Gerald and Hester, versus being in the middle of a bunch of trees and getting all turned around," Liam said. "But for now, we should keep our eyes open for birds. They're more likely to stay close to water sources."

It was then that Rachel realized she hadn't seen a single bird, or any creature for that matter. She intently listened for the chirping of birds, but all she heard was the rustling of leaves. When she was a sophomore in college her roommate was obsessed with scary movies. In most monster movies it was a sure sign the monster was near when all the animals had vanished. Rachel looked over her shoulder afraid she might find the Wolfman behind her. Nothing was there, of course. Her imagination was out of control. She looked to her left, towards the mountain and before turning frontward again she noticed something out of the ordinary from the corner of her eye.

"Hey, what's that?" she stopped to ask while pointing to the base of the mountain.

Cut into the mountainside was a small alcove—the beginnings of a cave, perhaps—manmade, like the cave where they started their adventure. What caught Rachel's eye were colorful designs on the alcove wall. From this distance—about fifty feet—the only thing Rachel could make out was a giant painting of a hand. The bright turquoise paint caught her eye.

"Let's take a look," Liam answered, and they left the tree line to investigate the alcove.

Standing in the alcove, Rachel observed it appeared to be about seven feet high by ten feet wide, and no deeper than six feet. The walls were covered in primitive painting. Besides the large hand, there were signs Rachel and Liam guessed were meant to represent water and food. Pointing to the water sign, Rachel said, "Hopefully that means there is water near."

"No, kidding," Liam answered, leaning against the alcove wall. "I am so thirsty."

Rachel stood looking at the water sign painted on the wall and thought she heard the casual splashing and burbling of a stream. She said to Liam, "I think I might be getting as delirious as Hester. I'm so thirsty I think I'm hearing water."

Liam looked at Rachel and then at the painted wall of the alcove in disbelief. He pressed his ear to the wall, then smiled from ear to ear. "There's water behind this wall," he said confidently.

"What? No way," Rachel said before putting her ear to the wall. She could clearly hear the sound she thought she'd imagined. Water. A relieved smile spread across her face before it dawned on her there was no path to the water. There was a wall between them and quenched thirst. She frowned and complained, "We've found water, but no way to get to it."

Liam stepped back from the wall. His eyes darted from corner to corner. He turned to Rachel with gleaming eyes and posed a question, "What if this were like the Great Pyramid of Giza?"

"What do you mean?" Rachel asked, confused.

"What if this," he said knocking on the alcove wall, "is a false wall? A door."

Rachel's pulse quickened with the thrill of discovery. "Of course. A door." She examined the wall again, and said, "If it's a door, there has to be a release or a trigger to open it."

Rachel pushed on part of the wall. Liam joined her. They both put their full weight against the wall, but nothing happened. They stood back and Liam said, "It was a valiant effort. I guess it's not a door."

Rachel scanned the primitive paintings again on the wall. Her eyes rested on the giant turquoise hand. From this close up it looked like a giant palm print—the sort kindergarten teachers have their students do as art projects—though no kindergartner, or grown person for that matter, could have a palm so huge. Rachel asked herself, "Could it be so obvious?"

She put her hand in the center of the palm print and pushed. The wall swung open, revealing an immense cavern. There were torches all around, like the torches from the cave. Barrels lined one wall, along with clay jugs, and earthen bowls.

Through the center of the cavern was a beautiful rushing stream.

"Amazing," breathed Liam.

They stepped through the opening in the mountain and were surprised by how cool the air felt. Looking at the supplies stacked against the wall and the torches, Rachel stated, "This is someone's hideout or home."

Liam walked to the wall and grabbed a bowl. "I hope they don't mind if I borrow this," he said before walking to the stream and filling it with water. Liam drank its contents, then filled it again and offered it to Rachel.

After both drank, Rachel suggested, "We should see if the jugs are empty. If they are we should fill them with water and bring them back to Hester and Gerald."

"Good idea, except we'll only need one jug," Liam said. "Gerald is a ghost, remember?"

Rachel laughed, "Oh, yeah." Somehow she had forgotten that Gerald would not need water the way the rest of them did.

The two checked the jugs and found that every jug was empty except one. The one full jug smelled of strong wine. Liam joked that they might pair the wine with some fish from the stream. Rachel thought to herself, "If there are any fish." She still hadn't seen or heard any animals.

Rachel and Liam began to exit the cavern, when Liam suggested, "We probably shouldn't both go. It could start getting dark soon, and it will be easier to find the entrance to this place if one of us stays outside with a torch."

"Good thinking," said Rachel, hoping Liam didn't mind being the one to go back for the others.

"I'll go back for Gerald and Hester," Liam volunteered. "It just makes sense. If Hester isn't strong enough to walk, I can carry her."

"Sounds like a plan," answered a relieved Rachel.

Liam filled one of the empty jugs with water from the stream then told Rachel he'd be back soon. Rachel waved to Liam until he had turned his back and was almost out of sight, then she reentered the cavern to explore. She expected to find more primitive art but found none. She guessed that the symbols they'd found on the alcove wall weren't supposed to be artwork, but simple directions indicating that it was a door. The water symbol was obviously meant to indicate the stream, and the symbols for food might represent the barrels. They looked like the sort of barrels that might hold grains. Rachel pulled the lid off one only to find it empty. "That's okay," she said to her growling stomach, "there are five more barrels. One might have food."

The next two barrels Rachel tried were also empty. She went to the fourth barrel both hopeful and doubtful. She opened it and inside she found ground meal. "Yes!" Rachel yelled, and her voice echoed through the cavern.

She scooped a handful up and held it to her nose to smell. "Perhaps cornmeal."

Rachel emptied the meal from her hand into the barrel and dusted her hand off on her jeans. She picked up and uncorked one of the empty jugs. She grabbed a torch from the wall and placed it—fire up—into the jug. "Instant torch stand," Rachel said triumphantly to herself, proud of her own ingenuity even if no one else was there to appreciate it. She took her improvised torch stand outside and set it near the alcove opening and sat facing the direction from which the others would come.

Rachel sat with her back against the stone and closed her eyes, willing herself to listen as closely as she could. All she could hear was the wind and the rushing stream. No birds. The idea made her stomach feel tight and squirmy. "It's okay," she told herself. "This isn't a horror film. It's really a very peaceful place, wherever it is."

Rachel could forget for moments at a time that they were lost and didn't know where they were. Other concerns became more important like water or food, and the idea they were lost who knows where was pushed from her mind. Now that she and Liam had found water, and she'd found the cornmeal in the barrel, she was no longer worried about dehydration or starvation. Her mind was speeding back to the idea she wasn't anywhere she recognized and the circumstances that had brought her here were unknown.

"You need a distraction," Rachel said to herself. She opened her purse and pulled out *The Mighty Arm that Built Egypt* and found the place where she had left off:

> *Malachi hurriedly searched for a place to hide. The heavy steps had almost reached the bedchamber when Malachi squeezed himself behind a massive wardrobe. His heart thudded. He held his breath and waited for any sound to indicate Ra had entered the room.*
>
> *Ra was the only one who would have such confident, powerful footsteps. Yes, the others were enormous like he, but none had his grandiosity, none matched him in pride.*

Malachi heard nothing but his own beating heart in his ears. He thought to himself, "I must have misheard. Perhaps it was just someone passing by." He let out his breath and spied around the side of the wardrobe.

Malachi's blood ran cold. He was eye level with two gigantic bronze legs and the familiar, extravagant golden sandals of Ra. Malachi instantly felt like he was flying. Ra had effortlessly lifted him up by the shoulders.

Crunch. Rachel looked up from her book. Such a small sound would not have normally stirred her from reading, but with the only sounds around her being the rustling leaves in the trees and the stream in the cavern, anything else stood out as though amplified over loud speakers. The crunch sounded like someone stepping on a twig or dry leaves. Rachel half expected to see Liam with Hester and Gerald approaching. However, there was no one there.

Rachel strained her ears trying to listen harder. "Just the wind in the leaves and water in the stream," she concluded. Rachel laughed when she realized she was holding her breath. "I am Malachi," she giggled. "I'm afraid whoever lives here or uses this place as storage is going to show up suddenly, find me here, and I'll be unwelcome."

The sun was setting, casting a dull orange hue over the ground between the mountain and the tree line. The leaves of the trees looked more like fall leaves in the strange orange light. Rachel thought to herself it was smart of Liam to suggest that she stay here with a torch at the entrance. It would have been difficult to find this place again in the dark.

Rachel placed her book back in her purse. There was no way she'd be able to stay focused reading with every little sound pulling her out of the story. She was too on edge.

Rachel stood and stretched her aching body. She paced the alcove and continued to scan the trees. Rachel couldn't quite shake the anxious feeling she had over the crunching sound that had roused her from her book. Had she heard birds chirping or seen squirrels scurrying up trees at any point that afternoon the crunch would not have even been perceived. Now every shadow in the trees before her seemed to hide a stranger watching her. "Paranoid," Rachel said aloud.

To prove her own paranoia to herself, Rachel addressed the trees. "Okay, if anyone is out there, just come on out. Obviously, I'm not very scary. I won't hurt you if you don't hurt me," she said toward the trees. No voice greeted her; no stranger emerged from the shadows.

"See, you're paranoid," Rachel accused herself again.

From a distance Rachel could hear a small voice almost squeak, "Who's she talking to? I can't see that far!"

Rachel's stomach dropped and she felt fear pulsating in every inch of her body. From a great distance away, Rachel could just barely make out three figures emerging from the tree line—Liam, Hester, and Gerald. From the sudden fright, then subsequent relief, Rachel felt lightheaded. She staggered against the alcove wall, then lowered herself to the floor. It was only Hester she had heard speak. It wasn't a stranger. She wasn't Malachi facing certain danger.

Rachel was relieved to have the others join her. It was now almost dark, and she was hungry from the day's exertion. "Hopefully one of them knows how to cook that meal into a palatable food source," she thought to herself.

When the others reached the alcove, Rachel stood and followed them inside the cavern. She showed them the barrel of meal and asked if anyone knew what to do with it. Gerald suggested they gather dry sticks and rocks to create a fire. He said if they added a bit of water to some meal and rolled it into a ball, they might be able to cook it on the rocks.

"Why don't we try to catch some fish?" Hester asked, peering into the stream.

"Do you see any fish, Hester?" asked Rachel.

"I don't have my glasses, so I don't see a lot," answered Hester spryly.

Liam walked to Hester's side and looked into the stream. "I don't remember seeing any earlier. Did you, Rachel?" he asked.

"Nope," was Rachel's answer.

"Cornmeal it is!" declared Hester.

She was much restored from the water, but Gerald still insisted his tiny wife not overexert herself. She sat against the wall with the barrels, bowls, and jugs. Liam and Rachel gathered a few stones and an arm full of dry sticks. Rachel found one almost perfectly flat rock which she stated was the perfect cooking rock. Liam smiled to himself remembering Rachel's confession of how non-outdoorsy she was.

The two brought the rocks and sticks inside the cavern and followed Gerald's instructions on how to make the best fire and cooking surface. Liam pulled his waterproof matches out of his pocket to light the fire, but Rachel stopped him. "Save your matches," she said. "You don't know if we might need them for later. For now just use one of the torches to light the fire."

"You should gather dry leaves to use as kindling, as well," remarked Gerald. "The fire will light easier with dry leaves than dry sticks alone."

Liam went back outside to gather leaves while Rachel filled a bowl with water from the stream and carried it over to the barrels. She set the bowl on top of the empty barrel next to the one that contained cornmeal. She placed an empty bowl beside the water bowl and alternated between filling her left hand with water and her right hand with meal. Rachel sprinkled water from her left hand into the meal in her right hand and formed small balls. She placed the gooey balls in the empty bowl.

After a few minutes, Hester looked up at Rachel and asked, "Can I help, dear?"

Rachel had almost finished filling the bowl with soggy cornmeal balls, so she said, showing the tiny old woman the nearly full bowl, "If you think we need to make more than this, then you can help me with the next bowl."

Hester smiled and said, "Let's try cooking those first. If we're still hungry, I'll help make more."

Rachel knew the little old woman wanted to be helpful, so her mind raced for an idea of something she could help with until it crashed into something. Her book!

"Hester, do you think you could do something for me?" Rachel asked.

"Of course, dear," replied Hester. "I would love to be of some use."

"Could you get the book and a pen out of my purse and sign it for me?" Rachel asked with a smile.

Hester giggled while rising to her feet. "You're just trying to tease me, I'm sure, but I like signing books so I'm going to take this as seriously as if we were at a Sci-Fi convention and you'd waited two hours in line to ask me to sign it."

"I am serious, Hester," protested Rachel. "I'm really enjoying *The Mighty Arm that Built Egypt*. Do people really wait two hours in line to have a book signed?"

"Sci-Fi fans are the best!" enthused Hester. She retrieved Rachel's book and pen and sat again on the floor of the cave. Hester's down cast head and busy pen suggested to Rachel she shouldn't interrupt the authoress while she worked, so Rachel continued rolling cornmeal balls in silence.

Liam returned with leaves before Rachel finished rolling the cornmeal balls. He quickly made the fire, and before long it was burning hot. Gerald informed them that the flat stone was probably warm enough to start cooking, so Rachel and Liam both carefully dropped squishy cornmeal balls onto the stone. Watching it cook, Rachel realized they had nothing to flip it over with or even retrieve it without risking getting burned.

Rachel turned to tell Liam, only to find him whittling a two-pronged fork out of a long stick with his multi-tool. "I completely forgot we'd need something to grab them with until we dropped them on the stone," he said while bits of bark fell to the ground.

Rachel was glad that if she were going to be stuck in some mystery place, at least she was stuck with Liam. Liam was resourceful. Rachel watched as he speared one of the balls, pulling it away from the flames. He turned it over in his hand, muttering, "Ow, ow, ow," then dropped it back onto the stone to finish cooking on the opposite side. He repeated this process with the cornmeal ball that was already cooking.

Hester carried an empty bowl to Liam and Rachel for the cornmeal balls they had cooked into cakes. Rachel and Liam continued dropping cornmeal balls on the flat stone to cook until the bowl of squishy uncooked cornmeal was empty and the bowl of cornmeal cakes full.

Rachel filled three jugs with water from the stream and placed the jugs next to the bowl of cornmeal cakes near the fire. Hester was already seated there, along with Gerald. Liam walked over to the wall where the barrels, bowls, and jugs were. His back was to the group when he said, "We can't forget this."

When Liam turned around Rachel observed he was holding the jug filled with wine. "We don't even know if that's safe to drink," she protested, her brow furrowing.

Liam uncorked it, smelled it like they had earlier, and said, "It just smells strong. I'm sure it's fine. And, seriously, we don't know if the water we've been drinking is safe to drink either."

"I'm game," Hester said, eyeing the jug of wine.

Liam and Rachel sat near the fire with Hester and Gerald. Liam placed the jug between himself and Rachel. "I'm not going to drink any of that," Rachel said stubbornly to Liam, pointing to the wine. "Put it between yourself and Hester."

"Party pooper," said Hester under her breath.

"I think that's extremely wise, Rachel," Gerald said. "You have no idea what could be in that wine or if it could be spoiled. I don't think you should drink it either, Hester."

Hester picked up the jug, held it to her mouth, and took a giant swig of the unknown liquid. After drinking it she stuck her tongue out at Gerald and Rachel, then winked at Liam before melodramatically clutching her throat and coughing like a soap opera actress. "Poison, poison," she jokingly moaned before breaking into a mischievous laugh. She passed the jug to Liam and he took a sip as well.

Rachel picked up the bowl of cornmeal cakes and held it out towards Hester and Liam while saying, "Would you like some food to go with your poison?"

Everyone laughed. Rachel, Liam, and Hester dug into the cakes. The party was mostly quiet while they ate and drank. Gerald, with a serious face, finally interrupted the feast to ask, "What happened to the medallions?"

"Our awards?" Liam asked, between sips from the wine jug. "What-what about them?"

"Someone stole them!" said a red faced tipsy Hester. "We should have never donated them to the university, Gerry!"

Gerald looked at Hester with a mixture of love and exasperation. "I don't know that someone stole them, Bunny. I was just wondering where they are. Do you all still have your medallions?"

"Mine's in my pocket," said Liam.

"Mine's in my purse," answered Rachel before adding, "Hester, isn't yours in your pocket?"

The inebriated octogenarian patted her lime green pantsuit jacket searching for pockets. "No, I swear someone took it!"

"Try your pants pockets, Bunny," suggested Gerald.

Hester pulled a butterscotch candy out of her right pants pocket and the medallion out of the left. "Bingo!" she exclaimed.

"Bunny, I think you should give your medallion to Rachel for safe keeping," advised Gerald.

"All right," she said, popping the butterscotch candy in her mouth, before adding with a note of defiance, "But if anyone steals it from Rachel, I'm gonna blame you."

Rachel took the medallion offered to her and placed it in her purse with her own medallion. Her book and pen were back inside her purse, too. She hadn't seen Hester put them back. Hester certainly was quick for a woman her age.

Slightly slurring his words, Liam suggested, "Do you think these medallions could have been like, uh, um, like homing beacons? Teleportation devices?"

"I think that's exactly what they were," answered Gerald with a confidant knowing look.

Rachel was quiet. They were back to talking about being beamed some place. Only now she didn't know how she could possibly argue with the premise. She didn't have any better ideas, and she wasn't going to argue with two drunk people and a ghost. Rachel stood, slung her purse across her body, and said, "I think I need some fresh air. I'm going to sit outside and read for a while, I think."

She got up and strolled outside. Rachel took her seat next to her improvised torch stand in the alcove. She sat cross legged on the ground in the torchlight. She was pulling her book out of her bag when she noticed movement at the entrance to the cavern. Liam was standing there, leaning against the wall.

"Hester just fell asleep," he said looking wobbly.

"That's good," Rachel replied, somewhat uncomfortable being the only one sober besides the ghost.

"I'm feeling pretty-pretty-pretty worn out," Liam admitted. "I think I'm gonna get some shut-eye, too."

"Sounds like a good idea. I'm going to sit out here and read. I'm sure I wouldn't be able to get to sleep yet if I tried," Rachel said.

"Shoulda had some wine," Liam grinned. He patted her on the head then staggered over to the wall with the supplies. He slowly eased himself down the wall, laid down, and instantly fell asleep.

Rachel smoothed out her hair. Being the sober one around drunks was never fun to Rachel. She was still glad she hadn't had any wine though. In stressful or foreign situations she wanted to stay as sharp and clear as possible.

The wind tousled the hair Rachel had just smoothed and made her torch flicker. For what felt like the millionth time that day she listened for the sound of wild animals. "Where are the owls?" she wondered before opening her book.

Rachel read the last paragraph she'd read earlier:

> *Malachi's blood ran cold. He was eye level with two gigantic bronze legs and the familiar, extravagant golden sandals of Ra. Malachi instantly felt like he was flying. Ra had effortlessly lifted him up by the shoulders.*

Crunch. For the second time that day Rachel's reading was interrupted by a crunching sound. She turned towards the trees half expecting nothing, half expecting finally to spot a wild animal, but Rachel's vision was completely obscured. Something large and warm had wrapped itself around Rachel's entire face. She lifted her hands to her face and tried frantically to pry it free, but she wasn't strong enough. Rachel couldn't see. She couldn't breathe. She tried screaming, but it came out as only a strangled mumble. She could barely make out the muffled voice of someone yelling, "Rachel! It's got Rachel!" before she felt herself lifted off the ground and away into the night.

CHAPTER 9

Liam awoke to the sound of Gerald's frantic yelling. It felt like it had just been seconds earlier that he'd fallen asleep. Liam opened his eyes but didn't see Gerald. "I must have dreamt it," he decided, before falling back into a deep sleep. In his dream he was floating on his back in a large pool. Everything around him was gold and turquoise. Luxurious and relaxing.

"Liam! Liam wake up!" Gerald's voice interrupting Liam's dream. "Liam, get up!"

Disoriented, Liam tried to stand, but found himself too unsteady on his feet. "What's going on?" he slurred while leaned back on his elbows. The cavern floor was hard and cold, but it still seemed to invite him to go back to sleep.

Gerald frantically paced. "Rachel was taken."

"Taken?" asked Liam. Nothing made sense. Why was Gerald yelling? "Taken? Like she disappeared? Like what happened to us in the ballroom?"

Liam pictured Rachel vanishing into thin air. One second there, the next gone. The thought drew him into his imagination. Liam closed his eyes and began drifting back to sleep.

"Wake up!" Gerald shouted.

Liam startled awake and muttered, "Sorry."

"Rachel was abducted," Gerald said, still pacing. "I couldn't stop it—him."

"It? Him?" asked a confused and still inebriated Liam. "Someone kidnapped Rachel?"

"Yes, that's what I've been trying to tell you!" Gerald insisted.

"Why didn't you stop them? Where did they go?" Liam inquired.

"Liam, I understand that you're drunk, but you've got to remember that I am a ghost," was Gerald's exasperated response. "I can't stop anything. I cannot touch anything. I was helpless to stop them."

"Oh yeah," Liam mumbled.

Gerald continued, "I tried to follow them. But the thing that took Rachel... It wasn't a man. It was giant! I couldn't keep up. I lost them in the forest. It was so dark I don't know which direction they went. When I was certain I couldn't find them, I turned around and came back here and woke you. You can at least pick up a torch and try to find your way through the forest to find them."

Liam covered his face with his hands and moaned. He ran his hands through his hair and cried, "I can't. I can't even stand, Gerald."

Liam wore self-loathing like a heavy coat. It weighed him down. Gerald paced. Hester snored.

"Rachel was right," said Liam. "I shouldn't have drank that wine. It was stupid. It was reckless. We don't even know where we are, and now someone has kidnapped Rachel."

Hester snorted in her sleep, then resumed snoring. She was still wrapped in Liam's blazer. She looked warm and content next to the fire Liam and Rachel had built earlier. Gerald stood over her, the bowl of cornmeal cakes sat close by, still a quarter full.

"Crawl over here and eat the rest of these cakes and drink a jug of water," commanded Gerald. "We need you sober. I'm powerless to help Rachel. And knowing my Hester, she won't be awake for hours—not that she'd be much help against a giant."

Liam obeyed. The word "giant" was now on repeat in his head. Giant. Giant. Giant. "Could Gerald mean an actual giant, or just a large man?" Liam wondered. He felt nauseated. "I think I'm gonna be sick," he told Gerald, before stumbling outside to throw up.

"That was a first," Liam told Gerald, as he staggered back into the cavern and resumed his seat by the fire. "I've never been glad to throw up before."

Liam ate the last of the cornmeal cakes and finished his jug of water. He didn't look one hundred percent, but he looked much improved. He stood shakily and walked to the stream to refill his water jug. With the jug in his left hand, he took a torch from the wall with his right, and asked Gerald to show him where Rachel had been taken into the woods.

"I'll take you the direction I followed them, but we'll need to be quick. I don't want to leave Hester alone for long," Gerald said, looking down at his sleeping wife.

Gerald exited the cavern, with Liam walking so quickly behind that sometimes he walked through Gerald's blue-green transparent heels. For a few minutes they walked in silence until Gerald spoke. "I think it was about here when I lost them. I'm not sure if they continued straight or veered left or right. I couldn't see them anymore, and the thing that took her seemed to move more quietly than a deer."

Liam felt sick. He wasn't sure if it was the alcohol still or his nerves. "Gerald, you've called it a 'thing' and a 'giant'..."

Liam gulped. "Was Rachel taken by an actual giant or just a large man?"

Gerald paused, looking around, as though he were afraid of someone overhearing. "I've never seen a man on Earth that large," he answered.

Liam stared at Gerald in disbelief. Liam was not a skeptic—he enjoyed reading sci-fi and fantasy and wasn't against the idea that some of it might be real. However, the last twenty-four-hours had proved a challenge for him to take in, even if he wouldn't have admitted that to Rachel.

"This has been one crazy day," he said to Gerald, staring off into the trees before him. "I met two authors, won an award, was transported to some unknown place, met a ghost, and now I'm going giant hunting."

"Good luck, son," said Gerald.

"Thanks," returned Liam.

Gerald turned and headed back to the cavern and his sleeping wife. Liam walked straight ahead, jug at his side and torch before him.

♦ ♦ ♦

Rachel slept on a cloud. She opened her eyes and found planets rotating in a figure eight above her. Their proximity overwhelming and wonderful. She watched angels float by dressed like Egyptian gods. They waved at her before flying away—up, up, up to the cycling planets. Everything was gold and sandstone and sunshine. A familiar smell surrounded her. *Sandalwood.*

The sun rising bright in her face was what woke Rachel from her dream. She faced an open window with white gossamer curtains drawn back. She felt too warm beneath the piles of sheets and blankets that covered her. Rachel's imagination traveled back to the night before. The last thing she remembered was being carried through the forest by something much larger than herself. Her feet dangling, her ribs aching, her air supply failing her. "I must have fainted," Rachel thought to herself.

Unlike the rotating planets and floating angels, the sandalwood was real. The air was thick with it. Rachel kicked off the sheets and blankets and sat up. She was in an enormous bed. "Perfect for sleep-overs," she thought, remembering nights from her childhood. When she was twelve, with a group of her friends she would take the cushions off the couches and all the extra pillows and blankets from the house to make a giant bed in the living room.

Rachel looked around. The room was beautiful. Like in her dream, she was surrounded by gold and sandstone. Everything was out of proportion though. Or perhaps it was she who was out of proportion to the room. Like she was a toddler in the world of adults. Everything seemed huge.

She slid out of bed and found herself barefooted. Though the room was warm, the stone floor was cool on her bare feet. Walking around the bed, she found her shoes and socks neatly placed at the foot of the bed. Rachel went to the window, hoping to get an idea of where she might be.

From the window Rachel saw a village—mostly mud huts with thatched roofs, some taller buildings made of stone. In the distance she could see water—"An ocean, maybe," she conjectured. The beach surrounding it backed up to large trees, most of which appeared to be evergreens from this distance.

The window from which she looked was high up, at least three stories, she guessed. It was high enough up to make her feel queasy looking down. Rachel tried to ignore her vertigo, so she could get a better idea of her surroundings.

She could see people in the streets below, going into buildings, carrying things, doing business, probably. She couldn't tell if they were her size or if they were large enough to fill the giant room in which she had awoke. Her perspective was skewed since she didn't know how high up she was. She stepped back from the window to allow her stomach to relax and stop the room from spinning.

Despite not knowing where she was, Rachel was calm. She was looking on the bright side—"I'm still alive, and I feel well rested," she thought while walking to the foot of the bed to retrieve her shoes and socks. Rachel sat on the floor to put them on, and from the floor looking up at all the large furniture in the room she felt even smaller. She imagined she was like Alice having eaten the side of the mushroom that made her smaller. "What was in that cornmeal?" she wondered.

The similarities of her situation and Malachi's in *The Mighty Arm that Built Egypt* hadn't escaped her either. Rachel considered the idea she was still dreaming or having a vivid hallucination. The cornmeal hadn't shrunk her like Alice, but maybe it drugged her. What if it was laced with hallucinogens? She tried to laugh at herself. She walked up to the large wardrobe against the wall next to the window and looked behind it saying, "Malachi, are you there?"

There was no Malachi. It was just her, alone in a room made for a giant. She stretched her arm up and pulled the wardrobe door open. Inside she found folded blankets like those that had covered her while she slept. She also found her purse sitting on the bottom shelf.

"Yes," Rachel said grabbing her purse and pulling it over her head so it hung across her body. She opened it to see if everything was still inside. She didn't notice anything was missing except *The Mighty Arm that Built Egypt*.

"Of course," remembered Rachel. "I was holding it when whatever attacked me grabbed me. I probably dropped it." Rachel was disappointed she wouldn't get to know what happened to Malachi.

For the first time Rachel thought about her friends and wondered if they were okay. She wondered if they'd all been attacked and whisked off into the night. Rachel remembered hearing a muffled voice yelling when she was taken—probably Gerald. Gerald, who as a ghost, would have been helpless. Rachel pictured Hester, tiny, frail, and in her eighties being roughly handled the way she had been. She was sure Liam would have been better at fighting off any attacker. Then Rachel remembered that both Liam and Hester were passed out drunk last night. "Anything could have happened to them," she realized.

Rachel pushed the wardrobe door shut and approached the giant door to the room. It reminded Rachel of the doors she'd seen on cathedrals in Europe. It was large, like everything around her, and ornate. Like she had done with the wardrobe, she stretched her arm up and attempted the handle. Unlike the wardrobe, however, the door didn't open. It was locked.

"What now?" Rachel asked herself.

She pictured all the movies she'd seen where kids had escaped groundings from tyrannical parents by tying bedsheets together and escaping through second story windows. If that was her only option, she'd try it, but Rachel wasn't feeling too confident in her knot tying skills. She also tried not to think about how high up she was. *Did she have enough sheets and blankets to make a rope?* Rachel began separating the many sheets from the blankets on the bed and took the extra blankets from the wardrobe. She had three sheets and five blankets. The sheets would be easier to tie together, so she'd start with them.

"This would work better if I had a knife," Rachel decided, eyeing a sheet that was at least fifteen feet long and twenty feet wide. "I just need a knife to start a tear, and I could rip it the rest of the way."

She looked around the room. Rachel knew it was unlikely her captor would leave a sharp object just lying around, but it didn't hurt to look.

Having already explored the wardrobe, Rachel walked passed it and up to the vanity that stood next to the ornate door. It had many drawers—four on each side. She couldn't reach the top two. "But maybe if I pull the bottom drawers out, I can climb them to reach the highest ones," she said to herself.

Rachel tried the right side first. She gripped the golden handle on the lowest drawer and pulled. The drawer squeaked, opening but a few inches. Rachel leaned back, allowing her body weight to do the work. The drawer screeched, opening a few more inches. The screech was loud though. "If anyone is near, they definitely heard that," Rachel thought.

The top of the drawer was waist level. Rachel leaned over the drawer to see what was inside. "Nothing sharp," she sighed. The drawer was full of glass bottles filled with yellow and amber liquids. "Probably perfume or cologne," Rachel assessed.

She reached up to the next drawer's handle—it was about eye level. Like the other drawer, it was also heavy. She could only budge it about an inch. Climbing up on the first drawer's edge, Rachel was able to peek into the second drawer. It looked like more bottles of liquid. "What good will perfume do me?" She aggressively put her shoulder against the drawer and pushed it closed.

Rachel climbed down. She tried the bottom drawer on the left side and it wouldn't budge. Neither would the drawer above it. She'd have to really climb to reach the top drawers, but it didn't look like she was going to find anything. Rachel kicked the open bottom drawer on the right. The bottles inside clinked and jingled.

"Glass!" she exclaimed. Rachel reached into the drawer and pulled out one bottle filled with amber liquid. The bottle was the size of a gallon of milk. Rachel took the bottle and threw it with all her might to the ground. It shattered, sending shards of glass everywhere. The same sandalwood scent Rachel had smelled upon waking permeated the room.

Rachel dragged one of the sheets near the puddle of perfume without getting it wet. She carefully used the edge of the sheet to pick up one of the shards of glass. With the shard half wrapped in sheet, Rachel shoved the uncovered point of the shard into a spot at the top center of one of the other two sheets, creating a hole. She put down the sheet wrapped shard and with both hands pulled at the hole she had made in the sheet. The sheet easily ripped, and soon it was two separate pieces.

As Rachel was tying the two pieces of the sheet together, creating her first section of rope, she heard a sound at the door. Rachel saw the door handle move, but before the door opened Rachel threw down her knotted sheets and grabbed the sheet with the shard of glass.

The door swung open, a large shadow loomed in the doorway. She couldn't see the creature's face, or any features. The light was shining from behind it obscuring every detail. All Rachel could make out was the thing's massive size. It matched the room. Enormous; at least twice the size of Rachel.

The thing stepped forward and closed the giant door. Without the light shining from behind, the immense man became clear. He looked like a regular man, only he might be as tall as a lamppost, probably twelve feet tall. All his features were in proportion to his height. His body was lean and tan. He was shirtless, but wore a sort of skirt or kilt made of linen, and he wore woven sandals on his feet. Against his bare chest rested a flat gold pendant. His head was shaved bald, and he had intense brown eyes so dark they were almost black. All of this Rachel observed in a second. Again she considered the idea she might be dreaming. It was like *The Mighty Arm that Built Egypt* had come alive before her.

The giant's gaze covered the room—the open drawer, the broken perfume bottle, the blankets and sheets strewn everywhere, including the ripped sheet. His unblinking eyes met Rachel's. She had never seen eyes so dark. He broke eye contact to assess again the scene before him.

He turned his intense eyes back to Rachel and asked, "Why have you made a mess of my quarters?"

CHAPTER 10

Rachel wasn't sure what she had expected the giant to say, but asking her about the mess she'd made certainly wasn't it. Still holding the sheet wrapped shard, she looked around the room.

It looked pretty bad. She remembered how immaculate it had looked when she awoke. Everything in its place. She wiggled her toes inside her shoes thinking about how she had found her shoes and socks placed neatly at the foot of the bed. The room had looked like it belonged in a fancy spa, only everything was obviously too large.

Rachel started to feel bad about what she had done, then she remembered she had only made a mess because she had been trying to escape—escape because she had been kidnapped. Looking at the giant's hands she guessed that was what had covered her face. The thing that covered her face had felt warm and soft like the palm of someone's hand, but it had seemed too large. But a basketball would look like a softball in this man's gigantic palm.

"I was trying to escape," Rachel stated. She was a little surprised by how brave she sounded. She was actually terrified, but if she were a stranger hearing her own voice she would have never guessed.

The giant disregarded her, turning his attention again to the disordered room. He picked up a sheet and began mopping up the puddle left by the broken bottle. Carefully pushing the pieces of broken glass into a pile, he muttered under his breath, "This wasn't necessary."

Rachel remained rooted where she had stood since the enormous man entered the room. She was glued to one spot, sheet wrapped shard held before her. The giant moved closer to her and she instinctually raised the shard higher and made her best "Don't mess with me" face.

The giant picked up one of the blankets from the bed and started folding it. "Put that down," he commanded.

Rachel didn't move. The giant sighed and rolled his eyes. He moved onto folding the next blanket. Rachel didn't know what to think. She had been kidnapped, locked in a room, and now instead of this enormous man hurting her or being mean to her, he was tidying up the mess she had made. He folded another blanket, then another.

He picked up the last blanket and started folding. Without looking at her he stated, "I said put that down."

Rachel still didn't move a muscle. She knew her shard of glass wouldn't do much against a being of his size, but surrendering it felt like giving up all together. She wasn't ready to give up. She still had her friends to think about. Rachel was worried about what had happened to Hester and Liam. Not Gerald so much since he was already a ghost. But she was very worried about Hester and Liam.

The gigantic man picked up the pile of five perfectly folded blankets, opened the wardrobe door, and placed them inside. He shut the door, turned to Rachel, and in two rapid strides was standing over her. Before Rachel knew it, he had yanked the shard out of her hand with a swift jerk of the sheet. The shard clattered across the floor out of her reach. The giant threw the sheet onto the pile of damp sheet and broken glass.

"I don't appreciate you threatening me," he hissed. Though hardly a whisper, his voice made chills run up and down Rachel's spine. A whisper from a man that size was as threatening as a yell from a normal man.

Rachel felt eclipsed in his massive shadow. He glared down at her. She lost track of time. *Had they been standing there a second or an hour?* Time seemed to lose all meaning. Rachel looked up into his impossibly dark eyes. She considered how different they were from Liam's eyes. Liam's eyes were the clear bright blue of a perfect ocean. You could see right to the bottom. Everything visible in them. This man's eyes were endless—their depth indiscernible. Rachel took a step back and time seemed to restore itself.

The giant man stalked across the room to the vanity. He closed the drawer Rachel had left open. He then produced a key from his waistband and unlocked the top drawer on the right. From the drawer he pulled something that looked remarkably small in his giant hand. He closed the drawer then walked back over to Rachel and took a seat on the bed near where she stood. His jaw was tight and his brows downcast as he held out the small object and asked, "Where did you get this?"

Rachel was flabbergasted. The small object the giant kept locked away in a drawer Rachel couldn't reach wasn't a weapon or a way out of the room, it was something that belonged to her. It was *The Mighty Arm that Built Egypt*. In his colossal hand it looked like it could be a doll's book.

Rachel stammered, "Th-th-that's my book!"

"Where did you get it?" demanded the giant.

"I got it at the airport gift shop," was Rachel's confused answer.

The giant looked incredulously at Rachel, stood, then began to pace the room. He crisscrossed the room several times before he stopped his pacing and said, "Why do you insist on defying me? Just tell me where this came from?"

"The Chicago airport," Rachel answered. She watched for the giant's reaction. He didn't seem angry, just frustrated.

"Apparently wherever we are doesn't keep a lot of H.H. Mays books on hand," Rachel thought to herself. "This might be Hester's *biggest* fan." Rachel smiled at her own bad pun.

"What? Do you find this humorous, human?" inquired the giant.

Human. Rachel let the word sink in. *Human.* It was hard to ignore the situation when it was made so plain to her. He would not call her "human" if he were one. *What was he? And where was she? Was this even Earth?* Rachel's panic was past simmering and was now nearing an uncontrolled boil. "What do you mean—'human'?" she questioned, trying to conceal her panic.

"Are you not a human?" asked the giant with a cautious yet probing glance.

"Of course I'm a human," insisted Rachel, her voice getting louder. She tried to hide her mounting hysteria, but the cracks in her calm facade were showing. Rachel questioned the giant, "What are you?"

One perfectly arched black eyebrow raised as he smirked. "What. Am. I?" He emphasized each word. "If you do not answer my questions with honesty, why should I answer yours?" he spat.

"Wh-wh-what?" stuttered a confused Rachel. "I told you I got the book at the airport in Chicago. In the gift shop. I don't know how I could answer you more honestly. It was an impulse buy. I figured it might be fun to read a silly book on ancient Egypt while waiting for my flight, and then on the plane to pass the time. It cost seven dollars and ninety-five cents. I used my debit card to buy it. I haven't finished it yet, so if you know the ending, please no spoilers."

When Rachel was uncomfortable she had two modes—shut down mode where she said nothing, and life story mode where she rambled until someone stopped her. Rachel was beyond uncomfortable right now. Rachel was in spiraling out of control "you-might-hear-about-my-seventh grade-crush-and-how-I-got-my-first-period" rambled story panic mode.

"I don't understand," the giant frowned.

"What don't you understand?" asked Rachel. Rachel was beginning to think she wasn't the only one struggling with something internally. Was this just as weird for the giant as it was for her, the *human*?

The massive man took a seat on the bed, opened the book, and read aloud:

> *Mighty Ra raised his fearsome muscled arm, and the earth shook. The people of Egypt cowered before his glistening bronze body. Ra wasn't a man, he was a god. And like most gods, he was immense and he was terrifying.*

The giant stopped reading to flip ahead in the book.

> *Towering over the crowd...*

He stopped to flip a page and read again.

He was twice the size of any human.

He flipped ahead again.

How would they defeat beings over twice their size...

Flip, flip.

...he was greeted by a bed larger than his own hut.

The giant closed the book and gestured to the bed on which he sat. He looked angry, perhaps a little hurt. "How do *you* have a book about *me*?" he asked carefully pronouncing each word, pointing at Rachel when he said "you" and at himself when he said "me."

Rachel was dumbstruck. She had already noticed the similarities between what she was seeing and what she had read in *The Mighty Arm that Built Egypt*. But despite the fact that she had been abducted and taken to an unknown place that looked exactly like what Hester described in her book, and despite all the other odd happenings of the last twenty-four-hours, Rachel was floored that not only had the person standing before her inferred he wasn't human, but he was now essentially claiming to be an Egyptian god. She laughed.

"Why do you laugh?" asked the giant, his dark brows furrowing. Rachel noticed how his muscles tensed all over his bronze body.

"Uh, um," Rachel stammered. "I'm just laughing at how absurd this is."

The gigantic man stared at her without moving or changing his facial expression. Rachel continued, "You stole my book from me—a work of *fiction*—and you're telling me it's about you." Rachel laughed again. "You're telling me you are the Egyptian god, Ra."

The giant remained unmoved. Rachel didn't think she could become more uncomfortable than she had when he called her "human." She took in the full size of the man. He was the exact description from the book. "Only the book didn't describe his endless eyes, or the fact that he was actually quite handsome if you liked the whole bald, giant, surly type," Rachel thought to herself. Without noticing it happen, Rachel had made unflinching eye contact with the giant again.

He spoke. "You deny what you see with your own eyes," he observed.

"Seriously?" she asked. "You seriously expect me to believe you are Ra?"

"Amun-Ra," he said. "Though I am known as simply Ra by many."

"The god?" Rachel scoffed, though her disbelief was a shield. She knew he was telling the truth.

"To some," Ra answered. "To myself I am..." He paused before saying, "Ra. Just Ra."

Rachel hadn't noticed she was holding her breath. She felt lightheaded. This was a lot to take in. She was standing in front of Ra. Before she knew it, Rachel's vision tunneled until it completely went black.

◆ ◆ ◆

Daylight shone through the entrance of the cave before Liam returned. He stalked heavily into the shady protection of the cavern, heading straight for the stream. As he filled his jug, Gerald bombarded him with questions.

"Did you find Rachel? Do you know where it took her? Is she alive? Why did you come back without her?"

Liam gulped down the contents of his jug. While refilling it he answered, "I don't know. I don't know."

He was frustrated and he looked exhausted. Gerald noticed Liam's shoes were covered in mud and sand. "You've got to know something," demanded Gerald.

From the wall of supplies, Hester piped up, "Let him catch his breath, Gerry. He's gonna tell us once he's had a moment, I'm sure."

Hester was rolling cornmeal balls like Rachel had the night before. She finished rolling one last ball before taking the full bowl to the fire that still burned. Liam looked at its size and guessed Hester had gathered more dry sticks and built it up. He watched her drop the mushy balls onto the flat stone.

Liam sat down next to the fire and took a long swig from his jug. He cleared his throat then began. "I continued straight in the direction you led me last night," he said to Gerald. "I walked a long time, never noticing any sign of another living creature. I listened closely to see if I could hear anything moving in the forest ahead of me, but I never even heard an owl. It was totally silent. Pretty creepy. I actually started getting afraid that I wasn't walking in a straight line—that I had been walking in circles—because everything looked the same. Just more and more giant oak trees. But then it changed. Here and there I'd see an evergreen tree—I'm talking enormous evergreens. Probably giant sequoias."

Liam stopped to take another sip from his jug. Hester continued cooking the cornmeal and Gerald impatiently asked, "Did you find Rachel?"

"No," Liam answered. "But after I was surrounded by the enormous evergreens, the ground became more wet—muddy. I started noticing foot prints. Like shoe prints, only I'd hate to see the guy who fit those shoes."

"That's what took Rachel," Gerald interrupted, his face grave and intense.

"I followed the shoe prints, and they led out onto a beach," Liam said. "From there I lost the prints. But at that point the sun was rising which revealed something pretty amazing."

"What?" Gerald and Hester asked together.

"A city," answered Liam. "There was a city or a village and what looked like a large palace. If I didn't know better, I'd compare it to Mesopotamia or ancient Egypt. If we didn't already know we're not in Texas, I think we've got our solid proof now."

"But you didn't find Rachel," Hester said quietly.

"I didn't know what to do or where to go," Liam said defensively. "I was alone and didn't know who I might encounter. I'm not afraid of going back. I will go back. I just thought it was better to come back here and let you both know what the situation was, at least. If I had just rushed into that city, banging down every door looking for Rachel, it's likely I would be taken, too." Liam sighed, "Maybe I'm just fooling myself. Maybe I'm just a coward coming up with excuses for why I didn't try harder."

"No, you were right to come back, Liam," assured Gerald.

"You did the right thing, hun," Hester agreed.

"For now you should rest," Gerald said. Liam started to object, but Gerald gestured for Liam to stop. The ghostly professor continued, "No, Listen. You need to eat something and try to get some sleep. We don't know what we're up against. If Rachel is still alive now, that means she'll be alive later. We're either too late already, or we have time to prepare. To find her and rescue her we need to be sharp and we need to be rested. We'll set out once it starts to get dark. That way we'll have the coverage of night to travel and we'll hopefully have more luck in spying out where in the city Rachel may be. My suspicion is the palace."

"Why do you think Rachel was taken to the palace?" asked Liam. He had honestly expected he'd have to go door to door. If Liam had thought it was as simple as looking in one place, he would have gone straight there instead of coming back to the cavern.

"Did the buildings in the city look large enough to hold a thing with the size of shoe prints you saw?" was Gerald's answer.

"No, they looked like normal sized buildings," said Liam, realization dawning like the sun across his exhausted face. He gripped his head with both hands and chastised himself, "How stupid could I have been not to have thought of that?"

"You were tired, son," Gerald said gently. "No one could blame you for not thinking of that. This is new territory. This is probably your first experience giant hunting." Gerald softly laughed and tried to coax a smile out of Liam.

"We should all get some rest then," suggested Hester, spearing the last of the cornmeal balls off the flat stone and placing it in the bowl with the other cooked cornmeal cakes. "Sounds like tonight we become heroes."

CHAPTER 11

For the second time in one day Rachel awoke in the giant room she now knew belonged to Ra, the Egyptian god. "*Supposed* Egyptian god," Rachel reminded herself as she sat up in bed. "I guess I passed out again," she said aloud.

Unlike earlier, though, her head pounded and her stomach ached from hunger. She looked around the room and noticed the soggy pile of sheets and broken glass had been removed, as was her escape plan—the ripped sheets she was fashioning into a rope. She got out of bed and observed that once again her socks and shoes were neatly placed at the foot of the bed. Rachel also noticed that sitting on an ottoman—which hadn't been in the room before—was a tray with a glass, a pitcher of water, and a plate of food.

Rachel contemplated the idea that the food could be poisoned. "That's incredibly silly," she argued with herself. "If he wanted to kill you, he wouldn't have to poison you."

The food on the plate was mostly fruit—grapes, melon, and figs. There were also olives, and a small loaf of bread. Rachel hungrily tore into the bread. She ate every bit of food on the plate except for the figs. At a conference she had attended with Dr. Goldblum, when Rachel was still an undergraduate student, she had tried figs at Dr. Goldblum's insistence. Unfortunately, the figs were bad, and Rachel got horrible food poisoning. It was such a bad case of food poisoning she was hospitalized.

Since then Rachel could hardly look at a fig without getting sick to her stomach.

After finishing the food, Rachel's headache subsided and her stomach no longer ached. She felt much refreshed, which made it easier for Rachel to focus once again on her escape.

She stared at the door. *How was she going to get out? Was she going to just have to wait for Ra to return to find out why he had her captive? What was he planning on doing with her?* Rachel sat on the ground and put on her socks and shoes. Her purse hadn't been put back in the wardrobe. It was on the bed near where she had been lying. She picked it up and pulled the strap over her head so that her purse hung across her body. She eyed the door again. Rachel knew it was ridiculous to think Ra would leave the door unlocked now, when he hadn't earlier, but she had to at least give the door a try.

Rachel walked to the large ornate door and stretched her arms up over her head to try the handle, like she had before. But, unlike earlier when she pulled the handle, this time the door handle swung down and the door creaked open.

Clang! The loud clang of a metal pitcher being dropped onto the stone floor nearly scared Rachel out of her skin. Instead of an open hallway before her, like she expected, there were three women who all looked just as surprised to see her as she was to see them. They stood holding various items—towels, bottles of oils and soaps. One was empty handed. She must have been carrying the metal pitcher. They were Rachel's size—that is to say, human sized—not giant like Ra. Two were slightly shorter than Rachel, while the other about four inches taller. The tall woman, the one carrying the mystery bottles, was the first to speak.

"We have come to direct you to the bath. We have orders to assist you in your evening preparations," she stated.

"Uh, preparations?" asked Rachel. She pictured old movies she'd seen where handmaids prepared the new concubine for her night with the king.

"I am Kesi," the tall woman said, then gestured to the other women. "This is Halima, and this is Mert. We are servants of Amun-Ra. You will follow us."

Halima bent down and picked up the pitcher she had dropped. Rachel looked from woman to woman. Mert averted her eyes, but Halima gave Rachel a friendly smile. Rachel could tell Kesi was all business. She was either a more important servant or older than the others, Rachel guessed.

"I was actually just leaving," Rachel tried casually. Stepping past the three women, she asked in her most nonchalant voice, "Would one of you mind showing me the exit?"

"Follow me," was Kesi's only response. Without waiting for further comments from Rachel, Kesi marched straight down the hall. Rachel, Halima, and Mert followed.

Rachel congratulated herself. "That was a lot easier than I expected."

The group turned down another hall, then descended a set of stairs—one, two, three floors—Rachel counted. She had been right. She had been captive on the third floor—just like *The Mighty Arm that Built Egypt.* This wasn't Egypt though. Rachel had been to Egypt many times, and though there were obvious similarities, this wasn't Egypt.

Kesi continued to lead the group down halls, turning left, then right, then right, then left. Rachel was glad she had a guide to show her the way. Without one it would be next to impossible to find it on her own. Finally the four women stopped in front of a set of two large double doors. Rachel smiled to herself. She was happy and surprised her directness was paying off; Kesi had led her straight to the exit. Kesi's hands were full, so she nodded to Halima. Halima stepped forward, and with her free hand knocked three times on one of the great doors.

"There must be guards outside," thought Rachel.

The doors opened, but instead of the steps to the palace, or a bustling city street, the scene before Rachel was what appeared to be a large indoor pool. Rachel's spirit sank. Kesi had led her to the bath and to her *preparations*.

"Leave us," Kesi commanded the male servants who had opened the large double doors. They left without a word, closing the doors behind them.

By the edge of the pool Kesi placed the bottles she carried, and the others followed her example putting down the metal pitcher and the towels. Rachel contemplated making a break for it. She was pretty sure she could take Halima and Mert, at least if she took them by surprise. Kesi didn't seem like the sort of woman to be trifled with though. "I could push Kesi in the pool, then run for the door," Rachel considered. She then remembered she had no idea how to get out of what she assumed was a humongous palace. And, if there were people just waiting to open the doors to the bathroom, there were sure to be guards at the entrance or exit.

Kesi was giving directions to Halima and Mert in a language Rachel didn't recognize. It occurred to Rachel that Ra and Kesi had both spoken English to her. "How did I not notice it before?" she wondered. Figuring she had nothing to lose, Rachel asked, "What language are you speaking?"

Kesi looked at her like she had asked a rude or ridiculous question. A laugh bubbled up from Halima. Mert remained silent.

Rachel repeated herself slowly, figuring that English was probably their second language, and they hadn't understood her question. "What language are you speaking?"

"Janusis, of course," Kesi replied haughtily. She had a proud face. She reminded Rachel of Dr. Holmes, only with dark hair and less polish. But if Kesi were given a Visa card and a manicure, she could be Dr. Holmes dark haired twin.

"Where are— " Rachel began before being interrupted by a violent pounding on the double doors.

All four women turned toward the doors. "Kesi!? Halima!?" came Ra's excited voice from the other side. "Tell me you are there and you have Rachel!" he demanded.

Kesi hurried to the door and opened it. Ra stood at the door way, a tower of distress. Rachel had somehow forgotten, while standing among these normal sized women, how immense Ra was. He did not move, he remained standing at the door. His eyes met Rachel's and the distress melted from his face.

"I assumed you had left," Ra explained. "I saw your satchel gone and assumed you had fled."

Rachel looked down at her purse, slung across her body, then back up at Ra. "I was going to leave, or try to, then these women tricked me into coming in here. I asked to be shown the exit."

Ra smiled a genuine smile. Rachel involuntarily smiled back. When she realized what she was doing she stopped herself and asked, "Why are you keeping me here?"

"I still need questions answered," replied Ra.

"Why the whole fancy to-do with a bath and whatnot?" Rachel asked, gesturing to the pool and servants.

"You've been traveling, I assumed you'd be more comfortable if you were allowed to bathe," answered Ra.

"So, I'm a prisoner, but a well-treated one," Rachel affirmed.

"Rachel, would you rather go bathe in the ocean and sleep in the dirt of a cave?" asked Ra, moving his hands to his hips, standing with his feet shoulder width apart. Rachel recognized his stance as a power pose. She had taken a leadership seminar that said if you wanted to assert your dominance in a situation you should adopt a power pose, or if you wanted to diminish someone else's power you should mirror them.

"How do you know my name?" she asked, placing her hands on her hips and moving her feet to shoulder width apart.

Ra laughed. "You know my name, why shouldn't I know yours?" he asked with an arch of his dark brow.

"I'm not against you knowing my name," she replied. "I just want to know how you learned it."

"The spirit of the old man was calling after you when I snatched you from the cavern entrance," said Ra. "And in your satchel there are several papers and small tablets with your name written or engraved on them."

"Tablets? I don't have any tablets in my purse," said Rachel.

"Yes, there are tablets," argued Ra.

Rachel opened her purse and looked inside. She saw her wallet and brush. She pulled out her wallet. Under it were her keys, a pen, deodorant, cellphone, and her lip-gloss. *The Mighty Arm that Built Egypt* had not yet been returned. Still holding her wallet in her hand she looked up at Ra and said, "You still need to give me back my book."

Pointing to Rachel's wallet, Ra said, "That holds the tablets and papers with your name."

Realizing what Ra meant, Rachel couldn't help but laugh. She opened her wallet and pulled out one of her credit cards and asked, "Is this a tablet?"

"Yes, of course," answered Ra. "It is tiny, but a tablet nonetheless."

"Okay," Rachel said. "Are you going to give me back my book?"

"Perhaps," responded Ra simply.

"Are you going to let me go?" asked Rachel.

Ra frowned. "You think you are a prisoner here, but that isn't exactly true." He paused, searching for the right words. "You are a detainee. I will not keep you indefinitely. But for now you will remain."

"And if I disagree? If I do not wish to 'remain'?" asked Rachel.

"You have no choice," replied Ra.

"Then I am a prisoner," said Rachel dryly.

"As you wish," he answered. "If you insist on being a prisoner, you are a prisoner. I will release you when the time is right."

Rachel was about to argue with him, but Ra abruptly turned, marched from the room, down the hall, and out of sight. Kesi closed the large door and acted as though there had been no interruption. She spoke in Janusis to Halima and Mert. They nodded and advanced on Rachel, Halima reached for Rachel's purse, and Mert began to attack the buttons on Rachel's plaid shirt. Rachel swatted them away.

"What are you doing?" she demanded.

"They are undressing you to bathe you," answered Kesi.

"Uh, um, I can undress and bathe myself," Rachel said, feeling already naked despite being fully clothed.

"We were commanded to see to your preparations," Kesi said in a voice that suggested she believed her word was final.

"Ra said I am not a prisoner, that I am a 'detainee.' If that is the case then I believe I have a choice whether I am undressed like a doll and bathed like a dog," Rachel replied. She tried to appear confident, but she felt panicked. Rachel had never had a stranger try to undress her. She felt embarrassed and scared. She wasn't prepared to give up her privacy so easily.

Kesi's facial expression was unmoving. She was a statue. Halima and Mert exchanged glances and both retreated from Rachel. Rachel looked from one woman to the next, addressing all three. "Ladies, I will comply to a degree. I will take a bath. But I don't want you giving me a bath. I don't want you watching me take a bath either. If you won't leave the room, then at least turn around so I can keep a little of my dignity."

All three women stared at Rachel. Halima and Mert looked from Rachel to Kesi, seeking approval from their leader to obey Rachel's guidelines. Kesi exhaled loudly. It was more than a sigh; it was almost a grunt—frustration, exasperation, resigned defeat. She walked to the edge of the pool and picked up one of the bottles. "Soap," she snapped. She put that bottle down and picked up another. "Shampoo," she spat. She repeated this exercise until she had listed the contents of the other bottles—body oil, hair oil, and perfume. Kesi sat the last bottle down, turned from the pool and strode to the doors while saying, "You will place your clothing in a pile by the pool's edge. It will be washed and returned to you later. After you have finished bathing, wrap yourself in a towel and we will escort you back to Ra's bedchamber."

Kesi finished her speech standing in front of the doors with her back to Rachel. Halima and Mert followed her example.

Rachel would have rather been left alone, but having no one staring at her while expecting her to get naked was better than nothing. She walked to the edge of the pool and slipped off her purse and her shoes. She undressed the rest of the way and did as Kesi said—she put her dirty clothes in a pile at the edge of the pool.

Rachel stuck a toe in the water expecting it to be cold, but the water was comfortably warm. Finding it warm, Rachel happily walked down the steps into the pool. She sat down on a step and allowed herself a moment to take in the room. It reminded her of an indoor pool you'd see at an expensive hotel. The rest of the palace Rachel had seen was stone. This room had elaborate tile in turquoise and various shades of blue. It was a beautiful room. There were several palm plants in woven baskets along the walls, which were covered in murals of more greenery. This room was quite a contrast to the rest of the palace Rachel had seen, which was mostly tan. Rachel liked this room.

She looked to the other end of the pool. "That has to be the deep end," she thought to herself. The bath was the size of a small swimming pool. Rachel imagined that it probably looked almost like a normal bathtub when Ra was using it, then she blushed realizing she was picturing him taking a bath.

Rachel dunked her head under the water and tried to clear her thoughts. When she came up for air, she grabbed the bottle of soap from the edge and began washing her arms. While lathering herself up she looked around and her eyes rested on her pile of dirty clothes. It finally hit her that Kesi hadn't said a thing about there being a change of clothes for her.

"She only said to put on a towel and that they'd take me back to *Ra's bedchamber*," the voice inside her head screamed. Her pulse raced. Rachel felt herself getting faint for what felt like the millionth time in the last twenty-four-hours. "Keep it together," she told herself. "The last thing you want to do is faint while naked in a pool."

Rachel took several deep breaths and told herself she could only face one thing at a time. For right now all she could do was wash off the dust from the adventures she'd had so far. "Later will have its own adventures, I'm sure," she said under her breath, before allowing her head to sink below the water's surface.

CHAPTER 12

Kesi, Halima, and Mert escorted Rachel back to Ra's bedchamber. Kesi opened the door with evident desire for Rachel to enter ahead of herself and the other two. Rachel complied, stepping across the threshold of what she hoped would be only a temporary prison—or a temporary 'detainee' room.

Rachel looked around the room, checking for any changes. Earlier when she awoke, she'd found the room cleaned of the mayhem she'd created—torn sheets, a broken bottle of perfume—and in its place an ottoman with a tray of food set out to appease her hunger. Rachel noted the ottoman remained, but the tray had been removed. The bed was freshly made, but unlike earlier there was only one sheet and one blanket—not enough material to make a suitable rope to escape through the window. Also unlike earlier, a set of clothes lay on the bed. A lightweight white cotton, almost gauze-like, dress lay on the bed, and a set of sandals sat where her tennis shoes sat before.

Mert shuffled across the floor and placed Rachel's purse next to the sandals. Her tennis shoes and clothes had been taken who knows where to be washed. Rachel insisted, however, that her purse not be confiscated.

After her bath, Rachel walked the corridors and up the stairs barefoot, wrapped in two enormous towels. One towel wrapped around her body, almost dragging on the stone floor, while the other towel she wore like a cape over her shoulders.

Rachel looked over her shoulder at the three women and wondered if they were planning on watching her dress or if they would leave. Without being asked, Kesi answered her question, "Halima will help you dress, if you need anything one of us will be in the corridor at all times."

Kesi turned to leave, as did Mert. Halima took one shy step forward. Rachel stopped them all in their tracks by stating, "I think I can dress myself. I've been dressing on my own for quite some time."

Halima deflated, disappointed to have such an important job taken from her. Kesi harrumphed and stomped off to the corridor, followed by Mert. Halima retreated with the others, but before walking through the doorway she meekly said to Rachel, "If you would like help arranging your hair after you are clothed, tap three times on the door and I will be happy to assist you."

"Thank you," answered Rachel with a smile. Halima seemed sweet. If Rachel were going to accept help from one of the three women, it would be Halima that she'd pick without a doubt. Halima gently closed the door after herself.

Though the three women didn't take up much space, once they had left and the door closed, the room seemed much larger to Rachel. She looked up and admired the tall ceilings. The room was impressive and large—"Like Ra," Rachel thought to herself.

Still wrapped in her two massive towels, Rachel walked to the window and looked out on the village. Rachel figured it was probably called a city, but it didn't look very large to her—a village or possibly a hamlet. At best a town. She watched people in the streets hurrying here and there. After meeting

Kesi, Halima, and Mert, and seeing the men who opened the doors to the bathroom, Rachel assumed those in the streets were also regular human size. She wondered if, like in *The Mighty Arm that Built Egypt*, there were others like Ra—gods or giants. The sun hung low over the ocean in the distance. Rachel's mind wandered to her friends. She hoped they were safe.

Turning from the window, Rachel walked to the oversized bed to examine the dress that lay out for her. It wasn't a complicated garment—it appeared to be a simple dress that would slip over her head—light and sleeveless. It was made of several layers of gauzy white cotton. "Thank God whoever made this knew to layer the fabric," Rachel observed, holding the dress up to the light coming through the window. If the dress were only one layer of fabric, it would be completely see-through.

Rachel placed the towel she was using as a cape on the bed and pulled the dress over her head without removing the towel she had around on her body. She eased the towel down along with the dress. She was afraid of having Ra or someone else enter the chamber while she dressed. Her trick of keeping on her towel—something she had learned in high school gym glass—ensured her modesty remained intact even if she was surprised by an unexpected visitor. After she dressed, she congratulated herself on carrying deodorant in her purse, pulled out the lucky antiperspirant, and applied it generously.

Rachel folded the towels and stacked them at the end of the bed. She pictured Ra's apparent disapproval earlier at the mess she'd made. It suddenly hit her she was seeking his approval. "Why?" she wondered. "He's my captor. My kidnapper. I don't need to impress him." Somewhere in the back of her mind a voice whispered, "But he's a god."

Rachel tried to clear her head of that thought by taking another look around the room. Perhaps she'd find something else new and helpful. Her eyes fell on the vanity. Sitting on top of the vanity was her book. "That can't be a mistake," she decided. "He must be returning it."

Rachel couldn't reach the top of the vanity though. It was just out of her reach. She quickly remedied that. She put her weight against the ottoman and pushed it across the floor until it backed up to the vanity. Rachel climbed on top of the ottoman—which was as tall as her waist—and stood. From this height she could easily reach her book.

After grabbing *The Mighty Arm that Built Egypt*, Rachel climbed down but left the ottoman where she'd pushed it. It was tiring work pushing furniture made for someone twice her size around. And she didn't need to impress Ra with how tidy she kept the room, she told herself.

Rachel took a seat on the bed. It only then occurred to her that the bed must be awfully low to the ground for Ra. Like an opened futon would be to her. The height of the bed to Rachel was just a little high—like the bed in her Aunt Tabby's guestroom. Rachel sat comfortably at the head of the bed, her back against the wall, and opened her book.

It took Rachel a minute to find her place. While searching she allowed her mind to ruminate on Ra and how he had asked her how she had a book about him. "Is it really about him?" she wondered. "The name is the same, obviously. But was there really a Malachi? Did the people of Egypt actually rise against him?" Nowhere in her study of Egypt did she find anything to support the idea that *The Mighty Arm that Built Egypt* was fact instead of fiction. Reading it, though, might give Rachel information on how to persuade Ra to release her, or on how to escape. She picked up where she left off:

Malachi's blood ran cold. He was eye level with two gigantic bronze legs and the familiar, extravagant golden sandals of Ra. Malachi instantly felt like he was flying. Ra had effortlessly lifted him up by the shoulders.

"What is this I find?" demanded Ra. "A pest? Vermin? Some annoying rat who slinks in the shadows of my bedchamber come to steal from me?"

Malachi's eyes were full of hatred for the god who had oppressed his people.

"Ah-ha," said Ra, his mouth curving into a menacing smile. "You haven't come to steal from me, have you, vermin? You came to murder me as though I were the pest."

Ra shook Malachi as he spoke. Malachi felt like a doll in the hands of so large a being. He expected at any moment to be hurled across the room by Ra in a rage, or to be crushed in Ra's powerful hands. But neither fate met Malachi, and his bravery wavered. What would be his fate? The unexpected fate was often worse than any imagined. Malachi was caught. Not just physically, but his plan discovered. He was there to murder Ra.

Breathless, Malachi asked, "What are you going to do with me?"

Ra's answer came in the form of a booming, cruel laugh. He shifted his grip and held Malachi away from himself with one strong hand as though he wanted to keep Malachi as far away from himself as possible. Ra kept this position, examining Malachi. Finally he said, "You came to murder me in stealth, little pest. It seems only fair and civilized that instead you meet me face to face as a man. If you want to kill me, you will have to best me."

It was Malachi's turn to laugh. His only advantage had been surprise. He had hoped to kill Ra as he slept. Hand to hand combat with a giant was basically a voluntary death sentence. Ra surprised Malachi by joining him in his laugh. "It is absurd," remarked Ra. "But would you rather die as a man or as a pest?" he asked.

Malachi stopped laughing, and soberly answered, "As a man."

Ra set Malachi on the ground, then marched to the door. He turned back to Malachi and said, "We will fight tomorrow at sunrise. I will send up nourishment. As a noble adversary, I will not face someone who is not at their own full advantage."

Ra disappeared through the door, which shut with a loud thud. Malachi heard a key clink in the keyhole, and knew he was locked in. It wasn't long before her heard the long low call of the war trumpet. A voice announced in the street, "At sunrise all are invited to witness a champion of the people face the Mighty Ra. The contest will take place in the palace arena." This announcement was repeated over and over until Malachi was certain he had memorized it himself.

Tap, tap, tap. Rachel looked up to see the door to Ra's chamber slowly opening. Halima's head poked into the room. "I'm sorry to disturb you, miss. The time is approaching for us to conduct you to the banquet hall. Are you certain you would not desire my help with the arrangement of your hair," Halima asked, her soft voice sounding uncertain but concerned.

Rachel's hair fell damp over her shoulders. She hadn't even brushed it since getting out of the bath. It had been over twenty-four-hours since she'd worried once about her hair. Rachel closed her book and climbed off the bed. "Yeah, I guess you might be able to help me," she said to Halima.

Halima smiled a radiant smile and slipped into the room. She closed the door behind her, then gingerly approached Rachel. Rachel picked up her purse, pulled out her brush, and began brushing her own hair. "What sort of thing did you have in mind for my hair?" asked Rachel.

Halima turned toward the vanity, saying "Excellent," as she crossed the room to climb the ottoman. She said to Rachel, "I am much gratified to find this ottoman. I feared I could not reach the drawer we needed."

Standing on top of the ottoman, Halima first lit a lamp that sat on top of the vanity with what Rachel guessed to be a flint. Until that moment Rachel hadn't noticed how dim it was in the room. Halima next produced a key from inside the sleeve of her dress. The key attached to a string, tied around her wrist. Halima unlocked the top left drawer, and from it withdrew a jar. She also took out a comb, hair pins, and ribbons. While she climbed down from the ottoman, she shared that she had once been Ra's official hairdresser. But that was before Ra had shaved off all his hair. "He had the most beautiful hair,"

Halima gushed. "Thick, shining like the sun, but dark as night."

Rachel noticed that Halima didn't seem afraid of Ra, instead she seemed to admire him. Rachel considered the fact that *The Mighty Arm that Built Egypt* wasn't about a god loved by his people. That book was about a god whose people feared and despised him. Besides having the same name, how could Ra think the book was about him?

Halima stood in front of Rachel, intently looking into her face and at her hair. "May I do as I wish with your hair?" she asked Rachel.

Rachel hesitated before answering. She liked Halima and naturally wanted to trust her. But at the same time didn't feel she should so easily comply with whatever her captors demanded. "You're not going to shave my head to look like Ra?" she teased.

"No, certainly not," answered Halima. "I would like to braid and pin your hair, if that is to your satisfaction."

"Sure," relented Rachel.

Halima invited Rachel to have a seat on the floor. She sat behind Rachel, and with the comb began separating sections of Rachel's hair. Rachel always had to fight falling asleep when she visited the hairdressers for a haircut or when she had her hair styled for special events like her cousin's wedding, or graduation. She felt her eyes slowly drooping while Halima's adept fingers worked on her tresses.

Rachel was startled awake by the sound of Halima's mild laugh. "I do not know how you fall asleep while having your hair arranged," giggled Halima.

"Sorry," mumbled Rachel between yawns.

"I am almost finished," said Halima.

When she had finished, Halima stood and offered her hand to Rachel to help her get up off the floor. "Come," she said, leading Rachel to the ottoman. "Look in the glass and see if you do not approve."

Rachel climbed the ottoman and took a good long look at herself in the vanity mirror. "I most definitely approve," Rachel said to Halima. Rachel found it hard to turn away from her own reflection; she had never seen her hair look so amazing.

Halima had braided Rachel's long hair into several braids—some large, some small. In a few of these braids she had added ivory, gold, and purple ribbon. Halima wove all the braids together and pinned them in an intricate up do. It was breathtaking in its design, and it made Rachel look more like a princess than an Egyptologist.

Without warning, the tall ornate door opened. "The sun has set, it is time for us to conduct her down to the great hall for dinner," said Kesi.

Halima helped Rachel down from the ottoman then picked up the remaining hair pins, ribbons, comb, and the jar of hair balm she had used to coax Rachel's hair into place. While Halima climbed the ottoman again, Rachel sat on the floor to put on the sandals that were set out for her. She also took *The Mighty Arm that Built Egypt* and put it back in her purse. Rachel placed her purse inside the wardrobe, but not before applying lip-gloss.

Rachel followed behind Kesi, and the group of four women again traveled down the stairs to the bottom floor. There were torches lit in every corridor—torches exactly like those Rachel and her friends had found in the cave and in the cavern. They alternated in height from being placed at regular human height to high above Rachel's head, suitable for someone Ra's height. The torches reminded Rachel of the cavern and her friends. *Were they safe? Were they still in the cavern? Had they been kidnapped, too? Had they figured out where we are?* Rachel firmly decided she would ask Ra all of her questions. "Not that asking him would guarantee his answering," she reflected as Kesi led them down another corridor. Rachel became discouraged. Escaping this place would be impossible. The palace was like a labyrinth. Without an escort, Rachel would get lost. She would have better luck answering whatever questions Ra had, and hope he'd just release her after she'd helped him.

As the group reached the end of one corridor, Kesi reached up and took a torch from the wall. When they rounded the next corner, a large open courtyard flickered before Kesi's out-held torch. In the dim light Rachel could just barely make out palm plants and exotic flowers, the fragrance of which floated to Rachel on a light breeze. Rachel looked around as they quickly followed Kesi, but couldn't see any doors leading outside. Rachel slowed her step to try to see through the dark, but Kesi turned and said, "We are late. You must hurry."

Rachel reluctantly followed. If she were to attempt an escape, the courtyard seemed the most likely place of opportunity. From her left, Rachel heard Halima's soft voice say, "We're almost there. Do not be nervous. You look beautiful."

Rachel actually hadn't thought about being nervous until Halima suggested she might be. "Why should I be nervous?" Rachel thought to herself. "We're just having dinner." Then it occurred to her that this might be something more than dinner—something like a date. "I did not sign up for this. I just want to have some dinner, and then get out of here."

Kesi led the women down another corridor that went from the courtyard into the palace, then through a doorway into another large open space. Far ahead, at the end of the room were a set of large double doors, more ornate than even the door to Ra's chamber. On either side of the doors stood guards holding impressive staffs topped with what looked to Rachel like golden hatchets. In the dim light the men looked like they were carved from the same stone that built the palace, though the armor they wore shone gold in the torchlight. Both stood motionless and frowning. Neither moved the slightest bit until the group of women stood directly in front of the doors. Kesi commanded in a voice that seemed unnecessarily loud, "Open." The guards bowed and in unison opened the impressive double doors. Kesi stepped aside and motioned for Rachel to enter the banquet hall. Before Rachel knew what was happening, the doors closed behind her, and she was left alone in a room full of giants—a room full of gods.

CHAPTER 13

"Holy cannoli, I'm tired," said Hester from behind Liam. Gerald walked alongside his wife as the group made their way through the forest.

"We can take a break if you need to," said Liam, stopping and turning to Hester. He gazed ahead to the horizon. Through the trees, he could see the sun was mostly set. It would be night by the time they reached the city.

Hester looked ready to protest taking a break, but Gerald jumped in, "Yes, let's take a break. You both should rehydrate and eat something to keep up your strength. And, Hester, you need to not push yourself too hard when you don't have an inhaler handy."

Hester stuck out her tongue at her husband then set down the bowl she was carrying—the bowl full of cornmeal cakes. Liam threw down the unlit torch he carried and began fiddling with the belt he had slung across his body. Before they'd left the cavern, Liam removed his belt and strung three jugs of water on it. He had then hung it over his shoulder and across his body. He now removed the belt and took one jug from it to share with Hester.

The group sat, and Liam and Hester ate a few cornmeal cakes and drank water from the jug they shared. When they'd finished the water, Liam set the unlit torch inside the empty jug the way Rachel had done the day before. "It will be easier to light if I have both hands free," Liam thought to himself as he dug in his pocket for his matches. He pulled the yellow box filled with waterproof matches out and lit a match. It sizzled into a flame. Liam held the match to the torch head, and it ignited.

"I think this is the part where one of us gives a rousing speech about how 'We can do it' or 'Good will triumph' or whatever," joked Liam. The idea of Rachel a prisoner somewhere weighed heavy on his heart.

"I know with the greatest certainty we will make it through this," Gerald responded. "We will triumph," he said in complete seriousness.

Liam laughed and rose to his feet. He strapped his belt with the two remaining jugs across his body, then helped Hester to her feet. Hester was still wearing Liam's blazer over her lime green pantsuit. Hester caught Liam looking her up and down after he helped her up. "I see you looking at me, young man. I'm spoken for, though, and don't forget it," she said with one hand on her hip and the other gesturing to Gerald.

Both Gerald and Liam laughed. "I was just thinking about how conspicuous you will be when we try sneaking through the village and into the palace. You're like a neon sign," Liam said.

"He's right," answered Gerald. "A beautiful neon sign, but still a neon sign, Bunny."

Hester picked up the bowl that still had a few cornmeal cakes in it saying, "We'll worry about that when we get closer. For now, let's just focus on getting out of this forest."

"How much further 'till we reach the beach, Liam?" Gerald asked.

"I'm actually not sure. I was so tired and out of it when I tried following Rachel and the thing that took her, and I was trying to move so fast. I, I have no idea," said Liam with frustration at himself.

Gerald tried to pat Liam on the back, but his hand passed through Liam's shoulder. Gerald paused, then said, "It's all right, son. We'll just keep walking. We'll get there soon."

Liam looked around at the trees that surrounded them. The only trees around were tall oak trees. "I remember that when I was trying to follow after Rachel, the further I traveled there were more evergreens. We haven't reached any evergreens yet, so we must be a little over halfway there."

"Good," answered Gerald. "If you two don't need another break before, then we should take a break when we reach the beach."

Liam nodded his head, bent down, and picked up the torch.

Hester answered, "Works for me."

♦ ♦ ♦

After watching Rachel pass through the double doors into the banquet hall, Kesi gave the guards the signal to close the doors. The doors shut and the large room grew infinitely darker and quieter. Halima asked Kesi, "Why did you do that? Shouldn't we have escorted her to her seat?"

Turning from the doors and stepping away from the guards Kesi answered, "Someone will direct her."

Kesi led the way again across the large open room and down corridors, left, right, left. Halima hurried to keep up with her, and Mert trailed behind. Halima did not like contradicting anyone, but it seemed cruel to leave Rachel alone without any direction or warning of what she was walking into. "It will be overwhelming for Rachel to be with so many of *them*," Halima whispered. "And she's not acquainted with our customs."

Kesi snorted. Annoyed and dismissive, she said, "Rachel is Ra's concern, not ours. We did not ask to be brought into this. We are not gods. We are not kings. We should not be forced to bear the weight or responsibilities of gods or kings."

Halima started to speak again but Kesi turned to her and said, "I am finished having this discussion. You may pity the human, but even you know Ra asks too much of us. He should not have brought her here. Had he left her alone perhaps she would have perished and she would be no one's problem."

Kesi's torch barely illuminated the dark corridor they traveled. Halima slowed her pace and fell back to walk with Mert. Kesi rounded a corner ahead of them and they were left in almost perfect darkness. Halima whispered to Mert, "Do you think we should have left Rachel alone like that?"

In the dark, Halima could just barely make out Mert turning her head to look at her. A long silence followed, just before the two reached the corner Kesi had disappeared around, Mert answered, her voice rusty from lack of use, "No. And Yes." She cleared her throat then added, "You are both right."

Halima understood Mert's answer—compassion for Rachel, but agreement with Kesi that Ra took risks that might negatively affect them all. "But that's what gods do," reflected Halima. "They make choices, with little regard to how those choices impact their people. So impulsive."

Around the corner was the kitchen, they found Kesi already seated at a long wooden table made for people their size, not gods. Kesi had a plate with grapes and bread. Halima and Mert joined her, each tearing pieces of bread for themselves.

"What do you think they'll do with her?" Halima dared to ask between mouthfuls of bread.

"Question her, most likely," answered Kesi.

"Feed her," suggested Mert, before popping a grape into her mouth.

"I do not think they will kill her, if that's what you're worried about, Halima," said Kesi, rising to bring a pitcher of water to the table. Halima got to her feet and collected three mugs from a cabinet behind her. Pouring the water from the pitcher, Kesi said, "It would make little sense for them to kill her. If they were going to kill her, why not kill her in the forest, or just leave her to starve?"

"You're right," said Halima. "Though the other gods might be unhappy at Ra for bringing her here. They might punish him by hurting her."

"True," was Kesi's only response.

The three sat in silence eating their bread and grapes and drinking their water. Halima's stomach was in knots from worrying about Rachel. She also worried for Ra. He was so kind to them. *What if the other gods were cruel to him for his indiscretion and carelessness? What would happen to the people if they lost Ra?*

CHAPTER 14

A long banquet table stretched the length of the room. Around the table sat a half dozen giants—beings the size of Ra. No one had told Rachel she would be dining with anyone besides Ra. Rachel suddenly felt self-conscious—like she'd felt when the high school kids on her block caught her playing dress up when she was in middle school. Five minutes before she'd felt almost beautiful with her hair done up and in the airy white dress, now she felt silly. She froze in her tracks, uncertain of where she should to go or what she was supposed to do next.

Rachel awkwardly waved at everyone. The group of gods looked at her without offering a wave or even a smile. Rachel wasn't sure what to do. She felt like she was staring at the popular kid table in the cafeteria, only there wasn't any other table for her to hurry off to and sit at alone. The screeching of wooden bench legs against the stone floor brought Rachel out of her high school cafeteria flashback. Ra had pushed back the bench he was sitting on and was now closing the distance between himself and Rachel. She was flooded with a sense of relief. She didn't know what to do around these other giants. She'd been faking confidence around Ra, but it felt like too much to keep up in a room full of Ras.

"Welcome, Rachel. You will sit next to me," Ra said in an unexpectedly quiet voice. Rachel found it odd he seemed to not want the others to hear what he was saying. It felt uncomfortably intimate. She nodded and followed him back to his bench at the head of the table. Ra picked up a large decorative bowl and a cushion from the ground near his bench. He placed the bowl on the bench and placed the cushion inside the bowl. Before Rachel could protest, Ra had lifted her off the ground and placed her atop the cushion.

Rachel felt ridiculous, like a child being put in a booster seat. Ra sat next to her and moved the bench closer to the table, careful not to knock Rachel off her cushion. Rachel did her best to sit as dignified as possible on the cushion inside the bowl. She looked up at the unfamiliar faces that ringed the table. She attempted a weak smile, which was met with frowns and eye-rolls.

"Is this necessary, Ra?" asked a man from the opposite end of the table. Like Ra he was tan and shirtless, but unlike Ra he was bulky like a bodybuilder and he had dark, curly hair that went past his shoulders. He gestured toward Rachel. "Can you not keep her in your room and let your servants feed her?"

"Reeeally, Ra. It's absurd that you put us through this," complained a woman in a voice that reminded Rachel of a bored cat. She sat next to the man, and they both exchanged knowing looks.

A woman seated to the left of Rachel—a statuesque strawberry blonde with billowing hair and sympathetic eyes—spoke in Ra's defense. "What harm does dinner do? Ra intends to rectify the situation. The least you can offer him is your cooperation."

"The least?" demanded the man. "No, that is the *most* we can offer. I am exhausted with Ra's impulses putting us at constant risk. What is his business with this human?"

He spat the last word—*human*—as though it were a dirty word. Ra cleared his throat and turned to Rachel on his left and said, "Allow me to introduce you to my friends."

"*Friends* must be a relative term here," conjectured Rachel.

Ra gestured to the kind woman on Rachel's left. "This is Sekhmet," he said. He continued clockwise around the table. "Mafdet, Horus, Bast, and Kuk." Horus was the man who had objected to Rachel's presence, and Bast the woman who sounded like an uninterested feline.

Mafdet spoke up in a bright clear tenor voice, "I hope your stay is pleasant and that you find we treat you in a just manner."

Horus and Bast rolled their eyes again and Sekhmet smiled at Rachel. Kuk said nothing. He just observed everyone at the table. The group ate off the golden plates set before them.

Rachel started to half believe again that she was hallucinating. She'd done extensive research on all the Egyptian gods and goddesses. It was inconceivable that she could be sitting at a table with so many of them. She had accepted Ra based on the idea that he *might* be a god, but was probably just a very large man. Now that Rachel was literally surrounded by beings twice her size and all sharing names with Egyptian gods, it was hard for her logical mind to make sense of it all. Her mind raced so much all of her questions seemed to blur. She looked from large face to large face, finally settling on Ra's—so close to hers and so handsome. Rachel remembered one of her questions. "Where are my friends?" she asked.

Ra looked at Rachel, temporarily confused. The second before Rachel had asked her question, Ra had taken a bite to eat, so he finished chewing before answering her question. He swallowed then replied, "I do not know. I assume they are where we left them—at the cavern."

"Cavern?" asked Kuk, his voice was deep and rough. "My cavern?"

"Yes, your cavern, Kuk," replied Ra.

"So, my friends weren't taken or harmed?" asked Rachel.

Horus guffawed from across the table. "Yes, Ra, tell us—did you kidnap any more useless humans?"

Ra scowled at Horus, which only encouraged him. "You haven't told us yet what you plan on doing with this one. For all we know you've decided to create a collection. You know we don't keep pets, Ra," he said, looking at Ra with unblinking eyes. "And even if we did, you know how this ends. Revolt, bloodshed, escape, etcetera, etcetera. You are weak, Ra."

"Enough," snarled Ra. His voice was low and quiet but exceptionally menacing. The others at the table quietly ate. All except Rachel.

Ra noticed Rachel hadn't touched her food. "Why do you not eat?" he inquired.

Rachel's cheeks flushed a becoming shade of pink. She felt her nerves causing her to change colors, which only succeeded in making her feel more embarrassed, so she stammered, "I'm a-a-afraid if I try to-to reach my pa-plate, I will tip the bowl and fall."

Ra chuckled good-naturedly. He liked the color in Rachel's cheeks and couldn't help but find her endearing. "Oh, if that is all," Ra said, picking up Rachel's plate and handing it to her. "You can hold it on your lap."

Ra was right, it fit on her lap. The plate was the size of the top of Rachel's nightstand at home, but it wasn't heavy, and she didn't mind resting it on her lap. Rachel sampled the food on her plate. There was bread and olives, like earlier, and more figs (which she skipped). The main dish was something different though. "It looks like mushrooms and something," Rachel concluded to herself. She watched the others using their bread to scoop up bits of the main course. There were no utensils at the table, and Rachel imagined if there had been they would look like exaggerated serving spoons and forks in her smaller hands. She copied the others and used her bread to move the mystery food to her mouth.

"Mmmmm." Rachel unintentionally voiced. The food was delicious. Ra smiled down at her, and Rachel felt herself turning red again. Rachel was right—the mystery dish was part mushroom. She couldn't identify the other ingredients. She had never been much of a foodie and she rarely cooked for herself. Rachel was certain the dish was vegetarian though. It then occurred to her she had still not seen or heard a single animal. *Were these giants vegetarians by choice or were there no animals here? And where was here?* "Now that's an important question I'd like answered," Rachel thought to herself.

She finished chewing a mouthful of mushrooms and bread before she said, "Um, excuse me, but could you tell me where we are?"

Everyone sitting around the table exchanged uncomfortable looks, everyone except Ra. Ra calmly answered "We are in the great banquet hall."

"No, I mean, I think it's pretty obvious we're not in Texas, or the United States," said Rachel.

All the faces around the table remained unchanged except for Mafdet, who chortled. Ra answered, "No, we are not in the United States."

Ra returned to eating his food as though he'd answered Rachel's question completely.

"Where are we?" Rachel asked again. She felt a bit like the annoying toddler asking a million questions. "But it's really not my fault," thought Rachel. "If he'd just answer me, I'd quit asking."

Ra turned reluctantly toward Rachel and said, "I will tell you later. Perhaps after you have answered my questions regarding the book."

Rachel sighed. She had already answered his questions about Hester's book to the best of her ability. She frowned at her food and wondered if she could lie about the book and that way find out where she was. In the middle of Rachel's thinking, Horus stared daggers at Ra. Something was boiling over in Horus, bubbling up until he could keep quiet no longer.

"You can't be serious, Ra," accused Horus from across the table, his eyes bright with rage.

Ra met Horus' glance. Something in Ra's eyes provoked Horus further.

"You put Janus in danger!" roared Horus, standing suddenly, knocking his own bench to the floor.

Rachel looked around. *Was there someone else she hadn't met? Was Janus another giant? Maybe the wife or girlfriend of Horus? Another god or goddess?* And how could she—someone half their size—be a danger to anyone? Janus. The name sounded familiar to Rachel. "There was no Janus in Egyptian lore," she silently remembered. Was it an Egyptian city? She racked her brain. The message above the cave had been Greek. Perhaps Janus was Greek? Then she remembered. "Janus wasn't Egyptian or Greek. Janus was Roman—a Roman god."

While Rachel ruminated, Horus yelled at Ra, "You are careless. You should have left this human to starve. Your fascination endangers not just us here in this room, but our father, the planet. What do you expect to come from this? You think you can just send this human home? The Earth will find out about us and then they will come to plunder our planet and wage war against us. You bring on our destruction!"

Rachel couldn't keep up. Somehow Horus believed she was dangerous. That she was a danger to everyone—and to their planet. It was all sinking in. Rachel wasn't in Texas or the United States. Rachel wasn't on planet Earth. Hester had been right—they had been transported to another planet. Rachel was surprised she hadn't fainted yet. This was definitely overwhelming information. Everything around her felt surreal—like she wasn't really living it, like she was just watching it through virtual reality goggles or something. It was a 3D movie. It was a play. It couldn't be real. Horus continued his tirade.

"We have done this before and each time you try a different more dangerous tact. How has that worked thus far? You change nothing for the better by interacting with this human. If you do not learn to avoid this decision, next time it will not be yours to make," threatened Horus.

Rachel's mouth gaped. She looked from giant person to giant person. Egyptian god to Egyptian god. It hit her—if this is a different planet then that means these people are aliens. Aliens. Rachel made a mental note to apologize to Hester.

Ra looked down at Rachel then back to Horus. "What is the point of your outburst? You will only frighten the human."

Horus laughed a long bitter laugh. "You don't want me to *frighten* the human, Ra?" Horus asked, putting special emphasis on the word 'frighten.' "You should have greater concern I do more than frighten," he added, placing his hands on the edge of the table and leaning forward. The position caused all the muscles in Horus' large shoulders and arms to bulge, the muscles on his back stood up like he was half mountain—more rock than man. In the torchlight the definition of Horus' muscles were like chiseled stone and immense like boulders. It was startling.

Ra's calm finally cracked. He assumed the same position as Horus. Ra was long and lean, so the effect was not the same. The light didn't throw Ra's muscles into terrifying relief. But Ra was taller than his opponent and more commanding. Despite having less muscle, he was more intimidating. Ra's voice shook the bowl in which Rachel sat. "Leave!" he boomed.

Horus remained unmoved for half a minute—a silent challenge to Ra. Neither man moved nor spoke another word. Horus relaxed and stepped away from the table. He bowed stiffly to all in attendance then marched to the set of doors. He grabbed one door handle and yanked the door open, causing it to bounce roughly against the wall. As Horus left, Rachel noticed he had a falcon tattooed across his back, wings extended from shoulder to shoulder—the first 'animal' Rachel had seen on this planet. Rachel remembered who Horus was—the god of falcons and war.

The room was silent for a beat. Bast rose to her feet and pushed her bench back from the table. She had the elegance and ease of a runway model and a panther combined. She brushed her silky dark hair over her shoulder and without looking around she covered the distance from the table to the door and exited the room.

Rachel wanted to ask more questions—about what planet they were on, why Horus was so angry, what he'd meant by basically everything he'd said, and did Bast hate her, too. But, by the looks of Ra's face and still tensed muscles, she decided she'd wait. Ra slowly lowered himself back onto the bench. Rachel couldn't remember having ever seen anyone or anything seeming to have so much precise control of their bodies. She watched him as he sipped wine from a beautiful gold goblet almost the size of her arm. Rachel stared like one watching a play. Ra turned to her and raised one eyebrow in question to her stare.

Rachel laughed at the absurdity of the situation. Ra impossibly smiled back. Somehow she felt like she was becoming friends with Ra. "Is this how Stockholm Syndrome works?" Rachel wondered to herself. "I've been captive less than twenty-four-hours and I'm already buddies with my kidnapper?"

It was hard for Rachel not to feel something for him. After seeing Ra behave so protective of her, and he seemed to wish her no harm. Though, inwardly she kicked herself for how easily she forgave kidnapping.

"You must be thirsty," Ra said, interrupting Rachel's inner monologue.

Ra handed Rachel a small cup that sat on the table out of her reach. Like his goblet, it was made of hammered gold and filled with wine. Rachel smelled it before taking a sip, trying to gage whether it was ridiculously strong the way the wine had been in the cavern. She did not want to get drunk like Liam and Hester.

"It's not poisoned, Rachel," Ra said softly, but not soft enough for everyone else to miss. Mafdet laughed. He seemed to be the one with the best sense of humor. He was obviously younger than the others, too. But, maybe Mafdet just looked younger because he was blonde. Rachel was reminded of a biology class where her professor had explained that only an exceptionally small percentage of men retain their blonde hair as adults. "That's why blonde hair makes everyone look younger, it's something associated with youth," Rachel reminded herself.

Rachel answered aloud, slightly embarrassed to have everyone staring again, "Oh, um, I wasn't trying to smell if it was poisoned. I was trying to see if I could smell how strong it is."

The group laughed and Sekhmet smiled at Rachel and answered, "This is very weak wine. We drink it for taste, not to get intoxicated."

"Oh, that's good," said Rachel with relief at realizing she wasn't going to get drunk from her small cup. "My friends drank some wine we found in the cavern and they got incredibly drunk. I would just rather not get drunk."

"They drank my wine?" asked Kuk sulkily.

"I will replace it," offered Ra.

Kuk nodded and went back to his food and drink. Rachel sipped her wine and was happy to find it was closer to grape juice than any wine she'd ever had before, and it was delicious. Everyone ate and drank, and it wasn't long before Kuk rose and said to the party, "I am finished. I will walk the grounds."

"Enjoy your darkness," replied Ra.

"Ah-ha," recalled Rachel. She had forgotten what Kuk was the god of, but Ra's comment reminded her. "Kuk is literally the god of darkness. Or he is darkness. Or whatever."

It wasn't long after Kuk left that everyone else finished with their meal. The four remaining—Ra, Rachel, Sekhmet, and Mafdet—stayed seated at the table. Sekhmet was debating with Mafdet whether it was wiser to execute a man who had tried to steal medicine, or heal him.

"He only became a thief out of necessity," argued Sekhmet. "We could just as easily heal him and release him."

"But our laws are in place for a reason," replied Mafdet. "I want the best for our citizens the same as you, but if he needed the medicine, he should have come to us and petitioned us for assistance."

"He was too proud," said Sekhmet, her brows furrowed. Rachel thought she looked noble, like the heroines from the books she enjoyed.

"And that's his biggest failing," answered Mafdet. "You know we would have helped him. But as it stands we have to act in accordance with our laws. I will see to his execution tomorrow."

Rachel wondered if there might still be a slight possibility she was hallucinating. The goddess of healing and medicine, Sekhmet, was arguing with the god of justice and execution, Mafdet. Rachel didn't doubt her subconscious could come up with this scene. It certainly felt real.

Sekhmet frowned. "Of course this is your call," she said to Mafdet. "It would have been mine had he asked for help. But now that he has committed a crime his fate lies in your hands."

"Too true," Mafdet smiled. His job as executioner seemed to be in direct opposition to his appearance which was cheerful and sunny. He shifted his glance from Sekhmet to Rachel and asked, "What do you think, Earth woman? Is our assessment fair?"

Rachel was about to answer, but was interrupted by a commotion outside the banquet hall. There was yelling and the sound of several voices excitedly mingled together. The doors to the room burst open, and Rachel saw the last thing she expected.

CHAPTER 15

The sun had set and it was night by the time Liam, Hester, and Gerald reached the beach near the village. While they were in the forest, the threesome were not aware that a full moon brightened the night sky. The canopy of trees blocked out all moonlight, making them thankful for the torchlight that led their way.

At the edge of the forest Gerald suggested to Liam that he snuff out the torch in the sand of the beach. "I imagine it will be easier to sneak through the town if we aren't carrying a beacon of light before us," Gerald said.

"And it's not like we'll need it," interjected Hester. "The moon is bright as a spotlight." With the word "spotlight," Hester improvised a cheesy dance complete with imaginary kick line and jazz hands.

Liam extinguished the torch and left it lying in the sand. He and Hester sat on the large rocks that separated the forest from the beach and ate the last of the cornmeal cakes. They each also drank a jug of water, quenching the thirst they'd built during their walk. While Hester and Liam ate, Gerald looked to the city and tried to figure out how long it would take them to reach the palace. "It shouldn't take us much time to reach the palace," he conjectured. "As long as no one stops us along the way."

"I should just go alone," suggested Liam. "Hester's outfit and you being a ghost, Gerald, might kind of make us stick out."

"Look at that architecture," Gerald said, pointing to the buildings in the distance. "We're not walking into a modern city, Liam. I have a feeling that you will stick out even without us. We might as well stick together."

Liam couldn't argue with that, so he suggested the group prepare to leave. They left their empty jugs and bowl on the beach and Liam laced his belt back through the loops on his pants. The distance between the beach and the city was a quarter of a mile, but it took longer to cross than expected because Liam had to help Hester every step of the way. Every time she took a step she sank into the stand almost up to her knees. The effort caused Hester to breathe heavy, and though neither Gerald nor Liam said a word about it, her breathing worried them. Often, Hester found it hard to free herself from the sand, and Liam ended up lifting her out of her self-made holes. He offered to carry her, but Hester would not allow it. "I'm not a baby, damsel in distress, or bride on her wedding day, so it's not proper." she argued.

Once the group reached the village, the streets were almost empty. They tried to keep more to the shadows as they walked, careful to avoid eye contact with the occasional stranger they encountered. They didn't speak a word to each other, again trying to draw as little attention to themselves as possible. From the beach, their path to the palace looked like a straight shot. Once in the city they found there was no such thing as a straight shot. The streets curved here and there, diagonal, crisscrossing—there wasn't any rhyme or reason to the city layout. After walking for a half hour, Hester broke the silence,

"We should ask for directions. We could ask someone which way to the palace."

"They likely don't speak English, Bunny. And it's in our best interest we don't draw attention to ourselves," answered Gerald.

"Typical," said Hester, rolling her eyes, a note of superiority to her voice.

Both Gerald and Liam stared at Hester, both confused what caused the tiny generally good-natured woman to sound so aggravated. Gerald asked her, "What's that supposed to mean?"

Hester issued an irritated sigh and said, "Typical man. You don't want to ask for directions."

As she made her complaint, from a side street on their right, a village woman entered the street. Without saying another word to Gerald or Liam and without even looking their way, Hester walked toward the center of the street, toward the woman. "Excuse me," Hester said politely, "could you tell me which way we should be walking to reach the palace?"

The woman froze; the proverbial deer in the headlights. She didn't say a word, she just stared at Hester. Hester turned to Gerald and Liam and said, "I guess you were right, they don't speak English here."

The woman followed Hester's glance to the two men waiting in the shadows. She locked eyes with Gerald. What followed next was a blood-curdling scream. The woman ran back down the street from which she'd came as fast as her legs could carry her, screaming in an unfamiliar language.

"That can't be good," muttered Hester.

"Come on, Bunny," Gerald called to his wife, already hurrying down a street in the opposite direction from the screaming villager.

"She's not screaming English, so you two were definitely right," said Hester, turning her speed walk into a jog. She could still hear the woman screaming from a distance.

"We gotta hurry," Liam insisted. He was much faster than Hester, her breathing seemed to make her movement slower and slower the more they ran. The stress of slowing his own pace for the old woman caused him to reach his breaking point. "Sorry," he said, picking up the tiny woman. "I know you don't want me to carry you, but we need to get out of this area fast."

Liam cradled Hester like a baby and he ran, down street after street. Hester didn't protest, she wheezed and coughed as Liam ran. Gerald only lagged a few paces behind Liam. Liam guessed that Gerald's ghost form made him impervious to becoming winded, but didn't make him any faster than a normal octogenarian.

Liam and Gerald ran until they met a dead end. Fortune had smiled on the threesome. The dead end was the tall stone wall which surrounded the palace. "We made it," Liam panted.

Not out of breath at all, Gerald looked down at Hester still in Liam's arms. "Oh, Hester, Bunny dear? Can you breathe?" Gerald asked, fear painted across his face.

Hester shook her tiny head from side to side, her fluffy white hair bouncing. "We need to get her help," said Liam.

"You saw how that woman reacted. Who will help us?" asked Gerald, his voice panicked. He clasped his own blue-green ghost hands in fear and worry.

Both men looked back down the street they'd ran. They could hear people yelling and the scuffle of feet on stony streets. The crowd was moving closer and closer to where they stood.

"We've got to keep moving," Liam said.

They looked down the stretch of palace wall and noticed a gate. "That," Gerald said, gesturing towards the gate. "If they are like typical subjects in a kingdom, they will not enter the palace grounds without express permission. It's the safest place for us now."

They hurried to the palace gate and found it unlocked. There were no sentinels or guards posted. Straight ahead were the large doors leading into the palace, but instead of attempting what would doubtless be a dangerous place to enter, they instead ran for what looked to be a garden courtyard. "We can wait here in the shadows and hope that Hester improves," Gerald suggested.

Liam could see the fear in Gerald's eyes. "He must be jumping to denial to avoid the true danger of this situation," Liam inwardly assessed. He said aloud, "Gerald, she needs an inhaler. We need help."

"Bunny, just try to think calming thoughts," Gerald whispered to Hester. Hester looked scared now, too.

"Calming thoughts can't fix asthma," argued Liam. He had never been so afraid in all his life. He was scared that Hester was going to die in his arms. He felt responsible for protecting her. He had already failed Rachel, he couldn't fail Hester, too.

While these thoughts raced through Liam's mind a slight movement caught his eye to the left of where they stood. Liam and Gerald had brought Hester to the shadows in the beautiful garden courtyard of the palace. The center of the courtyard was lit by the moon, but where they stood was almost as dark as the inside of a cave. Unnaturally dark. Liam looked up into the shadows in which they stood and noticed two dark eyes staring down at him. If it weren't for the whites of the eyes, Liam wouldn't have noticed. Before he could alert Gerald, a voice said from beside them, "Why do you lurk in my darkness?"

The voice startled Gerald, and he gave a small scream. To give Gerald some credit, in normal situations he wouldn't be so edgy, but at the moment given his fear for Hester, he couldn't be blamed for screaming. Having not been entirely taken by surprise the way Gerald had been, and feeling they had no other recourse, Liam gave a rambling, pleading answer, "We're sorry. We need help. I'm afraid we accidently frightened the villagers so they're after us. We tried running, and our friend has asthma and can't breathe. Please, if you can, help us."

"You are trespassing," answered Kuk. It hadn't been long since he left the banquet hall to enjoy the darkness in the courtyard. He had been disappointed by the bright moonlight, so he'd made due standing by himself in the shadows. While he stood there alone he meditated on how much he missed his cave and his cavern and that he should make it a point to visit both wonderfully dark places more often. His musings were interrupted by the human trio. He guessed these were the friends Ra's human had asked about. These were the wine thieves.

"We are sorry to trespass," Gerald said. Looking high above their heads to the eyes that seemed to float, he wondered if this could be the same giant that abducted Rachel. The shadows made it impossible for him to distinguish any features.

Kuk looked for a moment at the wheezing tiny woman in the young man's arms. He didn't like the idea of any creature suffering—even if they were wine thieves—especially when they could be enjoying the wonderful darkness which surrounded them in the shadows. He said to them, "You are criminals for trespassing and for stealing, but I will try to help you."

Without another word, he picked up Liam, who was still cradling Hester. Kuk tried to pick up Gerald, but his giant hand passed through Gerald's transparent body. "Neat," Kuk chuckled, before adding, "Follow me, spirit."

Gerald followed Kuk out into the middle of the courtyard, and then across it to a corridor that led into the palace. As they hurried, it became clear to Gerald it was not the same giant he had seen abduct Rachel. This giant, though still massive compared to a human, was smaller than the other. He also had wild black hair that seemed to reach out in all directions. It reminded Gerald of furling black smoke. As he followed the giant down the hall, Gerald wondered what the giant meant by "stealing," but the question evaporated next to his worries for his wife. They didn't know it, but Rachel's friends traveled down the same corridor Rachel had followed Kesi through earlier.

In Kuk's arms, Liam stared into Hester's tiny suffering face. In the light from the torches in the corridor, Liam noticed she was blue. He didn't want to alarm Gerald any further—he could hear Gerald nervously humming from somewhere below the giant's elbow. Hester was right that like Liam, Gerald was a nervous hummer, too.

Hester gripped Liam, like she were drowning and he was her life preserver. He looked into her eyes; they were mirrors reflecting his fear. Hester would die soon if she did not get an inhaler. Liam's heart sank. "What are the chances of finding an inhaler in a place like this?" he mused.

They reached a large open area, with impressive double doors at the far end. Two guards stood at either side of the doors. Gerald followed the giant across the room. Before reaching the guards, Gerald could see the alarm in their faces. The guards screamed as the group approached. Gerald stopped humming. Evidently, they did not fear the giant, but Gerald—the ghost.

Kuk bellowed, "He is spirit, he cannot harm you. Open!"

After nervous shouts of "Yes, Master," the guards obeyed, though their legs shook and their eyes bulged. Gerald remained close to the giant. He followed him into the enormous banquet hall. If he weren't so worried about his wife, the Egyptologist in him would have been ecstatic to note the similarities between his surroundings and ancient civilizations. As things were, he noticed nothing. Gerald was looking up to the giant who carried Liam and his precious wife—his Bunny.

"I found trespassers," announced Kuk to those seated at the table before them.

Rachel stretched herself up on her cushion to see what Kuk held in his arms. She locked eyes with Liam, and he exclaimed, "Rachel!"

Everyone at the table turned their attention to Kuk and the "trespassers." He walked to the table, and with his free hand pushed dishes aside, and placed Liam and Hester down in the space between Mafdet and Sekhmet. From where she sat, Rachel could see that Hester was blue. The breath caught in her chest, and she covered her mouth with both hands, horrified.

Gerald's view of Hester was blocked from his position behind Sekhmet, but he saw Rachel's reaction. "Bunny?" he called, now distraught. "Please, someone help my wife!" Gerald cried.

Without a word, Sekhmet placed one large smooth hand over the chest of the dying old woman. "Be well," she said.

The room was silent in anticipation. Not a soul made a sound. They all stared at Hester and Sekhmet. Hester gasped, breaking the silence—her first real breath since running in the streets of the village. She immediately went from blue to pink, and her breathing returned to normal. She smiled and said in a voice weaker than was normal for the feisty old woman, "Thank you."

"You are most welcome," returned Sekhmet, her smile broad and genuine. Her teeth gleamed white, despite the low lighting of the banquet hall.

Rachel was overcome with gratitude for the giantess. She opened her mouth to express her gratitude to Sekhmet, but was interrupted by the overly enthusiastic Liam. "Thank you so much," he said with tears in his eyes.

From below Gerald called up to the table, "Hester, dear? Is Hester okay?"

Kuk again tried to pick up Gerald and failed. He laughed about it, once more, and said with a shrug of his broad shoulders, "I would bring you to her if I could, but I can't lift spirits."

Seeing the clear solution, Sekhmet gently lifted Hester from the table to the ground to be closer to her husband. Overcome, Gerald tried to embrace his wife, but his ghostly arms passed through her. He finally broke down, blue-green tears streaming down his wrinkled blue-green face. "I love you, Bunny," he confessed to the tiny old woman, who returned his sentiments, then suggested they both sit on the floor for a minute.

Mafdet looked from human to human, with an amused smile on his face. "Of course, Horus would be all a twitter if he were here to witness this," he snickered.

"I could not leave the tiny woman to die," answered Kuk defensively.

"Absolutely not," agreed Sekhmet.

"I did good," asserted Kuk, still defensive and a little sulky.

"Yes, you did good, Kuk. Thank you," said Ra.

"I suggest you get these humans stowed someplace safe for now, though, Ra," advised Mafdet. "You know it won't be long until Horus gets wind of this. If he was as put out as he was earlier just about one human... can you imagine his reaction to three humans and a spirit?"

"Yes, you are right," Ra replied, looking from Rachel to her friends.

Ra arose and crossed the room to the double doors. He opened one door and murmured an order to the guards who stood outside. Rachel and the others could hear the clinking of a guard's armor as he ran across the large open room. Ra closed the door, returned to his seat, and informed the group, "I have sent Donkor for my servants. They will be here shortly to direct the humans to my chamber."

Ra's words were acknowledged with nods from everyone save Mafdet, who answered, "Excellent. I do have one question though. How do you propose I handle the matter of the humans trespassing? They have broken our law—no entrance without express permission."

"Mafdet, I believe you are splitting hairs," replied Sekhmet, her lips pursed and brows pushed together. Rachel admired Sekhmet. She was clearly a champion of the people.

"As we discussed before, we must be certain the people adhere to the laws we lay out. Without consistency we will fall into chaos," said Mafdet with a coy smile.

Ra was about to speak, but Gerald interrupted, "Excuse me, but are you suggesting we are breaking the law by being here?"

Mafdet turned on his bench to face the transparent Gerald seated on the ground. He smiled sweetly and gestured broadly. Mafdet both literally and figuratively spoke down to Gerald.

“Strictly speaking, yes. You were not invited. You did not come during standard visiting times. So, yes, you are trespassing and in violation of our laws,” said Mafdet in his crisp clear tenor.

“Your laws?!” Liam exploded, his excitement shaking the table upon which he stood. “Had one of you not kidnapped Rachel, we would never have even entered your city, let alone your palace.”

Mafdet nodded. He looked like a dashing young lawyer on a television show as he turned to Liam and asked, “So what you’re saying is, one law was broken, therefore that justifies another law being broke?”

“No, that’s not what I’m saying,” said Liam. “I’m—”

“Because that sounds like what you’re saying,” interrupted Mafdet, still all smiles and charm.

“Enough,” Ra ordered. “We will discuss this later. Do not trouble us with your semantics and games, Mafdet.”

“As you wish,” answered Mafdet, with a wink at Rachel.

Rachel was starting to wonder about Mafdet. He had seemed the friendliest of Ra’s peers, but there was something oddly confrontational about him despite his smiles and charm.

Just then the door opened and Kesi stepped into the room. “Master, I am here,” she stated.

“Take these humans to my chambers, Kesi. And see that food and drink is provided for the newcomers,” ordered Ra.

Kesi bowed. Without warning, Ra lifted Rachel from her cushion and lightly placed her on the ground. Since Mafdet was closest to Liam, he lifted Liam from the table and placed him on the ground next to Hester and Gerald before Liam knew what was happening. The group of four crossed the room to Kesi, all glad to be leaving the room full of giants. At least mostly glad. Rachel experienced mixed emotions. At the door, before leaving the room, she turned back to look at Ra. He was also staring at her, and for a brief second they maintained uninterrupted eye contact. Rachel's heartbeat accelerated and she felt her face flush. "What is this thing I'm feeling towards him?" she inwardly mused. She blinked, breaking the spell, and quickly turned and left the room.

CHAPTER 16

Once outside the banquet hall, Rachel saw that Kesi was not alone. Halima and Mert were again by her side. Kesi directed Halima and Mert to return to the kitchen and get plates of food for Ra's new guests. Without question, they turned and ran for the kitchen.

Kesi lead the group across the large open room, down the corridor, and into the courtyard where Kuk had found Liam and Gerald worried over Hester. When they were here earlier, Liam hadn't noticed all the beautiful flowers that surrounded them in the courtyard. He was too distracted by fear. With a relieved smile on his face he inhaled their rich fragrance.

"That's where we were hiding when the giant found us," he whispered to Rachel as they walked. Liam pointed to a shadowy area against a wall. This was the same courtyard Kesi had led Rachel through earlier. But earlier Rachel had seen no way of escape, despite the breeze she felt. Rachel now saw an opening in a hedge—probably the place where Liam, Gerald, and Hester had entered. "A chance of escape," she thought to herself. The thought was involuntary, and Rachel wondered why she felt guilty for thinking it.

But, attempted escape didn't seem wise now. Not with the knowledge the villagers were hostile. And somehow it didn't feel fair to leave without saying goodbye to Ra. And part of Rachel didn't feel like she was ready to say goodbye to Ra either—like there was something unfinished between them.

Before leaving the courtyard and reentering the palace, Rachel took a long look at Liam in the moonlight. He was handsome, though his time in the cavern and through the forest had made him look dirty and disheveled. He noticed her looking at him from the corner of his eye and turned to her and smiled. "I'm glad you're okay, Rachel. We were worried about you."

"Yeah, I'm okay. Thanks, Liam," Rachel whispered. "I don't know, it's almost like I think I should be more scared than I've been. But I'm okay."

"I think I know what you mean," said Liam. "I keep experiencing this déjà vu feeling. Like we've done this before, and it's all going to be okay, ya know?"

"Yeah," Rachel replied.

"I mean, except that thing with Hester. That was terrifying and like nothing I've ever experienced. And, really, I hope to never experience anything like that again," Liam said. He leaned in closer to whisper, "I thought she was going to die. I was so scared."

Rachel reassuringly patted Liam on the arm. They followed Kesi down corridor after corridor lined with torches. "Hey, those look like the torches from the cavern," suggested Liam, just like Rachel had observed earlier.

The group followed Kesi up the stairs. They took breaks on each bend in the staircase so Hester's breathing did not get out of control again. While they waited, Rachel wondered what new trouble the arrival of her friends might cause with Horus. "And what did he mean by saying bringing me here was a danger?" she wondered.

They reached the third floor, and after turning one corner and walking down one last corridor, they were at Ra's door. Kesi took a torch from the wall outside the room and ushered them inside the bedchamber. The room was dark except for the moonlight that streamed through the window and the lamp Halima had left burning on the vanity. In the semidarkness the large pieces of furniture loomed like hulking beasts. Kesi lit torches and lamps around the room, and as the light grew the space became more welcoming. Everything seemed cast in a warm amber glow.

As Kesi was leaving and closing the door, Mert and Halima arrived carrying a tray of food and a copper pitcher with four copper mugs. Of course, Gerald couldn't drink any water, but that hadn't occurred to Mert who carried the water and the mugs. As she entered the room, she tripped over her own feet and dropped all four mugs to the floor.

"Oops," she said under her breath, looking down at the mugs on the floor. Up to this point Rachel had assumed Mert was mute, but evidently she was just selective with her words.

"At least it wasn't the water," said Halima. Smiling, she set the tray of food on the ottoman, then hurried to help Mert pick up the mugs.

Kesi stood at the door waiting for the other two. Once Halima and Mert had left the room, Kesi said to Rachel and her friends, "We will be outside the door if you are in need of any assistance." She closed the door and Rachel, Liam, Hester, and Gerald were left alone in Ra's large room.

Hester was the first to speak. "Whoooooa," she said looking around the room.

Gerald also seemed surprised by something. One of his arms was wrapped protectively across the front of his transparent body while with his other hand he alternated between gripping his forehead and covering his mouth. Rachel and Liam looked from Hester to Gerald trying to figure out what their reactions meant.

"You two okay?" Rachel asked, trying to gauge if the elderly couple were both losing it at the same time.

"Look at this place!" exclaimed Hester, bouncing up and down, her shadow bouncing on the wall behind her.

"Uh-huh," answered Rachel. "What about it?"

"Don't you see it, Rachel?" Hester demanded. "You've read my book—it's just like *The Mighty Arm that Built Egypt.*"

"Yeah, I thought the same—" Rachel began, but was talked over by Hester excitedly addressing her husband.

"Gerry, it's just like your dream!" Hester shouted to Gerald, who had still not said a word.

"His dream?" asked Rachel and Liam at the same time.

"Yes. When we were first dating, Gerry told me about this crazy dream of his about all these Egyptian gods living on an undiscovered planet, and how they were giants and scary," said Hester. She held her arms out in front of her like Frankenstein's monster, and the shadow behind her looked just like the frightening giant she described. "His dream was so vivid, he was able to describe it in the minutest detail. I later used the idea to write *The Mighty Arm that Built Egypt.* Of course, I didn't base it on another planet—that seemed far-fetched—but I did make the Egyptian gods aliens still. That just made sense to me."

Rachel wasn't sure what to be more upset about—the fact that Hester had just spoiled the rest of *The Mighty Arm that Built Egypt* for her, or the fact that Gerald apparently already knew about this planet and its inhabitants. "This is another planet, and they are aliens," Rachel said.

"Woo-hoo! I knew it!" cheered Hester. Gerald still held one arm across his body, and one hand to his head. Rachel wondered if ghosts could experience shock.

"Why are you so happy about that, Hester?" asked Liam, his voice raising in pitch. "That means we're not on Earth."

"Where's your sense of adventure, dear?" inquired Hester with a twinkle in her eye.

"I've lost it bit by bit over the last twenty-four-hours. First when I tried to find Rachel and her kidnapper in a forest where I could have easily been lost, then the rest of it when I thought you were going to die in my arms," Liam confessed. He scratched at his beard, then added, "And giant alien Egyptian gods."

For the first time Rachel worried about Liam—that he might pass out or have a nervous breakdown. They'd all experienced a lot within the last day and a half, and it was starting to show on Liam.

"Liam, you must be hungry and thirsty. Why don't you try some of this food they brought for you?" Rachel suggested, leading Liam over to the ottoman and the tray of food. It was identical to the plate they'd brought Rachel earlier—figs, grapes, melon, olives, and bread—only there was three times as much food.

Liam obeyed Rachel and began tearing pieces of bread from one of the loaves. Rachel poured water into three of the four mugs. Hester was still looking around the room with a rapt expression. Gerald broke his silence and said, "Bunny, you need to eat something, too."

Hester crossed to the ottoman and browsed the food selection. "Oooh, figs!" she exclaimed.

Rachel and Liam both made disgusted faces at the mention of "figs." Even Gerald who couldn't have eaten them anyway looked thoroughly repulsed by the fruit. Seeing Liam's and Gerald's reactions to the figs, Rachel said to Hester, "They're all yours."

"Mmmmm," said Hester, pulling all the figs into a small pile. With a fig half chewed in her mouth she said, "Rachel, I like that dress on you. It suits you. You look like you could be an Egyptian queen."

Rachel had forgotten she wasn't wearing her normal clothes. The gauzy white dress and sandals were comfortable and felt natural.

"Your hair looks pretty like that, too," added Liam, smiling at Rachel from the other side of the ottoman. He seemed to be calming down with food in his stomach.

Rachel felt uncomfortable, almost ashamed. Her friends were dirty, tired, and had perhaps come close to death while she was basically being pampered like a princess. "You were kidnapped, though," she reminded herself, trying to ease her guilt.

She looked down at her dress and said, "That reminds me." She set down the mug she had been drinking from, walked to the door, and knocked three times.

Kesi opened the door. "Is everything all right?" she asked.

"Yes," answered Rachel. "I was just curious about when I'm going to get my clothes and shoes back."

"I will send Halima to see if they have been washed," said Kesi before closing the door.

When Rachel turned around, Hester was looking at her beaming. "This really is so exciting," the tiny old woman said.

"I don't see how you're so happy and so calm, Hester," said Liam. "You almost died, and we're on another planet. With aliens. Aliens who are giants! And clearly they possess special gifts, I mean, with what the lady giant did..."

"Sekhmet," interjected Rachel.

"It's all getting harder for me to wrap my brain around, honestly," admitted Liam. Food hadn't completely helped calm him.

"Yes," said Gerald, standing apart from the group. Both arms were now across his chest. He paced the length of the giant bed. Simultaneously Liam and Gerald both began humming.

Rachel looked from Liam to Gerald. *How had she become the only calm reasonable member of their party?*

Hester giggled, "You boys are so funny," and popped another fig into her mouth.

Rachel didn't think it was funny. She felt like she was witnessing the beginnings of two men ready to have nervous breakdowns. "Knock it off, all of you," she blurted.

Gerald, Liam, and Hester all stopped. Gerald stopped humming and pacing. Liam stopped humming and rocking himself back a forth (something he had just started doing to Rachel's horror). And Hester stopped chewing—one fig left half chewed in her mouth.

"You two," Rachel said pointing to Gerald and Liam, "need to calm down. Freaking out will not help us. And you," she said, looking at Hester, "you need to take this situation a little more seriously. We are stuck on a foreign planet. We don't know how we got here or how we're going to get home. We've been shown kindness, but we don't know how long that will last. Ra said he was keeping me to get me to give him answers about the book I was reading—your book, Hester."

"Yeah," Hester answered with her mouth full. She finished chewing her food, then continued, "I'm sure you've figured out by now he's the bad guy in the book."

"Uh-huh, that's how it seemed from what I'd read," said Rachel.

"He doesn't seem too bad in person, though," acknowledged Hester.

"Aside from kidnapping me, he's been fine. Polite, thoughtful even," Rachel agreed.

"Ra was who kidnapped you?" asked Liam. "If he's so nice, why would he kidnap you?"

"That's what I've been struggling with," answered Rachel. "He's been kind to me. He's just seemed focused on Hester's book. And, I don't know... at times it almost seems like he acts like we already know each other. It's hard to explain."

Gerald nodded his head in agreement. Liam saw him do it and confronted him. "What's that? What's that mean? Why are you nodding your head?"

Gerald looked from Liam to Rachel to Hester. His face showed there was something weighing heavy on his mind. Gerald sighed then admitted, "I've met Ra before. I've been here before."

Hester laughed, dismissing what Gerald had just confessed. "We know, Gerry. It's just like your dream you told me about."

"No. I've been here. In this room. I think I convinced myself it was a dream because it was too much—too overwhelming," the old man said.

Everyone was silent for a beat. Rachel knew the old man couldn't be lying though. He had no reason to lie. "How is that possible?" she asked.

"I don't know," answered Gerald. "But, I get the overwhelming feeling we aren't safe here. At least I know that the last time I was here it wasn't safe. We need to find a way out."

The room fell silent again until Liam suggested, "We could sneak out the window,"

"I was going to try that earlier. But we're three very tall floors up," said Rachel.

"Why don't we just open the door and walk out?" asked Hester.

"Yeah, we could knock those ladies out if we have to, and make a run for it," said Liam.

"We're locked in," Gerald said in a tone that inferred—*obviously.*

Rachel looked at Gerald in disbelief. Sure, she was locked in at first, but Rachel was certain they weren't locked in anymore. Ra was treating them has his guests, not as his prisoners. "No, we're not locked in," Rachel said and walked to the door. She stretched her arms up and tried the handle expecting the door to swing open. It didn't. Gerald was right—the door was locked.

"What?" Rachel muttered. She had been convincing herself she wasn't a prisoner—not a real prisoner. She was what Ra had said—a detainee. She and Ra had a connection. She was just here still to help Ra answer the questions he needed answered. She had convinced herself of all those things. But that wasn't the truth. Rachel and her friends were here because they weren't allowed to leave. Prisoners.

"I told you, we're locked in," said Gerald, with a tone that sounded more defeated than 'I-told-you-so'.

"We should try picking the lock," suggested Liam, looking around. "Maybe there's something in this room we can use to pick it."

"I searched earlier and didn't find much," Rachel confessed. As she causally took in her surroundings again, she stopped when her eyes fell on the vanity. "Wait a second," she said.

Without another word to her friends she lifted the tray of food off the ottoman, along with the pitcher of water. Liam figured out Rachel was trying to clear the ottoman, so he helped by removing the mugs. Rachel climbed on top of the ottoman—which was still shoved against the vanity. Earlier she had watched Halima use a key to unlock one of the top drawers, but didn't see Halima relock that drawer. Could there be anything inside besides hair styling products? Rachel knew it was a long shot that this drawer would hold a way out of the locked room, but it was her only hope at the moment. She opened the drawer and automatically had an idea—hair pins. She held one up, "Can we try picking the lock with this?"

"Why don't we just knock on the door?" asked Hester. "That one lady said she'd give us help. If they open the door, we can do like Liam said—knock them out and make a run for it."

"But what then?" Rachel considered. "Where do we run? How do we get home?"

As her thoughts spiraled into bigger fears, something caught her eye in the open drawer. From under ribbons like those Halima had woven through Rachel's hair, something shiny and bronze lay. Rachel moved the ribbons and was so surprised by what she found she almost lost her balance and fell off the ottoman.

"Are you okay, Rachel?" asked Liam, concerned.

Rachel steadied herself before turning back to the open drawer. Reaching her hand inside, she picked up the shiny bronze object she had found and held it out to her friends. "Guys, look!"

"No, way," said Liam.

Rachel pulled another bronze medallion out of the drawer. Two bronze medallions. It wasn't until that moment that she realized they were missing from her purse earlier. Rachel traced a finger along the engravings on one of the medallions—the familiar scarab. "I hadn't noticed they were missing. Ra had to have taken them from my purse."

"But that just makes no sense," argued Liam.

Rachel handed him the medallions so she could close the drawer, which only contained hair styling supplies aside from the bronze medallions. "What part of this has made any sense?" she asked, climbing off the ottoman.

"Fair point," he answered.

"Put the medallions in your pocket," Gerald commanded.

The others were surprised by Gerald's abruptness. Rachel and Liam looked at Gerald. The six foot tall ghost stared back at them with intense serious eyes. Both Rachel and Liam internally tried to make heads or tails of Gerald's behavior.

Rachel's eyes narrowed as she remembered the conversation they'd had in the cave. They had discussed the possibility that the medallions were some sort of transportation devices. Gerald seemed too sure, like the idea of the medallions being keys or homing beacons of some sort was inarguable. *Did Gerald know more than he was letting on? Did this have to do with what he said—that he had been here before?*

Rachel was about to interrogate Gerald when Hester beat her to the punch. "Gerry, what's going on? Those medallions were yours. *You* were the one who donated them to the university. And you say you've been here before. This all isn't adding up for me and I don't like it. You said you got those medallions at a swap meet and you told me you had a dream about this," she said gesturing to the room around them. All signs of the giggly bouncy Hester gone, in her place a somber version who looked disappointed. She shook her head and continued, "Now you say you've been here before, and lo-and-behold, those same medallions were stolen, then hidden in this very room. You and I don't keep secrets and this feels like a big secret to me."

"Bunny, it wasn't my intention— "

"Don't 'Bunny' me. Just tell me the truth, Gerry."

Rachel and Liam looked back and forth between the elderly couple. Gerald swallowed loudly, then spoke, "Hester, I never intended to lie to you. Most of the time I thought I had dreamt it. I convinced myself I had dreamt it. And when I didn't believe it myself, there were times I thought I was most likely certifiably insane because of the memories I had."

Gerald looked pleadingly at Hester, then at Rachel and Liam. "I mean, giant aliens twice the size of regular men! With the names of Egyptian gods!" Gerald paused, collecting his thoughts. "I have been here before, and I escaped. My memory of the ordeal is foggy. It always was foggy—like a dream. But, the longer we've been here and the more we've traveled here the clearer my memories become. I think the shock of it the first time I was here left me with holes. I still don't remember everything. For example, I don't remember how I got back to Earth. I just know when I returned to Earth, I had those three medallions in my pocket. Knowing you were all holding them when we were transported here makes me feel positive they are keys between planets. I don't understand the science behind it, but it's what makes the best sense."

"But you lied to me, Gerry," Hester said in a monotone.

"Bunny, I wasn't trying to lie to you," Gerald maintained. "When I met you I knew I wanted to spend my life with you. That I was supposed to spend my life with you. What would you have said if I'd told you I'd been on an alien planet and escaped but I wasn't sure how I'd escaped?"

"I don't know, Gerald. You didn't give me a chance," replied Hester, with tears in her eyes.

"Bunny... Hester, I have always loved you," he said, his voice getting rough and shaky. "That is the greatest truth I know. If I lived forever the only thing that would stay the same is my love for you."

Gerald reached out as though to touch her, but froze. The group watched as the remembrance of his inability to touch his wife dawned on his sad wrinkled face. He let his hands fall to his sides and said, "I am sorry for lying to you, Hester. I'm sorry I didn't give you a chance at hearing the truth before now."

Hester's bottom lip trembled. The tears that had been standing in her eyes brimmed over and trickled down her soft wrinkled cheeks. "I wish I could hug you, Gerry."

"Me, too, Bunny," he answered. Gerald looked over to Liam and Rachel. "Liam, will you, please, hug my wife?" he asked, his voice shaking.

Liam put the medallions in his pocket, crossed to the tiny old woman, and gave her a comforting hug. Her white head rested against his chest and the tears continued to stream down her face, leaving a wet mark on Liam's shirt. Liam soothingly patted her on the back and said, "It's okay, Hester. Everything is going to be okay. We'll figure it out. We'll get home and everything will be okay."

Rachel, touched by the scene before her, joined Liam and made a Hester sandwich. The little old woman laughed, "I guess if I'm going to be stuck on an alien planet, you two kids and my Gerry aren't the worst company."

"I thought you liked aliens," teased Rachel.

"Not when they're holding me prisoner, I don't," returned Hester, wiping her eyes on the sleeve of Liam's blazer.

"They don't all seem bad, though," said Liam. "The lady one and the funny one who found us in the courtyard seem nice."

"Yeah, they *seem* nice," answered Rachel, crossing to the door again and giving the handle a tug. "But why are we locked up?"

Rachel turned her back on the door and leaned against it. A second later she felt the door opening, causing her to lose balance and fall to the floor. Kesi stuck her head into the room and asked, "Is everything fine? Do you need something?"

From the floor Rachel exhaled, "No."

Kesi looked down and said undisturbed and matter-of-factly, "I have sent Halima for your belongings."

"Thank you," responded Rachel, not knowing what else to say to Kesi. Rachel tried to look like she chose to sit on the floor. She folded her hands in her lap and smiled up at Kesi. This entire situation was making Rachel like Kesi even less. Kesi had already seemed unfriendly, but now that Rachel knew Kesi was part of keeping her prisoner, it was hard for her to put on even the facade of friendliness to Ra's servant.

Kesi closed the door. This time Rachel heard the faint *clink* of the lock. At that moment she felt more like a prisoner than she had since being kidnapped. In the morning, when she'd first awoke, she knew she was locked in a room, but she thought all she had to do was escape. She thought all she needed to do was make it back to her friends. Now her friends shared her prison. *If they were to escape, to where would they escape?* Rachel's thoughts were interrupted by Liam's voice.

"Gerald, what do you remember about being here before?" he asked.

"Let's see," Gerald said, pausing to think. "I remembered the cave and the cavern, and the city, though I hadn't remembered the streets being so confusing."

"Seriously, Gerald?" Rachel interrupted, getting off the floor and back onto her feet. "I can't believe you didn't say anything earlier."

"Like I said before, it was all hazy. It doesn't really come back to me until I'm standing in front of it," he claimed.

"Can you think of anything now that might help us?" asked Rachel, trying to keep the irritation out of her voice but not quite succeeding.

"Off the top of my head, no," Gerald said. "Though, I feel very uneasy. We are not safe here."

"That's helpful," snapped Rachel sarcastically, choosing the wall to lean against this time instead of the door.

"Hester said you told her about this—that's how she got the idea for her book," said Liam. "Is there anything from the book that maybe you told her that would be helpful now?"

"Oh, I've got the book," offered Rachel. She walked to the wardrobe, stretched her arms up over her head and opened its door. From inside she pulled out her purse, and from her purse she pulled *The Mighty Arm that Built Egypt*. Pushing the wardrobe door closed she said, "Maybe there is something you remember that would give us a clue what's bothering Ra so much about this book."

"Let me see that," said Hester, grabbing the book from Rachel.

She turned to the table of contents where the chapters were listed. Each chapter was titled things like "Confrontation," "Confession," and "Revolt."

"Gerry, if I read you my chapter titles do you think you'd remember the parts you inspired? Or do I need to jog your memory better by telling you what happens in each chapter?" Hester asked her husband. She squinted at the page in front of her, her eyes having trouble making out the print.

"It will probably be more helpful if you just run through what happens in the story big plot point by big plot point," he said, as he again started pacing.

"Can one of you kids read what each chapter title is?" asked Hester. "I can't see it so good—between not having my reading glasses and the dimness of the light in here. If you tell me the chapter title, then I will be able to remind Gerry what happens in the book."

Hester handed the book to Rachel, and Rachel took a seat on the bed. She read aloud, "Chapter one—Dynasty."

"That chapter just gives a history I made up of how Ra and his fellow gods came to power. Nothin' Gerry told me there," answered Hester, waving her hand in a manner that suggested Rachel continue to the next chapter title. "Well, except the descriptions of how big and scary the gods were," amended Hester. "I got that from Gerry."

"The next chapter is 'Control'," said Rachel, trying to keep the old woman on track, hopeful they might discover something helpful.

"Umm, I think that chapter talks mostly about the awful lives of the Egyptian people. How the gods controlled them through fear or whatever," Hester answered. She looked eagerly at her husband and asked, "Ringing any bells, Gerry?"

"I know their size and the fear they instilled is obviously from what I told you about them, but you'll need to be more specific about the story for me to know if it came from my memories of my time on this planet," he said.

"That's the chapter where Ra kills the villager," said Rachel. She pictured the scene where the elderly citizen stands up to the enormous god, only to be struck down by a blow from Ra's staff. Rachel expected Gerald to say that was something Hester had created from her imagination, but instead he answered, "Yes, that happened."

Rachel was looking down at the next chapter title, ready to read it to Hester. Gerald's answer took a minute to sink in. When it did, it caused Rachel's head to snap up. She was shocked. Appalled. Something in her revolted against the idea that the person she knew could be so cruel. Ra was immense and frightening, but he had never seemed that callous—he had never struck Rachel as a vengeful murderer. Gerald saw the horrified look on her face and added, "I mean that happened when I was here last time—to a villager—but I don't remember which one of *them* did it. It might have been Ra, or it could have been any of them. My memory isn't clear."

Rachel took a deep breath. She didn't know if she should ask Gerald more about that particular incident or if she should read the next chapter title. Liam saved her from making the call by asking a question.

"Do you remember if it was a god or a goddess?" asked Liam.

"Yes, I am certain it was male. A god, if that's what they are," answered Gerald, sounding doubtful.

"I guess we don't even know that," Rachel said.

"I thought you said they're aliens," chirped Hester.

"This is a different planet and they're obviously not human, so I guessed they were aliens," replied Rachel.

"We should ask them," said Hester enthusiastically.

"Yeah, we'll ask them that right after we ask them to stop locking us in rooms and kindly to send us back to Earth," said Rachel, rolling her eyes.

Hester frowned and when she spoke again, all the excitement had left her voice. The tone it now took reminded Rachel of her mother when Rachel had disappointed her. "We're in this together, dear. Don't forget that."

Rachel looked at the three faces in front of her—from Hester's disappointed face, to Gerald's serious face, to Liam's tired face. "Sorry," Rachel muttered, half embarrassed, half frustrated. She stared at the book in her lap, not wanting to see what she saw in her friends' faces.

"They have the same names as Egyptian gods, so I guess a part of me just assumed that confirmed the mythology," Liam said to Gerald. "It hadn't occurred to me to question that."

"I don't believe they are gods. I can't fathom a god as cruel as some of the beings I've met on this planet," said Gerald.

"And that's another question," added Liam eagerly. "What planet are we on?"

"Janus."

CHAPTER 17

The answer came from behind Hester, Gerald, and Liam. Soundlessly Ra had entered the room and was standing behind Rachel's friends. They each gave varying reactions of fear and surprise—gasps, jumps, and jolts. Rachel's heart skipped a beat and her breath caught in her chest. Ra stood before them holding Rachel's washed clothes and shoes in his hands.

Hester clutched her chest and looked up at Ra thoroughly annoyed. "Dang it, you almost gave me a heart attack! A little warning for us mortals if you don't mind!"

Ra looked from human to human, and said sincerely, "My apologies."

He closed the door behind him, then placed Rachel's clothes on the bed and her sneakers at the foot of the bed where she'd found them before. "Here are your possessions," he said politely.

"Thank you," Rachel answered. She wanted to say more—to get angry at Ra for keeping them prisoner. She wanted to ask him a million questions about where they were and why they were here and how to get home, but her tongue felt too big and her mouth was dry. Her biggest question of whether he was the cruel monster who so easily and thoughtlessly killed people weaker than him seemed to stick in her throat, making it impossible to talk.

"So, this is Janus," Liam said in response to the question Ra had surprised them by answering.

"Yes, this is Janus," Ra said without inflection.

The torch and lamplight flickered with the slight breeze that came through the window. Rachel tried to ignore the way the light accented Ra's chiseled chest. She focused instead on his answer—Janus. Rachel remembered she'd heard that name earlier in the great banquet hall. Horus had called "Janus" their father and had acted as though she, a tiny human, might cause it danger. It seemed the biggest source of his anger—Ra putting Janus in danger.

"I thought Janus was one of Saturn's moons," Liam said to Ra.

"This is no moon," Ra answered, looking down at them, concern painted across his face. Without another word, he sat gently on the bed next to Rachel.

Ra sharing the bed with her so suddenly surprised Rachel. Ra noticed her raised eyebrows and wide eyes. "Pardon me," he said. "It occurred to me that it might hurt your necks looking up at me. I will sit so you and your friends do not have to strain your necks."

Again, Rachel felt confused and conflicted. She thought to herself, "We're prisoners, but our captor is endlessly polite, even concerned that our frail human necks might get strained."

"Thanks," Hester said to Ra. "That was pretty high to be looking up at."

Ra nodded in response to Hester, then turned to Rachel and said, "I see you are examining the book. Perhaps you will now be able to help answer questions about its content." Rachel was about to answer she would help him with whatever she could, but that she didn't know what exactly the problem Ra was having with the book, besides being a character—the villain—in the story, when Liam interrupted.

"We'll answer questions if you answer questions," Liam boasted, obviously trying to appear tough. Rachel didn't think this was a wise way to approach someone who was literally twice their size. She doubted Ra would respond well to a "you scratch my back, I'll scratch yours" philosophy.

Ra turned to Liam, a half smile slowly turning up the left side of his mouth. Rachel noticed that the teeth under his full lips were bright white and perfectly straight. Ra turned back to her and asked, "Does this human man speak for you, Rachel?"

There was something more to Ra's question. Rachel tried to determine exactly what the undertone was—*Was Ra trying to imply she was weak and needed a man to speak for her? Or was he implying that she had a relationship with Liam where speaking for her would perhaps be acceptable? Was Ra asking her if she was dating Liam?*

Rachel stuttered her answer. "Uh, um, Liam is my friend. As is Hester and Gerald. We see ourselves as strangers in a strange land—a group of lost friends—so I guess you could say that we all speak for each other." It was the most diplomatic answer she could give. For some reason she didn't want Ra to think she was romantically linked with Liam—Liam, whom just the day before she had been developing a crush on. When Rachel realized she was intentionally making it clear she was not an item with Liam she blushed.

Even in the low light of the room Ra noticed, though he did not comment on it. Instead, he turned back to Liam and said, "You desire a question for a question—or more aptly, an answer for an answer?"

"Yes," agreed Liam.

"Since I have already answered a question of yours—what planet this is—then I believe I should get to ask the next question," said Ra.

Liam looked to his friends to gage how they felt about the arrangement, but couldn't tell either way, so he answered the best he could. "I guess that sounds fair."

"Good," replied Ra. "All of my questions are about that book," he said and gestured to the book in Rachel's lap.

Rachel looked down at the book. She had closed it the moment she was aware Ra was in the room. Looking down at the front cover, in her head she read the familiar book title and below the title, "H.H. Mays." Rachel's stomach dropped. It hadn't occurred to her until that exact moment it might be dangerous for Hester to have anyone here learn she was the author of the book. Ra was not happy about his negative depiction in *The Mighty Arm that Built Egypt. What would his reaction be if he knew the author herself was standing before him?*

Ra looked straight at Liam and asked, "Do you know about this book? Have you read it?"

Liam began to answer, "No, but..." when Hester interrupted.

Hester started to say, "I..."

"Hester has read the book, as well!" Rachel blurted.

Everyone turned to Rachel. She hadn't meant to shout. Rachel had just known she had to stop Hester from saying she had written the book. Hopefully the others knew better than to contradict her, and tell the truth that Hester had done more than read the book. Before anyone else said another word, Rachel added, "And Gerald has read parts of it."

Ra looked at Rachel for one long moment, like he was weighing what she had said by an internal scale. "Then three of you might be helpful," Ra said, looking from Rachel to Hester to Gerald. His eyes traveled to Liam as he said, "And you will need to remain quiet."

Liam didn't say a word, and as far as Rachel could see he wasn't taking offense to the way Ra had treated him. Rachel considered what a good guy Liam really was. "So good natured. He came to rescue me, and he's been so sweet to Hester," Rachel reflected while looking at the tiny old woman in her lime green pantsuit and Liam's blazer. Looking back at Liam, Rachel saw his shirt was dirty and ripped. But even dirty and disheveled he was still cute.

"My question for the three of you is," Ra began. Rachel turned her head to look up into his dark eyes as he spoke. He paused, taken off guard by her sudden eye contact. This wasn't the first time they'd locked eyes like this, and Rachel wondered if his culture was one where eye contact was taboo. *Was she committing some major social faux pas every time she looked him in the eye?* Ra regained his composure and continued, "My question is, where did this book come from?"

"I've already answered that question. I told you I bought it at the airport," answered Rachel.

"I understand you purchased it. But how did it come to be?" asked Ra.

Hester answered calmly, more calm than Rachel was used to seeing the tiny octogenarian, "Someone wrote the story, and someone else bought the story. It was then printed in large quantities and sold to the public."

Ra reached out and took the book off Rachel's lap. "There are more of these?" he asked, shaking Rachel's copy of *The Mighty Arm that Built Egypt* at Hester. His brow was deeply furrowed, and his free hand clinched.

"That's another question," Liam said under his breath.

"He doesn't have an answer for his first question, so we'll allow it," Rachel said, trying strongly to imply not to nitpick an unhappy twelve foot tall Egyptian god.

Ra scowled at Liam and said in a controlled whisper, "I have shown you more kindness than you deserve, human. I will only answer your questions if you can answer mine. I have no answers yet, and therefore it is not your turn to ask questions."

The giant looked like he wanted to throw the book across the room, or at Liam, or perhaps throw Liam across the room and tear up the book. He spoke to Hester. "You said there are many of these books?"

"Yes. It was printed, then reprinted," Hester answered, looking into Ra's endless eyes. "Hundreds of thousands of copies."

Rachel wondered what Hester saw there, and she wondered why Hester was being so honest. *Did Ra really need to know there were hundreds of thousands of copies of this book about him on a planet he wasn't living on?* Hester looked sad staring into Ra's eyes. The more Hester stared, the sadder she became. "I'm so sorry," the old woman muttered and tears ran down her face.

"You see," Ra's words rushed out. "You see that this isn't true. I am not a monster. This book is lies mixed with truths. But mostly lies."

"I'm so sorry," Hester said again between sobs.

Liam patted Hester on the back, but remained silent. Gerald looked concerned at his wife, but just as confused as Rachel. Rachel was sure he had the same fear she did—that Hester was about to confess to writing *The Mighty Arm that Built Egypt.*

Ra stood, walked to his vanity, and unlocked one of the drawers with the key he had hiding in his waistband. From the drawer he pulled a handkerchief the size of a baby's blanket. He locked the drawer and walked back across the room. Standing over Hester he crouched down to her level and handed her the giant handkerchief. She smiled at him and thanked him. Ra stood. He returned to his seat on the edge of the bed. Hester dabbed her eyes with the cloth she could have used as a headscarf.

"I will answer a question now," said Ra, his elbows rested on his knees.

Rachel and her friends looked at each other. *What question came next? Who would ask it?* Rachel could think of a half dozen questions off the top of her head—*Where is Janus? How did we get here? How do we get home? Why are we being kept as prisoners? Why does Horus say she's a danger to Janus? And, even if bad things were said about Ra in the book—like the scene with the villager—why does it matter so much if it isn't true?*

Rachel and Liam started asking questions at the same time.

"How did we—" Liam began.

"Why does the book—" Rachel started.

They both stopped once they realized they were talking over each other. Ra laughed. He said to Liam with a smile, "I said you did not get to ask questions since you could not answer them."

Above his beard Liam's cheeks turned a barely perceptible shade of pink. Rachel wasn't sure if it was embarrassment or anger that caused Liam to change colors. She guessed that if it wasn't for his beard, Liam would look incredibly young—younger than his actual age (which Rachel realized she didn't know).

"Rachel, what was your question?" asked Ra.

"Oh, uh, um," Rachel stammered, then stopped. She wasn't sure now if she was asking the best question. *What if they didn't get all of their questions answered?*

"Yes?" asked Ra.

Rachel decided she'd just ask her question anyway. Maybe her question would help answer Ra's next question, too. "Why does it matter that this book was written with you as a character? I mean, I understand that it says bad things about you. But, it's just a story. How does it hurt you? You don't even live on the planet on which it's published."

Ra looked from Rachel to Hester. He looked like he wanted Hester to explain it to Rachel, like he was sure Hester understood why it bothered him.

"This book," he said handing the book back to Rachel, "says I am a terrible and cruel god. That is bad enough. That is not fair to me. But if that is all it said I would dismiss it as a stupid story written by someone who is uninformed. The thing I most strongly object to in this book is its truth. The perfect description of this room, of this palace. The descriptions of things that have happened on this planet, and not on yours."

"I still don't understand," said Rachel. "Why does it matter?"

"It matters because it changes my actual story," replied Ra.

Ra looked at Rachel and she felt like she was falling into the endless depth of his eyes. She could feel his sadness mixed with anger, but she didn't understand it. Rachel still didn't get what Ra meant. She looked around at the others to see if they understood something she didn't. Rachel felt stupid saying she still didn't understand, so she was silent. Ra could read it on her face, though, so he tried to explain. "Someone who has been here has recorded histories and presented them as fiction. I dislike the lies the book says about me, but you are right—how does it hurt me? 'What does it matter?' as you say. It matters because this book has changed time, I believe."

Rachel looked at Ra blankly. He spoke English to her but he might as well be speaking Janusis or Greek. Liam forgot he wasn't allowed to ask questions and asked, "What do you mean—the book has changed time?"

Ra allowed Liam's question. He answered, "What is time to you? A straight arrow endlessly going out before you?"

Liam nodded. Ra continued, "But that is not true. That is not how time works. Time is not a straight line—it is not linear. Time is a circle. It is infinite like the line you picture, but it is, was, and will always be. What has happened today has already happened, and what will happen tomorrow has come before, as well, and yesterday will repeat itself."

Ra looked around at his audience to make sure they were following him. "Perhaps you have experiences where you feel as though you've been in that exact moment before?" Ra asked.

"Yeah, I felt that way earlier," Liam answered. The others nodded in agreement.

"You feel that way because you have been in that exact moment," said Ra. "Every moment. Every moment has already taken place. Everything has already happened, and it will infinitely continue to happen. Those moments feel strange to you because you are not usually aware that it has already happened. But, that is mostly because you do not understand that time is a circle."

"What does the book have to do with that?" asked Hester.

Rachel noticed Ra didn't seem bothered that he was answering more questions than he was asking. She made a mental note to answer more questions for him if she could.

"The book is new to the circle," Ra said in response to Hester's question. When he said circle he made a circle in the air with his pointer finger.

"Is that possible?" asked Rachel. "I mean, if everything has essentially already happened, how does something change? Wouldn't everything be fixed? Wouldn't it be like we're reliving the same TV episode over and over again?"

Ra looked confused. "What is 'TV episode'?"

"Oh, um, do you have plays? Theatre?" she asked.

"Yes."

"It's like that. Wouldn't time be like reliving the same play over and over again, only not being aware of it?"

"For most creatures, yes," Ra answered. "But not for me and my friends you met tonight, and not for other higher beings. We are aware of time. You might say we are outside time. It does not apply to us."

"So, you've lived this exact moment before?" asked Rachel.

"What do you mean 'time doesn't apply' to you?" Liam asked on the heels of Rachel's question.

"One question at a time—though I do believe it should be my turn to ask the questions," said Ra with a teasing grin.

"We will answer every question we can, we just need to understand what you're saying better first," said Rachel.

"Of course," answered Ra. He took a deep breath and continued. "Time does not apply to me in the way it applies to you. I remember what has happened before and what will happen. It is not bright and fresh like the memory of yesterday, but I remember it nonetheless. I have met you all before."

"You've met us before," Rachel stated more than asked, before repeating her previous question. "You lived this exact moment before?"

Ra shook his head. "No, that is why I have a problem with the book," said Ra. "I have not lived this moment before. Pieces of it are the same. But it has changed. I believe it is the book that has changed it. I believe the book has changed time."

"Holy cinnamon and sugar sandwich!" exclaimed Hester. "I think I need to sit down."

Hester took a seat on the stone floor with her back against the wardrobe. She looked pale like she might faint. Rachel watched her, worried Hester would reveal herself as the author of the apparently cataclysmic novel.

Ra took Hester's reaction as a sign of sympathy. He tried to reassure the tiny woman, "It might not be terrible. For the time being it is just different. Unpredictable. I have intentionally changed time before. For example, every time I have encountered the four of you our interactions have been slightly different. I alter the circumstances marginally each time to see if the end results change. They have not. But this time I encountered you—I watched you at the cavern—I noticed you had something new in your possession. You had that book. That is what is different this time—something outside of myself has changed time."

"Horus accused you of putting all of them in danger. He said you try something different every time, but it didn't matter," Rachel said then paused before continuing. "You said you've met us multiple times and you try something different every time. Is that what Horus was talking about? And why try something different? Are you intentionally trying to change something that takes place in the future, or are you just bored or something?"

Ra laughed. "Perhaps I do get a little bored," he admitted. "My friends would like me to ignore your presence on our planet altogether. You have greatly fascinated me, however. Each time I relived your arrival, I snuck closer and closer to your encampment in the cavern. I finally started revealing myself to you to varying degrees of success. Sometimes the group of you screamed. Sometimes you tried to scare me off with fire."

Ra broke into a long hearty laugh. He pointed at Liam and Rachel and choked out between laughs, "You two miniscule humans tried to frighten me off with torches."

Ra laughed so much, tears streamed down his face. He wiped them on the back of his large tan hand and smiled at Rachel. His teeth gleamed in the low light from the torches and lamps. She couldn't help but laugh a little at the thought of her and Liam waving torches at the giant. Rachel remembered earlier when she wouldn't relinquish her shard of glass. Ra was apparently used to being threatened by her.

"You," Ra said breaking into another stream of laughter and pointing at Hester, "threw wet cornmeal at me."

Gerald and Hester both laughed at the picture Ra's statement elicited. "You probably deserved it," teased Hester with a wink at the oversized god.

"True. I did frighten you," conceded Ra. "There was a part of me that hoped you'd remember me the way I remembered you. The time you threw cornmeal mush at me I hadn't given you much notice before I entered the cavern. I thought I'd just join you at the fire the way I had the last time I'd seen all of you. But the time before I didn't surprise you inside the cavern. I'd met you outside first. Or, I met Rachel outside the cavern and then she introduced me to the rest of you when you arrived."

"In every version of you meeting us, were you hiding somewhere outside the cavern?" asked Rachel.

"Yes. Every time I've met you, I first watched you and Liam find the cavern. I've then watched him leave and you take a seat at the entrance alone waiting for their return," said Ra.

"When I was outside waiting for them I thought I heard an animal stepping on a twig or leaves or something, but I never saw any animals. Was that you?" asked Rachel.

"Yes, the sound you heard was most likely me. We do not have animals on Janus."

"Why don't you have animals?" Hester asked.

"That is complicated," Ra answered. "I think it is better we continue talking about this concept first, and after that I might explain why we do not have animals on Janus. For example, as I was saying, every time I met you it was the same. Rachel was waiting for the rest of you at the entrance of the cavern. This time was different, however. This time when she sat alone waiting she pulled out a book. I crouched almost over her shoulder and read the title of the book, and then when she opened the book I saw my name in print."

"Wowee, those are some impressive eyes you've got!" exclaimed Hester. "I need a pair of glasses to read it when it's right in front of my face."

"I am blessed with exceptional vision," Ra confessed.

"I get it that you say things were different—time was changed—and that you hadn't done it. You were a little freaked out to see your name in the book Rachel was reading. But why kidnap her? Why not let the story play out like it normally would? You know, let us try to scare you with fire or whatever?" asked Liam, his hands on his hips.

"I don't know. Perhaps the best explanation is I panicked. I saw something change that I hadn't had a hand in and I needed to know more. I almost took Rachel and the book back to my palace when she was alone, but I convinced myself not to. I attempted to convince myself to behave as I always had with you. Befriend you, invite you to the palace, and all the other things we had done before. But I spent so much of the evening debating what to do that it was past nightfall and I had not even introduced myself to you yet. I decided the only thing I could do was take Rachel and her book back to my palace and ask her to explain its existence. We had gotten along well all the other times I had lived this experience. I thought it would go smoothly. But it seems that this adventure is not meant to go smoothly," Ra finished sadly.

"We've been friends every time we've met?" Rachel asked with a smile.

"Yes, after you stopped waving a torch at me, we have generally gotten along well," Ra smiled back.

"Can we go back to the animals?" Liam asked. He was getting bolder. Rachel wondered if Liam was the sort who got cranky when he was tired, or if he had just decided he didn't like Ra because of the kidnapping thing.

Regardless of whether Liam's attitude could be attributed to tired crankiness or not, Rachel wanted to know about the animals, too, so she asked, "Yes, why don't you have any animals?"

"Surely it should be my turn to ask questions again by now," Ra attempted with a smile at Rachel.

"Why are you avoiding that question?" Liam asked.

Ra shot Liam an annoyed look, then turned to Rachel and answered, "We do not have animals on Janus because we frighten animals."

"What do you mean you 'frighten animals'? Like your size?" asked Liam.

"We tried to have animals here and most died of fright. I can only guess we seem unnatural to them," Ra answered with a grave look.

"They think you're monsters," Rachel said in a whisper, as though the quieter she said it the less offensive it might be to Ra.

"Yes," answered Ra. He stood and walked to the window. The moonlight shown on his face and the front of his bald head. He intently looked at something below. "That is not good," he muttered.

"What? What is it?" Rachel asked. She stood and joined Ra at the window. The others followed and crowded around to see what Ra had seen below. Outside, below in the streets, a crowd of villagers gathered. They had torches and they stood at the gate. The proverbial villagers with pitchforks, sans the pitchforks. The sound of their voices carried up to the window, but their words were indistinguishable.

"Those must be the villagers who chased after us," Gerald said. When he spoke Rachel realized he hadn't said a word since Ra had entered the room.

"Yes, and that means Horus will soon know you are here... if he has not already been made aware," said Ra with a sigh as he turned and stalked from the window. He stopped in front of the vanity, the ottoman, and the tray of food that had been left on the floor. He picked the tray up and placed it on the ottoman and helped himself to some grapes.

"What's Horus' problem? Why does he think I'm dangerous? Does he think they're dangerous, too," Rachel asked, pointing to her friends.

"Yes, you are all dangerous by virtue of the fact that you lead to the destruction of Janus," Ra replied flippantly.

Ra's statement hit Rachel and her friends like a ton of bricks. They were all silent. Not one of them knew how to respond. They each had several questions pop into their heads, but no one seemed capable of communicating those questions. Hester was the one to break the silence.

"Ra, sweetheart, you're gonna have to be a little more clear with us. You've told us that time is a loop, that you've met us before as friends, and now you say we cause your planet's destruction. All that seems pretty contradictory to me, and I'm guessing for everybody else, too."

The others nodded in agreement. Rachel added, "Are you leaving anything out that might make it clearer?"

"What do the Egyptians say about me?" he asked. Rachel couldn't decide what his voice sounded like. Sad? Irritated? Misunderstood?

"The Egyptians?" asked Rachel. She reflected for a minute and then answered. "If we've met before then I can only assume that I told you I am an Egyptologist, and that Gerald told you he is an Egyptologist. I'm sure we've told you about what the Egyptians have written about you. I can't imagine spending time as friends with the Egyptian god, Ra, and not telling him what I already know about him."

Ra smiled. "The Egyptians called me the god of the sun or the king of gods," he said with a chuckle. "I am no god. At least not that I know of. I am not human, though, and to Egyptians that makes me god enough, I suppose."

He ate a few more grapes and looked across the room at the humans still huddled at the window. "Why don't you sit and make yourselves comfortable?" he asked, his hospitality returning.

Liam took a seat under the window and Gerald followed Hester back to where she had been sitting against the wardrobe. Rachel's sandal's made a slapping noise as she quickly crossed the room to where Ra stood, in front of the vanity. She looked up at him, the lamp on the vanity casting his face in strange shadows. "Why are you talking about the Egyptians? What does that have to do with us being a part of the destruction of Janus?" she asked.

Ra towered over her for a minute before answering. He slowly lowered himself to the floor and sat cross legged next to the ottoman. With Ra seated on the floor and Rachel standing, his gaze was only slightly above hers. He answered her by saying, "The Egyptians thought I was a god. I am not. I am, however, endowed with a certain gift."

Ra paused and turned his attention again to the tray of food. Rachel wondered at how he could so quickly go back and forth between extreme curtesy and oblivious rudeness. He ate grapes with no apparent intent of continuing the conversation.

"What is your gift?" Rachel asked, trying to keep the annoyance out of her voice. *How could Ra seem so aloof when the fate of his planet might hang in the balance?*

"Oh, that?" he asked. He picked a bunch of grapes from the tray and pulled five from their stems. "Time. Like I said earlier, I influence time."

"By changing things? Like you said before?" Rachel asked. "Like by changing the way you interact with us?"

"Yes, and by slowing it or stopping," he replied. He threw the grapes he had plucked from the bunch in the air. They froze mid-flight, in front of Rachel's face. They did not drop to the ground. "I will it, and it is so."

"Wha-what?" Rachel stared at the grapes in front of her. "No way."

"It is real. I am no magician," Ra said.

"Guys, do you see this?" Rachel asked turning to her friends.

Hester, Gerald, and Liam didn't say a word. "Hester? Gerald?" she asked, looking to her friends in front of the wardrobe. "Liam?" she asked, looking directly at her friend seated under the window. Not one of her friends answered or moved.

Rachel felt her stomach turn to lead. Her friends weren't moving. Were they breathing? She felt panic pulsating throughout her body. Rachel turned back to face Ra. With the slightest incline of his head the grapes fell to the floor. Rachel heard Liam yawn.

Hester asked, “Why’d you throw those grapes on the floor?” To the others it had looked as though Ra threw the grapes in the air and they followed the typical law of gravity by falling to the floor.

“You can control time,” Rachel whispered. “You can will it stop.”

“Yes,” Ra answered.

“If you can will time to stop, then couldn’t you will it to stop before Janus is destroyed?”

“You’d think I could,” he said with a melancholy sigh, his dark brows almost meeting in the middle.

“Why can’t you?” she asked.

“I keep hoping it will end differently,” Ra said with a smile, his head cocked slightly to the right.

Rachel felt herself blushing. She thought to herself, “In the middle of these circumstances that are impossible on so many levels, is this handsome giant creature flirting with me?”

Ra added, “And I can only stop time for a moment. My abilities have their limitations. I can stop the sun from rising or setting. But not forever.”

“You can stop the sun in the sky?” Rachel marveled. “Did you do that in front of the Egyptians? Is that why they say you were the sun god?”

Outside in the corridor, there was the sound of loud footsteps and a sudden loud voice. “WHERE IS RA?!” it bellowed.

Ra held his finger to his lips, indicating for everyone in the room to remain quiet. Rachel and her friends held their breath while they tried their best to hear what was happening outside the door. They could hear Kesi calmly speaking to the source of the yelling, but couldn't make out what she was saying. A minute later, they heard the loud footsteps heading away from the door, toward the stairs.

Kesi opened the door and stuck her head inside. "Horus is looking for you, Master. He is unhappy."

"He has most likely heard about my additional guests. What did you tell him?" asked Ra.

"I said I believed you had gone with Master Kuk to walk in the courtyard," replied Kesi.

"Thank you, Kesi. If you fear your safety is in jeopardy, feel free to retire to your quarters. Otherwise, remain guarding the door while I go handle this matter."

Kesi bowed and closed the door. Ra stood and looked around at his guests.

"What are you going to do?" asked Rachel.

"I am going to try to find Horus—away from all of you—and attempt to calm him. At the very least I will try to find Mafdet and Kuk to help me persuade him to calm down." Ra said the last bit with an arch to his eyebrow. Rachel guessed that "persuade" meant brute force. She hoped it wouldn't come to that. She hated to think she might be partly to blame for any act of violence.

"What about us?" asked Liam. "Are we safe here?"

"I will lock the door behind me. I cannot imagine Horus would attempt to force his way into my chamber," said Ra. He turned and left the room. They heard the lock clink and felt the shadow of uncertainty and fear drape over them like a cloak.

CHAPTER 18

Ra placed the key back in his waistband. He was alone in the corridor. Kesi had returned to her quarters, as Ra had given her permission. Mert undoubtedly followed her lead and returned to her quarters as well. He knew Halima had already returned to hers. When Ra had apprehended Halima downstairs with Rachel's clothes and shoes, he relieved her of her duty and dismissed her for the evening.

Ra took a deep breath and hurried down the corridor to the stairs, walking fast enough to make the torchlight wave violently as he passed. At the top of the stairs he paused to remind himself to appear calm. "Do not rush," Ra told himself. He took the steps two at a time, not because he hurried but because they were in proportion to normal human size. Had he still been hurrying he could have taken the stairs four at a time, no trouble. Ra knew it was important to appear calm when he encountered Horus. Give Horus no reason to assume him guilty of anything.

"Am I guilty of anything?" Ra wondered as he made it to the bottom of the stairs. He turned corner after corner in the labyrinthine halls of the palace. "I did not invite them to the palace this time. They came on their own. How is that so different from before? There is an angry crowd. But there is always an angry crowd in this story."

Ra rounded a corner and was confronted by darkness. Not a single torch glowed gold in the corridor that stretched before

Ra. It was a hall in the center of the palace, so it had no windows. Usually at least one torch was left lit. "Kuk?" Ra asked the darkness.

Ra saw two eyes appear in the darkness, then a smile. The darkness receded slightly. "Yes, Ra," said Kuk in his husky voice.

"Do you mind if I light a torch?"

"Not at all. I was about to look for you," replied Kuk. Before Ra had a chance to search out a flint, Kuk had lit a torch himself. "Horus is on the hunt for you. He did not see me, but he walked through this hall a few minutes ago cursing your name under his breath."

"I believe he has been alerted to the presence of the additional humans," said Ra. "I need to find him and talk reason to him. I fear he will not have patience though. Will you search for him with me?"

"Let us find Mafdet first, then search for Horus together as a team," suggested Kuk.

"Wise plan," agreed Ra. He had considered the idea of strength in numbers earlier, but decided the faster he found Horus the better. However, Kuk was right. He needed a team to approach Horus.

Ra followed Kuk down the hall in the direction Horus had traveled. They reached the corridor that lead right to the bath chamber and left toward the main entrance to the palace. "I doubt he'd go for a bath," mumbled Kuk, before heading left toward the main entrance area.

The giant gold plated doors to the main entrance opened into the same large room Rachel and her friends had traveled through to reach the banquet hall. Had Rachel realized how close her escape had been when she'd been ushered to the bath chamber or when she'd been escorted to the banquet hall, she might have considered making a break for it. But, with the angry crowd of villagers before the main entrance now, she was safer where she was in Ra's bedchamber.

As Ra and Kuk reached the giant gold plated doors, one opened slowly and Mafdet stepped backwards through it, waving to the crowd outside before closing the door. He looked to his right at the two who had been searching for him and gave them a friendly smile. "I was just checking in on our adoring subjects. Let's just say they're not in the adoring mood. It seems the old man spirit gave one of them quite the fright. They demand we rid them of this curse."

"The spirit is harmless," said Kuk.

"Of course, I know that," replied Mafdet. "But you know how these villagers can be. They're positively simple. They insist on justice."

"Justice for what?" demanded Ra. "The old man did nothing. He is incapable of doing anything to anyone."

"Nevertheless," said Mafdet.

Ra shook his head, trying to free it of the idiocy he felt Mafdet was inflicting on it. Ra despised petty behavior, and this stank of pettiness. He decided to ignore what Mafdet was suggesting and focus on what he felt was the most pressing. "Mafdet, we need you to join us in our search for Horus. I am afraid he has discovered that the other humans are in the palace and he means them harm. We believe he will be more easily convinced if it is three rather than one who approaches him."

"Mmmmm, I don't know," Mafdet whined, slowly deliberating whether he wanted to get involved. He looked away from Ra to inspect his nails. "What is your endgame, Ra? Do you plan on keeping them as pets? Or allowing them to escape and tell Earth all about our planet? I certainly see

Horus' side." Mafdet paused to rearrange the golden caplet he wore. He looked up to see Ra's face creased with worry and anger. Feeling half guilty, half frightened, he responded, "Oh, all right. I will help you. Where should we start?"

"He came looking for me at my quarters less than ten minutes ago and my servants said I was with Kuk. Perhaps we should try the courtyard?" suggested Ra.

Ra led the way across the large room that was essentially an oversized entryway, down the corridor that led to the courtyard. The moon still shone brightly. Kuk looked to the sky and gave a sad sigh.

"Why can't you just enjoy a full moon, Kuk?" asked Mafdet, giving Kuk a teasing elbow to the ribs.

Kuk scowled, looked around the courtyard and said, "He is not here. What now?"

"The east wing? We could see if he returned to his own quarters?" proposed Mafdet.

"Yes, but let us hurry," Ra said. He was becoming increasingly worried the more time eclipsed between when he last saw Rachel and her friends safe. Horus had sounded enraged. Ra did not want that rage unleashed on Rachel.

Another set of doors led them into yet another dark corridor. Kuk lit a torch and took it from the wall so they would not have to stop repeatedly to light torches if they encountered more dark halls. They turned from left to right, to left to left, to right again before reaching the east wing and the section of the palace where Horus' chamber lay. The door was closed and not a sound issued from within. Ra knocked loudly three times.

The door opened a hair and from inside a woman's voice said in a purr, "Horus isn't in."

Ra pushed the door open. The only person in the room was Bast. Seeing the group standing before her, she laughed. Her laugh was high pitched and musical, but mocking.

It took all of Ra's self-control to remain calm. Without the influence of Horus, Bast was harmless, helpful even. But Horus brought out the worst in Bast. "Where is Horus?" Ra demanded.

"He's gone to find where you're keeping those humans," Bast smirked. "The villagers told him they were here. Apparently one is a spirit and nearly scared a poor woman to death. They say he's an evil spirit come to kill their children. Or was it kill their crops? I don't know, you know how foolish and superstitious they can be."

Bast crossed to the bed and made herself comfortable. She curled up on her side using her arm as a cushion for her head. Her long black hair fanned out around her like a pinup girl or a Hollywood starlet. Bast smiled up at Ra, unafraid.

"Where is Horus now?" Ra again demanded.

"I don't know," drawled Bast. "I'm not his keeper."

Ra slammed the door then hurried down the hall. "Where to now?" inquired Mafdet, his golden hair bouncing as he skipped behind Ra.

"Servants quarters?" asked Kuk as he struggled to keep up with the others. He was the shortest of his peers. Ra was the tallest at more than a head taller than Kuk. Most of that extra height was in Ra's legs, which meant when Ra hurried Kuk had to break into a jog to not get left behind.

"We will pass that way and enquire with the servants, but now I feel uneasy leaving Rachel and her friends alone. I believe I should return to my chambers to ensure their safety," said Ra.

When the three reached the servants hall Ra rapped on a door. It was as tall as his door, but had a handle closer to the ground. The room belonged to his three female servants—Kesi, Mert, and Halima. Mert answered to door. When she looked up to find Ra, Kuk, and Mafdet standing before her, her eyes widened for a moment, before taking a step back and saying simply, "Kesi."

Kesi came to the door and before Ra asked a question she spoke, "Horus passed Mert and I in the hall. I believe he was going—"

"Back to my chamber," Ra said finishing Kesi's sentence.

"I believe he knew—"

"I wouldn't leave Rachel alone," said Ra finishing Kesi's sentence again. "He will assume I'm in my chamber."

Without another word Ra ran down the hall, followed by Kuk.

Always the charming gentleman, Mafdet said to Kesi before turning to run after his friends, "Thank you for your assistance."

The halls echoed with the sound of their sandals slapping against the stone floors. Torches flickered as the giants streamed by. Kuk still held his torch out before him, like an Olympic torch bearer. Mafdet effortlessly outpaced Kuk and was running neck and neck with Ra. He smiled up at Ra. "This is quiet exhilarating," he said, his blonde hair waving and his blue eyes shining.

Ra didn't reply. He ran to the stairs and took them four at a time up to the third floor. When he reached the third floor, he stopped and listened. He heard nothing. Mafdet then Kuk reached the top of the stairs, and stopped behind Ra, waiting on his command. Ra soundlessly walked down the corridor, followed by Mafdet and Kuk. They carefully turned the corner to the corridor that housed Ra's chamber. When they were ten paces from the door to Ra's chamber they heard Horus' voice.

Ra ran towards it.

♦ ♦ ♦

It had been at least five minutes since Ra had left Rachel and her friends alone. "Maybe it's been ten minutes," she guessed before asking aloud, "How long do you think it's been since Ra left?"

Her friends all answered simultaneously different answers—2 minutes, 7 minutes, 15 minutes. "Apparently not one of us has a good internal sense of time," Rachel concluded.

She paced the room listening to the *slap, slap,* slapping sound of her sandals on the stone floor. Liam stood and walked to her without making a sound. He gently grabbed Rachel by the arm and she stopped. The room was instantly quiet. Liam leaned in to whisper in her ear, "We should probably try to be quieter. Can you either stop pacing or take off your sandals?"

Rachel looked down at her feet, and then at her dress. "I should change. Jeans and sneakers will be better attire for if I need to run or hide or fight even," she decided. Though the idea of trying to fight someone the size of Horus was laughable.

She whispered back, "Thank you. You're right. I'll change back into my regular clothes. Can you ask Hester and Gerald not to look while I change?"

Liam nodded then went to the elderly couple and whispered Rachel's request. They closed their eyes and covered their faces with their hands. Liam remained facing them, away from Rachel.

Rachel unstrapped her sandals and placed them next to her sneakers. She grabbed her clothes from the bed and pulled her panties and her jeans on while still wearing the dress. Pulling her arms into the dress, she kept it around her shoulders while she maneuvered her bra under the dress and put it on under the cover of its gauzy white layers. She knew her friends weren't watching her change, but she was still concerned that Ra or one of his servants might surprise her when she was topless. After Rachel fastened her bra, she pulled the dress off over her head, then put her shirt on and buttoned all the buttons, starting at the top and working her way down.

After Rachel was fully clothed, she placed her dress on the bed where she had found it and tip-toed to her friends to whisper they could look now. Still barefoot, she took a seat on the floor next to her shoes and put on her socks and sneakers. She tied double knots in her laces. She kept picturing herself having to run from Horus or villagers or some other unknown danger and tripping and falling over her own shoe laces. Rachel had never been too coordinated, she needed all the help she could get. Double knots were a must.

Liam came and sat next to Rachel at the foot of the bed. He sat quietly for a minute before leaning closer to her ear and saying, "You smell really nice."

At first Rachel didn't know what to say. This seemed like an awkward moment for Liam to be making a move. This didn't seem like the time or the place—Rachel took a deep breath, readying herself to rebuff his advances. When she inhaled, she smelled what Liam must have smelled. To double check, she lifted one of her sleeved arms to her face and inhaled deeply. Whatever her clothes were washed in smelled delicious—like sugar cookies or vanilla. Something about the scent made Rachel think of cozy holidays by the fire under a blanket or Christmas morning—comfort and happiness. She whispered back to Liam, "Oh, wow, you're right. I smell amazing."

Liam chuckled. He smiled and teasingly whispered, "You're so modest." He added with a self-deprecating grimace, "Please don't smell me." Liam smelled himself and made an overdramatic disgusted face.

Rachel smiled at Liam. She was amazed at his ability to put her at ease even at a moment like this where she should be scared. Instead of focusing on the fact that an angry giant alien could come for them at any minute, Rachel was focused on not laughing too loudly. "Liam is pretty special," she conceded to herself.

She watched Liam yawn then roughly scratch his beard. The scratching left his beard looking messy—like bedhead, but on his face. Liam saw Rachel watching him so he scooted closer to her to tell her something. He whispered, "If we ever get home—back to Earth, that is..."

Liam paused. Rachel waited for him to finish his sentence, but he seemed intent on something.

"If we ever get home *what*?" asked Rachel in a breathless whisper. *Was he about to suggest they go out? Be a couple?* Her mind raced.

"Shhhh," Liam whispered. "I think someone is coming."

Rachel focused on listening, and sure enough she could hear heavy footsteps coming down the corridor. They stopped in front of Ra's door. Rachel held her breath.

Thud, thud, thud, came a powerful knock upon the door. "I know you're in there, Ra!" shouted Horus. "There isn't a chance you left your human pet alone by herself."

Thud, thud, thud.

Rachel and Liam watched the door shake on its hinges. "He's going to break it down," whispered Rachel.

"We need to hide," Liam breathed. He jumped up and crossed to Hester and Gerald and told them to hide. Liam reached up and opened the door to the wardrobe and helped Hester inside. Gerald followed her. Liam closed the door on them.

Rachel tried to pantomime to Liam to ask where they should hide. He shrugged his shoulders and looked around the room. The thudding against the door had turned into a sound they could only guess meant Horus was now throwing the entire weight of his body against it. They could hear the door begin to splinter, separating from its hinges. Rachel grabbed her book and ducked behind the side of the bed that was hidden from the doorway. Just before her head disappeared behind the side, she saw Liam scramble behind the wardrobe.

Rachel instantly felt nauseating déjà vu. *Had she seen this happen before?* No, she hadn't. But she'd read it. *Could it be a coincidence that Liam picked the exact same hiding spot as Malachi?*

Rachel pushed herself flat against the side of the bed. She heard the loud and unmistakable splintering of wood and prayed that if Horus entered the room, he would perceive the room to be empty and leave without a thorough search. Rachel listened, but all she could hear was the sound of her own heart beating in her ears. Then Rachel once more heard the powerful sound of Horus throwing his body against the door. The door practically screamed on its hinges before falling to the floor inside Ra's chamber.

The heavy sound of the door hitting the stone floor made Rachel's heart jump, and she hoped her movement was hidden from the angle of the door. She squeezed her eyes shut, like a child who thinks they become invisible the moment they can't see others.

Horus breathed heavy. He sounded like an angry bull breathing through his nose. His large feet clomped across the room. Right foot, left foot, right foot. He paused. "There are too many lamps lit for this room to be empty," Horus bellowed.

He was greeted with silence. Horus took two more steps forward. He was almost to the foot of the bed and the front of the wardrobe. "Ra is not here," He said, lifting the blanket on the bed, upsetting the dress Rachel had left there. "The question is who is here?"

Horus laughed, deep and menacing, like every cartoon villain Rachel remembered from her childhood. "Such a foolish hiding spot, human," Horus drawled. "You human vermin always pick the same stupid place."

Rachel braced herself for what she guessed would be Horus' discovery of her hiding place behind the side of the bed. But instead she heard Liam yell then ask, "What are you going to do with me?"

Rachel was frozen. This was *The Mighty Arm that Built Egypt. Horus called Liam a vermin and hadn't Ra done the same to Malachi?* Rachel wouldn't just lie there while Liam was hurt or dragged off to some unknown misery. She sat up and peered over the edge of the bed, willing herself to jump up and fight for Liam's freedom. She would kick or even bite Horus' legs if it would do any good. Rachel looked around for something to use as a weapon. "A torch, maybe?" she considered. She set the book on the floor and slowly stood on shaky, nervous legs. Horus' back was to her, the falcon tattoo stretched across it staring at Rachel. She saw Liam's legs dangling. Rachel soundlessly eased backwards, stepping silently toward the closest wall with a torch.

Horus sneered in response to Liam's question. "What am I going to do with you?" he asked sarcastically, repeating Liam's question. "I should just kill you here and now and avoid any possible future problems. I didn't invite you here. I would have left you to die in the cavern or the forest, or I would have hunted you and killed you as the pest you are."

Rachel stepped in front of the torch to remove it from the wall. Standing in front of the torch threw her shadow on the wall opposite—the wall Horus was facing.

"What is this?" he thundered, turning to face Rachel. He slung Liam around like a rag-doll. Rachel saw Liam wince in pain.

Rachel stood her ground, torch in hand. "Let go of my friend," she said in her best attempt to sound unafraid.

At that moment Ra rushed through the doorless passage to his chamber, followed by Mafdet and Kuk.

CHAPTER 19

Ra looked from Horus, holding Liam carelessly by his shirt front, to Rachel standing fearless with a torch. "Unhand my guest," Ra said in a surprisingly calm and polite voice.

"Guest?" spat Horus. "I can only assume this *guest* is among the humans who caused trouble in the village earlier."

Horus waved Liam at Ra as he spoke, giving him an extra violent shake on the word "guest."

"The villagers are over-reacting," said Ra.

"I don't care if the villagers have made it all up," growled Horus. "The villagers expect action from us. We are their masters—their protectors. And what I care about more than the perception of the villagers is the future of Janus. This little pest," he said shaking Liam, before point at Rachel, "that little pest, and whatever other pests you've got hidden up here are a threat to Janus. The situation with the villagers only complicates things where complication is unnecessary."

"What do you suggest?" interjected Mafdet.

In the lamplight and torchlight of Ra's chamber Mafdet looked otherworldly to Rachel. "Of course, this is another world," she reminded herself. *Hadn't he been in torchlight in the great hall? What made him look so different now?* Perhaps it was the lights flickering so close to his golden hair and fair skin. He contrasted in such an extreme to the other gods—other aliens. His build was boyish, too, where the others had obvious muscle. Even Ra, who was leaner than Kuk and Horus, looked muscular in comparison.

Kuk placed his torch in an empty torch stand before taking his place behind Ra. He folded his arms across his chest, waiting for Horus' answer to Mafdet's question. He looked like he might be a nightclub bouncer, only he was probably ten feet tall. Horus looked from Mafdet to Kuk to Ra. Horus answered, "I was thinking about throwing him out the window."

Horus moved swiftly to the window and dangled Liam outside. The villagers, still gathered at the gate, cheered. Rachel gasped. Ra yelled, "Horus, no!" as he lunged forward.

"Tsk-tsk, Horus. Now is that very sporting of you?" asked Mafdet, as he crossed the room and coolly took a seat on the bed facing Horus at the window. Mafdet crossed one thin leg over the other and with this motion the lamplight glinted off one of his gold plated sandals.

"What do I care if I am being sporting, Mafdet? You turn everything into a joke, you fool!" yelled Horus while he shook Liam, causing the crowd outside to cheer wildly.

"A joke? Goodness, no," replied Mafdet. "We do have our rules and laws to consider, though."

It shocked Rachel to hear Mafdet again touting the importance of their laws. If it saved Liam, it would make her happy, but Mafdet's obsession with rule following was bordering on pathological. She understood that he was the god of justice, but something about his manner struck Rachel as off. *Did he not have a moral compass outside their laws? Was that what bothered her about it?*

To Rachel's surprise and relief, Horus pulled Liam back inside. The villagers at the gate booed. "To which laws do you refer, Mafdet?" asked Horus.

"Of course, they've frightened villagers. That should be considered, though we don't have a law against scaring people. But, more importantly they trespassed on palace grounds without an invitation. That is in violation of our law, as you know. Everyone knows admittance to the palace after hours is by invitation only," finished Mafdet with a broad smile.

"This is absurd," said Ra. "They are my guests."

"Did you invite them, Ra?" asked Mafdet.

"No, not yet," he said. "But you know I have before."

"It might sound like a technicality to you, friend, but as they say 'the devil is in the details'," replied Mafdet.

"What do you suggest then? What do we do with these law breakers?" Horus asked as he shook Liam. Rachel wasn't sure if it was her imagination or if Liam was starting to look green from all the shaking.

"Our laws are quite explicit in the acceptable protocol in such events. We let the perpetrator pick his fate. He can either opt for a swift execution or he can ask to compete with one of us in hand to hand combat, face to face," said Mafdet. He looked serenely authoritative from his seat on the bed—like nothing pleased him more than administering what he believed to be fair justice.

Rachel heard Liam breathe the word, "Seriously?" She felt the same way. Mafdet's verdict was a kick in the gut. Both options were a death sentence.

"What was that, young man?" asked Mafdet, who looked younger than Liam, though much larger.

Liam repeated himself. "Seriously?"

"Yes. Which option do you choose? Execution or hand to hand combat?" Mafdet answered.

"This is insanity," muttered Ra. Rachel wondered why he didn't do anything. *Couldn't he intervene and stand up for Liam? Or did the law forbid that, too?*

"Tut, tut, Ra. Let the boy answer," said Mafdet.

"Put me down," responded Liam.

"Oh, of course. Put him down, if you will, Horus. It must be difficult to make an important decision while dangling about," said Mafdet with a loose wave of his hand.

Horus dropped Liam to the floor. Liam slowly got to his feet. He looked up at Horus in anger. Horus put his hands on his hips, towering over Liam.

"Well?" prodded Mafdet.

Liam turned to Mafdet and decided, "Hand to hand combat."

"Excellent choice!" rejoiced Mafdet. He clapped his hands in celebration then stood. Mafdet turned from Liam and Horus and began to exit the room. Before crossing the threshold he turned. "Come along, Horus," he said, "there is much to be planned for tomorrow."

Liam jumped back to avoid being walked on by Horus. Mafdet and Horus exited the room.

After they were gone Ra sighed heavily. "Our laws state you will fight tomorrow at sunrise," he stated.

"Where is the funny tiny lady and the spirit?" asked Kuk.

"Oh my goodness, they're in the wardrobe," Rachel said in a rush. She crossed to the wardrobe and tried to reach up to open the door while still holding the torch. Seeing the evident effort this took, Ra stepped in and relieved Rachel of her torch with his right hand and opened the wardrobe with his left hand.

"What in the blazes was happening out here?" asked Hester, wide-eyed. She stumbled out of the wardrobe followed by Gerald.

"How much could you hear?" Liam asked as he plopped down on the floor.

"Not as much as you would think. These walls are pretty thick," Hester said, knocking on the door to the wardrobe with her tiny hand. "Mainly it just sounded like jumbled mumbles."

Liam looked up at Hester while he rubbed his neck, which was sore from all the shaking he'd received from Horus. He was about to answer when Rachel answered for him.

"The short version is Liam is Malachi," she said.

Liam stopped rubbing his neck to look dumbly up at Rachel.

"Huh?" replied Hester. "I don't follow."

Instead of Rachel, it was Gerald who replied, "He was found by one of them and challenged to hand to hand combat."

Rachel noted that Gerald didn't ask. He told. *Was Malachi's story Gerald's story?*

"Who is Malachi?" asked Kuk, who was doing his best to keep up with the rapid conversation shared by the humans.

"Malachi is a character in the humans' slanderous book," answered Ra. "In the book, the human—Malachi—is hiding behind my wardrobe. I can only assume Liam selected the same poorly chosen hiding spot." Rachel and Liam nodded. Ra continued, "And, like Liam, Malachi is given the option of an honorable death via hand to hand combat."

"Is Liam fighting you?" Hester asked Ra.

Ra shook his head in answer. "Horus is who challenged Liam," Rachel said, clarifying things for Hester and Gerald. Rachel's mind raced, trying to find the solution to their problem. "I haven't finished reading the book yet. I only got to the chapter where Malachi is found and challenged. What happens? Is he killed, or does he escape?"

"He escapes." Rachel assumed Hester would be the one to answer, but the answer came from Ra. Apparently Ra had gotten through more of the book than Rachel had.

Ra picked up the door to his room, which lay on the floor hingeless and splintered. He leaned the door against the wall next to the wardrobe.

Rachel looked from Hester to Ra, asking both, "How does he escape?"

"He banishes me to my home planet by using the 'mysterious pendant' I always wear around my neck," Ra answered, pointing to the actual pendant he was wearing.

"Is that something we could do? Would that work?" asked Liam.

"Banish me to my home planet?" smirked Ra.

"No, um, can we use your pendant to send Horus away?" Liam asked.

"No," Ra said with finality. "Where would you suggest Horus be sent? His home planet? This is his home planet."

"Liam will have to face Horus like a man," interjected Gerald, "and hope for the best."

Ra and Kuk nodded in agreement. Rachel was speechless. *How could they all so easily go alone with Liam's certain death?* "This isn't right," she thought to herself. "This isn't fair."

Wind blew through the window, causing the curtains to dance and draw everyone's attention. From down below a voice announced, "Friends, fear not, justice will be served!"

Liam jumped to his feet and loped to the window. Rachel and Hester followed to stand on either side of him. The others stayed where they stood and listened.

Rachel recognized the voice before she saw the giant standing several paces from the villagers. It was Mafdet. Behind him stood Horus with his massive arms across his broad chest. An attendant carried a torch for them.

Mafdet continued, "We have apprehended the invaders—including the spirit that so frightened some of you. At sunrise one among them will face one among us. You are all invited to watch the pair face off in hand to hand combat at the palace arena tomorrow morning."

The crowd cheered and Mafdet and Horus returned to the confines of the palace. The double doors to the palace closed with a heavy thud, and the attendant who carried the torch approached the gate. He stood before the crowd and repeated Mafdet's message, "At sunrise a match of strengths will be held at the palace arena between one of the invaders and one of our masters. All are invited. Tell your neighbors!" The attendant repeated the message over and over until the crowd dissipated and he was left yelling the message to himself.

Liam, Rachel, and Hester turned from the window. "So, I'm fighting a giant Egyptian god tomorrow," said Liam. "No biggie." He attempted a weak smile.

Rachel put her hand on his arm. She tried to think of something encouraging to say since she couldn't think of a way out of the situation. Liam looked her in the eyes and said softly, "It's okay, Rachel. Really. It's okay."

Before Rachel knew it, her eyes welled up with tears. Her emotions took her by surprise. She wiped her eyes on the back of her hand and tried to gain control of herself, but the tears kept flowing. Liam pulled Rachel into his arms for a hug. While he held her he whispered, "I really have a feeling this is all going to work out okay."

Rachel didn't believe it. She didn't see any way out of this situation. It wasn't going to be okay. *Is that what this crying was? The sound of her own hopelessness? The sound of her giving up?* Rachel heard her own sobs. It didn't feel like those sounds were coming from her. She continued to cry, and Liam gently rubbed her back as he held her. He repeated, "It's okay," a dozen times.

Rachel's sobs eventually quieted and Liam let go of her. Looking around the room, she found every face focused on her. She thought to herself, "I can add that to my list of 'Things Worse than Symposiums'—crying hysterically in front of a group of people."

Rachel walked to the bed and sat down. She suddenly felt exhausted. Hester climbed up onto the bed next to her and patted her knee encouragingly.

"Is there anything I can get you?" asked Ra. His face concerned; his eyes serious.

Rachel shrugged then looked at her travel weary friends. "I don't need anything, but maybe you guys want to get cleaned up a little?"

"Mercy me, that would be nice," squeaked Hester. "I don't need anything fancy. But if I could at least wash my face and run a comb through my hair, I would be pleased as a peach."

"Yeah, me, too," said Liam.

"I will show you down to the bath chamber and find what you need to be more comfortable," said Ra.

"I will be in the center corridor, Ra, if you require any more help," said Kuk, before slinking off into the shadows.

Hester stood and said to Ra, "Lead the way, mighty Ra."

Ra arched one dark brow in response. Rachel wasn't sure if he was annoyed or amused, until he smiled, "Follow me, tiny Hester."

CHAPTER 20

The group of four followed Ra down two corridors, down the stairs, and through hall after hall. Rachel thought she should know the way by now, but she knew if left by herself she would still be easily lost. When they reached the bath chamber Ra opened one of the double doors and invited them all inside. The attendants who were posted inside earlier were gone. Rachel imagined, like Ra's other servants, they were dismissed at night.

The room was mostly dark. Only two torches were lit in the giant room, and the moonlight didn't seem to penetrate the windows which were high off the ground. Had Rachel not known there was a pool sized tub in the room, it would have been easy to walk right into it before knowing what had happened. She pictured Hester doing just that, so she warned them all about it to avoid having to try to do CPR on the old woman. Rachel had never actually taken a CPR course, so it would all be guess work based on what she'd seen in movies.

Ra walked to one of the torches and took it from its stand. He walked along the walls lighting torch after torch until the room was lit in a golden glow.

Rachel watched Ra. He searched the one small cupboard in the room and looked behind the many potted plants. He finally turned to Rachel and asked, "Do you know where my servants put the soaps and oils? Or do you know where the towels are?"

Rachel laughed. Ra—an Egyptian god, or at the very least giant alien master of this planet—didn't know where the towels were kept in his own palace. Rachel answered him, "No, they were carrying them when they came and got me."

Ra sighed. "I will return shortly." He strode to the doors and closed them behind himself.

"Where's he going?" asked Hester.

"He doesn't know where anything is to help you two get clean. He's probably going to his servants' quarters to ask them," answered Rachel.

"This place is amazing," said Liam. He gestured to the pool before them, and then the beautifully tiled walls.

"It really is," said Rachel, smiling back at him.

"I was just thinking I'd wash my face or something, but if he'll let me I think I'd like to swim in that pool," Liam said, walking to the edge.

Rachel noticed Gerald staring at Hester. Hester was looking around the immense room in childlike awe, but he was looking at her with eyes that professed a love that transcended the grave. Rachel wondered if she would ever find someone who looked at her like that—with so much love, with unadulterated adoration.

Rachel's musings were interrupted by a spray of water against the right side of her face. She looked to her right, to find Liam suppressing a laugh. He'd splashed her with water from the pool.

She laughed back at him. With her hands on her hips she threatened, "I'd push you in if I didn't think you'd like it."

"Do you think Ra would mind if I stuck my feet in?" Liam asked as he grinned good-naturedly at Rachel.

"Just wait a minute. I'm sure he'll be back soon," she answered.

As though they were waiting for Rachel's cue, the door opened, and Ra appeared, followed by Kesi and Halima. Kesi's arms were full of soaps, oils, and lotions again, and Halima carried a stack of towels. Ra directed them to set the supplies on a table near the sink Rachel had brushed her teeth at earlier after her bath. Under the sink was a cabinet that earlier Mert had pulled a small brush that looked almost exactly like a modern tooth brush and a jar filled with minty powdered soap. After setting the things she carried on the table, Kesi opened that same cabinet and pulled out 3 small tooth brushes and the jar of mint soap and placed them on the table. Rachel walked over and found that one of the brushes had a white ribbon tied to it.

Kesi pointed at that toothbrush and said to Rachel, "That one is yours."

From a pocket somewhere in the folds of her skirt, Kesi brought out an orange ribbon and tied it to one of the other toothbrushes.

"Hey, Ra, is it okay if I swim in the pool?" Liam asked. He had taken his shoes off near the pool, he stood looking up at Ra like a child asking his parent for permission.

"You want to bathe?" Ra asked.

"I don't need to go full on bath time," Liam bargained. "I could just strip down to my boxers and go for a swim. You know, use some soap while I'm in there, I guess."

Ra looked to Rachel. "What is he asking?"

"He wants to know if he can swim in your bath, but not take off all his clothes," she answered.

"If that pleases him, yes," Ra answered, though he looked confused.

"Thanks," Liam said as he began unbuttoning his shirt.

He was out of all of his clothes except his boxers in seconds. Liam jumped into the pool with a splash, startling Kesi and Halima.

"If I had my swimmin' suit I'd join you," Hester giggled, watching Liam swim from one end of the pool to the other.

Rachel tried not to stare. Liam was fitter than she expected. In her experience most of her colleagues who studied ancient civilizations weren't big on fitness or working out. They were typically more interested in reading books or examining ancient artifacts. "Liam looks like he would pull off the shirtless look of the Egyptian gods just as good as the rest of them," Rachel decided, picturing him dressed like them.

"He's a good-looking boy, isn't he?" Hester said next to Rachel. She startled Rachel and made her blush. Apparently Rachel hadn't been succeeding in not staring at Liam.

"Believe it or not, Gerald once looked a lot like that," confided Hester. "He was what you kids would call a 'hottie.' He filled out a pair of swim trunks like no other. All the girls were jealous of me because he was mine."

Rachel tried to picture Gerald young and handsome like Liam, but she just couldn't do it. She looked the blue-green ghost up and down and wondered if she'd be able to picture him better young if she'd seen him alive and in living, breathing color instead of as a ghost.

"What color eyes did Gerald have?" Rachel asked.

"The brightest prettiest blue eyes you ever seen," answered Hester with a sad reminiscent smile.

"Liam has really pretty blue eyes," Rachel said, turning her attention again to Liam in the pool.

"Really?" asked Hester. "Huh. I hadn't noticed."

Hester looked across the room at Gerald. He looked back at her and they shared one long unspoken moment of love.

Halima approached Rachel and Hester with a tentative smile. "Do either of you seek assistance in your nightly preparations?"

"What's she mean, dear?" Hester asked Rachel.

"Yes, please, Halima," Rachel answered Ra's servant, before turning to Hester to say, "She's just asking if she can help us get ready for bed."

"Oh, in that case, yes, yes, yes," said Hester full of her trademark enthusiasm. "I'd like to wash my face and comb my hair. And brush my teeth if I can."

"Right this way," said Halima. She led Hester to the sink and the table full of supplies. Rachel watched from a distance as Halima explained the tooth powder and gave Hester the tooth brush with the orange ribbon. Halima also gave Hester a towel the size of a dish towel, presumably to wash her face, soap, and a wooden comb.

Rachel turned back to Liam in the pool. She approached the edge and sat down. While Rachel had been talking with Hester, Kesi had brought shampoo and soap to Liam. He was busy lathering his hair when Rachel sat.

"Is it weird that I'm basically taking a bath in front of you?" he asked, swimming closer to the edge where she sat.

Rachel hadn't thought about it like that until Liam said it. She blushed uncontrollably and hoped he didn't notice. Blushing reminded Rachel of earlier when they had been sitting quietly in Ra's bedchamber before Horus started pounding on the door. Before Liam was interrupted it had sounded like he was about to say something important to her.

Rachel ignored Liam's question on the awkwardness of him bathing in front of her to ask her own question. "What were you going to say earlier before Horus broke the door down?" Rachel asked.

"Huh?" Liam rubbed shampoo into a lather on his hands before adding it to his beard.

Rachel couldn't help but laugh at the sight before her. Liam was a soapy Santa Claus with the shampoo lathered on his head and his beard. Rachel didn't allow Liam's ridiculous appearance to derail her train of thought, though. She rephrased her question for clarity.

"Before Horus interrupted with his pounding on the door, you were in the middle of saying something. Something like 'if we ever get back to Earth...'"

"Oh, that," he said.

Rachel's heart thudded in her chest. *Had she foolishly let her curiosity get the best of her? What would she do if he did suggest they be a couple? Would that make things weird if they were stuck on this planet forever? Or would that make them a couple now? What would Ra think? And why did she care what Ra thought?*

Liam dunked his head under water, washing away most of the bubbles in his hair and beard. He emerged and swam even closer to the edge where Rachel sat. He gripped the edge with his hands and looked up at Rachel with his beautiful sparkling eyes that still reminded Rachel of pristine blue oceans.

"I was just thinking if we survive this and we ever get back to Earth," said Liam, he paused before finishing his sentence. "If we ever get back, I think I'm going to change my emphasis. I don't think I want to be an ancient civilizations generalist anymore. I really think I want to switch to Egyptology."

Rachel felt herself blushing again, only this time it was with embarrassment. *How could she think Liam was about to profess his love to her—his need to be with her?* They'd only known each other for a day and a half or however long it had been. It was still difficult to figure that one out with the obvious time difference between Earth and Janus. It was night when they were transported, but they arrived during the day. So deep in her self-reproach and embarrassment, Rachel had hardly noticed that Liam was still talking.

"After this experience it's impossible not to want to know more about Egypt. I figure with what we've seen here, if I focused my studies more, I might make some really ground breaking discoveries," he said. "You know, try to separate the reality from the myth."

"Mmm-hmm," Rachel answered. She was so unprepared for what he had told her, she didn't know what to say. She settled on, "Yeah, that sounds like a good idea."

"I'm glad you think so," said Liam. "Your opinion means a lot to me."

Rachel told herself to not read too much into anything Liam said. "My opinion probably doesn't mean that much," she told herself.

She said to him, "Yeah, Egyptology is great."

Liam dunked his head again before lying back and floating on the surface of the pool. Their chat was over. Liam was enamored with Egypt not Rachel.

Rachel stood and turned so that her back was to Liam in the pool. When she glanced up, she became aware that Ra had been watching her. He leaned against the wall between two palm plants. Unlike humans would if caught staring, he didn't turn away. He kept looking at Rachel. He held eye contact.

Rachel decided she'd break this weird staring match by crossing to him and having a conversation. She walked over to him and copied his stance. She leaned against the wall, too, a little closer to a palm plant than she found absolutely comfortable—its frons brushing her cheek.

In one swift motion, Ra sat on the ground next to her. She followed his example and sat, too. She felt like a kitten next to a tiger.

"Are you and he betrothed?" Ra asked Rachel, with a jerk of his chin toward Liam in the pool. "Because you weren't last time."

Rachel marveled at how direct Ra was. "He just jumps right to it," she thought, but reminded herself that she was wrong about Liam being interested in her and she was probably misreading Ra, as well.

"Uh, no," she answered Ra. "We're just friends."

Ra sat stoically not asking another question. Questions. It occurred to Rachel that she answered a question of his so perhaps he'd answer one of hers.

"Are we still playing 'a question for a question'?" Rachel asked, coyly smiling up at the giant god.

"Perhaps," he answered. "What is your question?"

Without thinking, Rachel instinctually tried to run her hand through her hair, but was stopped by the intricate braided hairstyle Halima had fashioned. "Oh, I forgot about that," she said patting her head.

"About what?" asked Ra.

"My hair," said Rachel. "I forgot it was done up like this. I need to get these braids out before going to sleep tonight or I'll wake up with a terrible headache." Rachel began unbraiding the small braid near her left ear.

"I will help," said Ra.

"But, uh—", Rachel began.

"What was your question?" interrupted Ra. His large hands gently and adeptly unbraided the larger braids twisted around the back of Rachel's head.

"This is Janus," she said.

"That's not a question," he interrupted again, pointing a hair pin at her.

"Yeah, I know," Rachel said. "This is Janus. But... where is Janus? Is it in our galaxy—my galaxy?"

"Yes," Ra answered, starting on his third braid.

"Is it in our solar system?"

"Yes."

"No way!" Rachel almost yelled.

In the pool, Liam looked up. She had also inadvertently gotten the attention of Hester, Gerald, Kesi, and Halima. Rachel smiled awkwardly at everyone. She was sure that, besides her uncalled for raise in volume, the sight of Ra helping her with her hair probably looked strange. Rachel said loudly for everyone to hear, "Sorry, didn't mean to get that loud."

Rachel whispered to Ra, "How is that possible? How has it not been discovered by our scientists?"

"It's amusing, isn't it, how one doesn't always see things hidden in plain sight?" Ra answered.

Rachel looked at Ra, waiting for him to continue. He looked around the room then back at her. "Would you know this room were here if I had not directed my servants to show it to you? How is it you know about the other planets in your solar system besides Earth?"

Ra looked deeply into Rachel's eyes. "At any moment you walk the earth you could be missing buried treasure just feet below you. Literal treasure is underfoot, inches away, covered by dirt. Janus is buried treasure. This planet is nestled between two other planets in your solar system. You did not know because no one told you. And no one told you because they did not know either."

"But where?" was all Rachel could ask.

Ra handed her a handful of ribbons and hair pins he had pulled from her hair. He gave Rachel a careful smile. "I have told you enough, have I not?" he asked with an arch of his brow. "I'm afraid if I tell you more, you will feel compelled to tell others, and before I know it, Janus will be overrun by Earth men."

"Who am I going to tell besides them?" Rachel asked, pointing to Liam, Hester, and Gerald.

"Mankind, I'm afraid," answered Ra as he stood. He crouched again, low, and offered a giant hand to Rachel to help her to her feet. Rachel knew if he'd wanted to, he could have easily picked her up and set her on her feet like a doll. She appreciated that he didn't, that instead he acted as a gentleman. An enormous gentleman, but still a gentleman. A gentleman who had just helped take down her hair.

CHAPTER 21

Rachel asked nothing more of Ra while in the bath chamber. He had closed that conversation, and even if she persisted in questioning, Rachel knew for now Ra would not answer more questions.

After Rachel and the others had finished with washing, combing, and teeth brushing, Ra's servants returned to their quarters and Ra led the way back to his bedchamber. Rachel tried to memorize the path this time, just in case she needed the bathroom in the middle of the night. From the bath chamber, it was down the hall, then left, right, right, left, three flights of stairs, turn right down the hall until it hits the end, then left and straight down the hall to Ra's room on the left. Rachel memorized the sequence then reminded herself she'd have to reverse it going from Ra's room. After having it memorized, she wondered how she had considered it confusing before.

In their absence, someone had come up and straightened the room. Rachel guessed it had been Mert since she had not been with Kesi and Halima to help in the bath chamber. The door still sat off its hinges, leaned against the wall, but the rest of the room was restored to perfect order. The tray of food had been taken away and replaced with a tray that only contained a fresh water pitcher and mugs. The dress and sandals Rachel had left out were gone, and the bed was neatly made—no longer rumpled from when Horus had pulled up the blanket looking for hiding humans. Atop the bed lay extra blankets. Beside the bed, where Rachel had hidden, there was a pile of cushions long and wide enough for someone Ra's size to lie comfortably.

"I hope you all will be comfortable tonight," Ra said as he walked around the room extinguishing the many torches that lined the walls.

"Can we keep a few lamps lit?" Rachel asked as Ra started to extinguish the light from the lamps, as well.

"Of course," he answered. "Are two enough, or shall I leave more?"

"Two works," said Rachel.

After bringing the light low in the room, but leaving two lamps lit for Rachel, Ra addressed his human guests again. "My bed is quite large and I believe you all can lie comfortably on it without disrupting each other. Does this arrangement satisfy you, or do I need to acquire more bedding?"

Rachel looked from Liam to Hester, and they all exchanged looks that implied, "It's okay with me. How about you?"

"That works for us," Rachel answered.

"I will remain with you tonight. One of my servants has made me a bed on the floor," Ra said gesturing to the pile of cushions on the side of the bed. "If you need anything throughout the night, or if anyone enters the room meaning danger to you, wake me immediately."

Rachel and her friends agreed and began making themselves comfortable. Hester shrugged out of Liam's blazer. "Hun, I'm just going to put your blazer in the wardrobe, if that's all right," Hester said to Liam.

"Sounds good. I won't need it while I sleep anyway," he answered.

Something on Hester's lime green lapel shined in the lamplight. Hester's "I Believe In Alien's pin," Rachel remembered. She'd been wearing it at the awards ceremony. It seemed like such a silly fashion choice then, but now it couldn't be more appropriate.

Rachel pulled off her sneakers and placed them at the end of the bed, the way she'd found them before. Liam and Hester followed her example, and soon they were claiming sections of the bed. Liam called the foot of the bed, as to not make the ladies feel uncomfortable with him sleeping too close. Hester asked Rachel if she minded which side she slept on. Rachel answered in the negative, so Hester took the side closest to the window. That left Rachel with the left side of the bed—the side closest to Ra.

There was a bedside table on that side with one of the two remaining lit lamps. Rachel was glad Hester had wanted the other side of the bed. Having the lamplight meant Rachel could stay up for a while and try to get through more of *The Mighty Arm that Built Egypt*. She thought to herself, "Maybe if I read more, I can get a better idea of how Malachi avoided his fight with Ra, and by learning that I can help Liam avoid his fight with Horus. It's got to be more than just a magic pendant. There's got to be something in this book that can help us."

Rachel looked for her book where she'd left it—on the floor—but it had been moved. She found it safely tucked inside the wardrobe. She grabbed it and one of the blankets and made herself comfortable on her side of the bed. Ra was already lying on the pile of cushions. He looked up at her at the same moment she looked down at him. Seeing the book in her hands he rolled his eyes.

"What?" she asked defensively.

Ra answered with a sigh.

At the foot of the bed—his head on Rachel's side, his feet on Hester's side—Liam propped himself up on his elbows. "Um... Ra? I'm trying not to make a big deal about tomorrow," he began. "Though, seriously, who would blame me if I were? But, just out of curiosity—what should I expect?"

Rachel felt terrible. She hadn't asked Liam once how he was feeling about his impending fight with Horus. She hadn't tried to reassure him. She hadn't even told him she was going to search for clues in the book. "Of course, he must be scared," she realized. "And he must have a million questions. Poor guy!"

Ra answered, "The bells will ring before dawn to awake the people. I will direct you to the palace arena. There, a ritual cleansing will be done to your hands and your feet. As the sun rises, you will be asked to take your place at the center of the arena. When the sun has broken the horizon, a trumpet will sound announcing the start of the fight."

Rachel pictured it all—the crowd, the sun, the fighters. It all seemed so clear in her head, she wondered if this was something she might have lived before, too, like the previous meetings with Ra that she didn't remember.

"So, that's it? I'm really expected to just fight Horus with nothing but my own two hands?" asked Liam, an edge of panic to his voice.

Ra nodded.

Liam pressed his face into the bed. Rachel wondered if he was stifling a scream.

"I'm reading more of this tonight," she said, waving the book. "I'm seeing how it all went down for Malachi. Maybe there is some trick I can find in it for you that will help you tomorrow."

Liam looked up and smiled weakly at Rachel. It was obvious he was trying to look hopeful. "Thanks, Rachel."

"Don't give up," Rachel added softly.

Liam rolled over onto his back. He pulled his blanket up over his shoulders and said, "I'm trying not to. I mean, if Gerald made it off this planet there's still hope for us, right?"

"Right," answered Rachel.

From the corner of the room, near the window Gerald said, "You're going to make it, Liam. Just try to get some rest."

"Thanks, Gerald," Liam said.

Ra eyed Gerald's ghostly form at the window but didn't speak. Hester snorted in her sleep, then broke into a steady rhythmic snore. Her snore seemed to signal it was no longer time for talking, but for sleeping.

Rachel opened *The Mighty Arm that Built Egypt* and quickly found where she had last stopped reading.

A voice announced in the street, "At sunrise all are invited to witness a champion of the people face the Mighty Ra. The contest will take place in the palace arena." This announcement was repeated over and over until Malachi was certain he had memorized it himself.

He paced the room, uncertain of what he should do. Escape was out of the question. If he didn't face Ra—if he were to escape and hide some place far away—Ra was certain to seek justice somewhere. He would most likely inflict some sort of new cruelty against his people. Escaping and running weren't options. He had to face Ra as a man.

Tap, tap, tap.

Malachi stopped pacing and turned to where the tapping sound came. The giant door to Ra's chamber slowly opened and in walked a young maiden carrying a tray. Malachi automatically recognized the maiden. It was Kesi—

In utter shock, Rachel stopped reading. "What?!" she whispered to herself. "How is that possible?" she wondered.

It was Kesi, the daughter of the disgraced farmer who could not fulfill the high quotas set by Ra and his fellow gods. The poor farmer was forced to offer up his daughter in place of his missing crops.

Malachi stared at Kesi. She was beautiful beyond words—of noble bearing, though just a farmer's daughter. She was proud with intense, dark eyes.

Wisps of jet black hair fell around her face, loose under her headscarf. Had she not been taken by Ra, Kesi might have been Malachi's bride.

"Kesi," Malachi said passionately.

"Malachi," Kesi answered back, "I didn't know it was you."

She looked pained. Her brows knit together and her bottom lip trembled.

"Please, do not look so sad, my dear," begged Malachi. He rushed toward her and lifted the tray from her hands. He placed it on the bed and turned to face the woman who might have been his if their lives were not ruled by tyrants.

"May I hold you?" he asked.

Tears streamed down Kesi's face as she nodded her consent. "Why is this our life?" she sobbed.

Malachi held her in his arms. He felt her heart thudding against his chest and wondered if she felt his, as well. His heart sang, "This is what life would be without Ra and the rest. This.

Love. Embraces. Family. Freedom. Kesi."

"I'm sorry I failed tonight," Malachi whispered in Kesi's ear. "I'm sorry I failed our people."

Kesi answered with a heartbreaking sob.

"I face Ra at dawn," he went on. "Though I should have no hope, seeing you—feeling you in my arms—it gives me hope that perhaps a miracle can happen. Perhaps I can defeat Amun-Ra. Perhaps I can set our people free."

"I wish it were possible," Kesi said between sobs.

"Do not give up on me," Malachi implored.

"I will never give up on you, Malachi," she said.

With one arm around Kesi's waist, he took her face in his hand and looked down into her warm brown eyes. "I love you," he said. She smiled back at him a sad smile. She was speechless, but not without action. Kesi stretched herself up as tall as she could and kissed Malachi. In her kiss he felt all the feelings that overflowed from her—

> *grief, sadness, pride, hopelessness mixed with hope, and love. Deep, deep, unending love.*

"Wow," Rachel whispered to herself. She looked around the room at her sleeping friends to make sure she hadn't awoken them. She noticed Gerald still standing by the window. He was looking out it, absorbed in his own thoughts.

"Gerald?" Rachel whispered.

He turned towards her and waited to hear what she had to say.

"Gerald, did you meet Kesi the last time you were here?"

"Yes," he answered.

"What did you think of her then?" Rachel asked.

"I thought she was the most beautiful woman I'd ever seen," he said.

Rachel was taken aback by his honesty and straight forward answer to her question. She weighed whether it wise to ask him more questions or whether she should leave Gerald in peace to gaze out the window.

"She didn't recognize me this time," Gerald said flatly, interrupting Rachel's musings of whether she should ask him more. He turned back to the window and looked out into the empty streets. All the villagers had dispersed and gone home once they'd been told there would be justice for the fright they'd experienced.

Rachel pondered his answer. She thought back to earlier when he claimed he didn't remember much from being here before—that he only remembered once confronted with something. His answer regarding Kesi didn't seem to fit that narrative. "You don't forget the most beautiful woman you'd ever seen," decided Rachel.

Rachel cleared her throat. Gerald turned from the window again. His glance traveled from Rachel to his sleeping wife, back to Rachel.

"Gerald, I'm not trying to be pushy, but are you sure there isn't something else you might remember from being here before that might help Liam tomorrow?" Rachel asked.

Gerald hesitated then said, "Yes. I'm sure."

He started to turn back to the window, but stopped when Rachel spoke again. "I'm just worried about Liam."

"I understand," Gerald said. He turned back to the window and said in a voice barely audible, "Liam will be okay."

"But you can't know that," Rachel responded. Gerald's mix of stoicism, mystery, and nonchalance was wearing her down. This was Liam's life they were talking about.

"Rachel," Gerald said with an authority she hadn't heard in his voice until now, "if I can make it off this planet, then Liam can."

"But—"

"Liam will survive," he foretold. Gerald didn't look at her, he just continued to stare out the window. Rachel resumed her reading. She reread the passage where Malachi and Kesi kiss, just as she was about to start the next paragraph Gerald spoke.

"For the record, I did not have a romance with Kesi. I know you're thinking I'm Malachi now, and I know Hester wrote it as Malachi and Kesi being an item. We weren't. We never kissed. I just thought she was beautiful, and I told Hester about it. So, that's how Kesi ended up a character in the book."

Rachel didn't know quite what to say to Gerald's confession. A long silence followed, before she said, "Okay."

"Most of that book was made up," Gerald added, a little defensive.

Rachel reflected for a minute before answering. "Are you saying I'm wasting my time looking for clues in it?"

"I don't know, but sleep isn't a bad idea," he said gruffly.

"Okay, Gerald," she conceded. "I'm just going to finish this chapter then. How about that?"

"Sounds smart."

Gerald sat on the floor near the bed next to Hester. Rachel watched him reach his arm up and place his ghost hand over Hester's solid hand. Rachel looked away, not wanting to invade a private moment. "How sad to love someone so much and not be able to touch them," she thought to herself.

She opened her book and read:

> *In her kiss he felt all the feelings that overflowed from her—grief, sadness, pride, hopelessness mixed with hope, and love. Deep, deep, unending love.*
>
> *"Kesi!" Ra boomed outside the chamber and down the corridor. His voice reverberated in the floors and through the walls.*
>
> *Malachi reluctantly took a step back from Kesi. The absence of Malachi's hands on her face and waist made Kesi instantly aware that she was*

cold. She longed for the return of his warmth.

Ra boomed again, "Kesi! Here! Now!"

Passion and revenge glowed in Malachi's eyes. "You will not always be his slave," he vowed.

Kesi took two steps toward the door before turning back to Malachi. "If only that were true," she breathed before running from the room.

Malachi was left alone with his thoughts, his fears for himself, and his unwavering resolve that Egypt deserved to be free.

The chapter was over and it had offered no new information besides sparking the conversation with Gerald that revealed he'd previously known Kesi. Rachel decided Gerald was right though. She needed sleep. Rachel closed her book and placed it on the nightstand beside her.

She looked down at Ra spread out on his pile of cushions. "He is not the Ra of *The Mighty Arm that Built Egypt*," she concluded. "This Ra is kind. Would the Ra in the book sleep on the floor and give his bed to tiny humans?"

Rachel guessed that there were other rooms in the palace where Ra could have either put them or taken a bed for himself. But, Ra chose to stay in the same room as them to keep them safe, even if that meant sleeping on the floor. For all that, he could have made them sleep on the floor and taken the bed for himself.

Rachel thought back to earlier—to when she had accused Ra of keeping her as a prisoner. She didn't feel like a prisoner at all now. She felt like a royal guest, or like some other important individual with a twelve foot tall bodyguard. Her feelings sure seemed to change rapidly here on Janus. Nothing seemed to be what it was to begin with, and everything seemed up in the air.

What would become of Liam? She glanced down at her feet where he lay. He lay on his side, facing her. He must have turned over while Rachel was absorbed in her book. Liam was asleep and looked far more peaceful than Rachel felt. Rachel had known him for such a short time, but it felt like longer. She didn't want him to get hurt, or worse die. Rachel focused on what Gerald said—he had made it off this planet. Liam was going to survive. "Liam is going to survive," she repeated to herself in her head. The question was still—*how*? Rachel closed her eyes and fell asleep while the question repeated in her head. *How? How? How?*

CHAPTER 22

Rachel awoke to the loud clanging of bells. The room was still dark. It was lit by just the glow of the two lamps Ra had left burning for her. Rachel sat up and found she was the only one left in bed. The others stood gathered around the ottoman eating a light breakfast that Rachel guessed the servants had brought up while she slept. Ra sat on the floor while Rachel's friends stood.

"Good morning, sleepy head," Hester said with a mouth full of bread.

"Why didn't you guys wake me?" Rachel asked with an edge to her voice. *Were they planning on waking me at all?*

"I was certain the bells would wake you without our help," answered Ra. He saw the concern didn't leave Rachel's face, so he added, "Those are just the first bells. You still have plenty of time to eat before we make our way to the arena."

Rachel climbed out of bed and joined the others at the ottoman. She poured herself a mug of water and grabbed a piece of bread. As Rachel chewed her bread, she considered what Ra had said—*first bells.*

"How many bells will there be before we're supposed to be down there?" she asked.

"We should be at the arena by roughly the fourth bell. The fifth bell signals the start of the ceremonial cleansing, then the trumpet signals the start of the match," he answered.

Liam, Gerald, and Hester seemed unmoved by this information. Rachel assumed Ra must have already told them before she awoke. Rachel looked at Liam. He seemed cheerful. She watched him entertain Hester and Gerald by throwing grapes into the air and catching them in his mouth. Hester clapped and cheered "again!" with another mouth full of bread.

Rachel sipped her water and contemplated if it was smart to eat anything. Food wasn't usually a wise choice for her when she had an uneasy stomach. She'd thrown up her cereal the mornings of her SAT and GRE tests. She'd thrown up before her first job interview. She'd thrown up the first time she met with a publisher. This was a lot bigger deal than any of those events. If they didn't figure out a way to stop Liam from having to fight Horus, Liam would probably die. Rachel took another bite of bread and prayed she wouldn't see the bread for a second time that day.

"I'm gonna need to tinkle," said Hester, interrupting Rachel's spiraling thoughts. "Can we make a pit stop at the bathroom before heading to the arena?"

Ra nodded in assurance.

"Does, uh, Horus have any weaknesses I should know about?" Liam half-jokingly, half-seriously asked Ra. "Trick knee? Bad back? Irrational fear of dancing?"

"His weakness is that he does not care about any life but his own," Ra imparted solemnly.

"Yikes, big guy," replied Hester, slapping Ra on his large knee which was almost eye level for Hester, since Ra was sitting on the floor. "That's not exactly encouraging."

With Ra's response about Horus, Rachel decided eating anything more was strictly out of the question. She put down her unfinished piece of bread, drained the last of the water from her cup, and sat on the floor near her shoes. She put her sneakers on and once again tied double knots in the laces just in case running was in her future.

Hester and Liam followed her lead. They put down their food and sat to put on their shoes. Just as they'd both finished, the second set of bells tolled. Rachel grabbed *The Mighty Arm that Built Egypt* off the bedside table and shoved it in her purse. She pulled her purse over her head and across her body. Ra suggested, "We should depart for the bath chamber."

Liam took a deep breath, nodded, and said, "Okay."

He knew each successive bell led him closer to his potential death. It was a lot to process. On their way out of the room Liam grabbed a piece of bread. He turned his head in time to see Rachel watching him.

"Nervous eater," he confessed and flashed Rachel what she'd come to know as his almost constant good-natured smile. Rachel thought back to the symposium when Liam had entered the room late. He wasn't daunted by the icy Dr. Kathy Holmes, and apparently he wasn't intimidated by the fiery Horus either.

They left Ra's chamber and walked the path to the bath chamber—down the halls and stairs and more halls. The palace had been quiet the day before, but today the silence felt foreboding. When they reached the bath chamber's corridor, Kesi, Halima, and Mert were waiting for them.

Halima and Mert looked uncomfortable and Kesi looked anxious. She spoke rapidly and in a whisper. "Horus is in the bath chamber."

Ra nodded his head slowly, stood silent for a moment, then commanded all three servants to go to the palace arena. They bowed and hurried away.

Once the servants were out of sight, Ra turned to Liam and said, "Pay no attention to Horus. He will attempt to unnerve you and frighten you. Do not engage with him."

Ra didn't wait for a response from Liam. He took the remaining long steps down the hall to the doors of the bath chamber. Rachel and Liam almost jogged to keep up with Ra's pace. Hester and Gerald trailed behind. Just as Ra reached for one of the door handles, both doors swung open from within. Horus stood before them, his long hair dripping and his chest glistening.

"I guess Horus is too macho for a towel," Rachel discerned.

For the first time Rachel felt like she was in a book that wasn't Hester's. Instead she felt like she was in one of the trashy romance novels Dr. Goldblum always tried to get her to read. Dr. Goldblum would tell Rachel, "If you can't have a boyfriend, at least you can have a book."

Rachel never understood how a serious academic could enjoy the equivalent of literary junk food. Dr. Goldblum told Rachel on more than one occasion, "Everybody needs some down time. Mine might as well include sweaty hunks and raunchy sex."

Horus looked like one of Dr. Goldblum's sweaty hunks—unnecessarily wet, hard-bodied, and barely clothed. But, unlike Dr. Goldblum's hunks, Horus wasn't there to please anyone. He was counting the bell chimes until he could kill someone.

Ra shouldered past him, creating a path for the others to walk. Horus smirked at Ra, but Ra wouldn't give him the satisfaction of meeting his gaze. Rachel and her friends followed Ra's example and ignored Horus. Horus watched the parade of humans that passed him by without acknowledgement.

"Small human, I look forward to destroying you," he jeered at Liam.

Liam ignored Horus and asked Ra whether it was okay if he brushed his teeth. Horus didn't like being ignored. Like Ra predicted, he had been intentionally trying to unnerve Liam. Instead Horus was the one becoming unnerved by the lack of response he was getting from the humans. *How infuriating! They should be afraid! They should tremble with terror!*

"Human, I'm talking to you," Horus said louder to Liam.

Liam bent down to get his, Rachel's, and Hester's tooth brushes from under the sink, along with the tooth powder. He didn't acknowledge Horus.

Horus scowled at Liam, then at Ra. Anger boiled up inside the hulking giant. Rachel looked over at him just as he lunged toward Hester. Rachel jumped in his path, and as gently as she could, pushed Hester into Liam. Horus' right hand slammed into Rachel, causing her to go flying against the wall of potted palm plants. Thankfully one of the plants broke her fall. She blinked and the scene before her quickly shifted. Ra held Horus by the throat against the beautiful tiled wall.

"DO NOT ATTACK HER! DO NOT ATTACK WOMEN!" he shouted in Horus' face. "I SHOULD CALL FOR YOUR EXECUTION THIS MOMENT!"

"Under what authority?" croaked Horus, his fingers clawing at the powerful hands wrapped around his throat.

"MINE!" Ra boomed, his face inches from Horus'.

"You are not my god." Horus choked out the words, his face turning a reddish purple. It reminded Rachel of the not-quite-ripe plums she preferred to eat. Not that she wanted to eat Horus' face. Sitting among the palm plants, Rachel tried to clear her head of plums. *Were Ra and Horus going to have a full blown fight right now? Was Ra going to kill Horus? Could that stop*

Liam from having to fight? Or would that just mean someone else would insist on fighting Liam? The villagers would undoubtedly demand it. As Rachel watched Ra hold Horus against the wall, she realized she was impressed. Horus appeared more muscular than Ra, but evidently Ra was stronger.

Ra looked away from Horus. For a half a second his eyes locked with Rachel's. Then in one swift unexpected movement, Ra flung Horus from against the wall out the doors of the bath chamber. Ra closed the doors then turned to his guests.

"My deepest apologies for that display," said Ra. He walked to Rachel still sitting among the palms and lifted her to her feet. "Are you injured?"

"Uh, I don't think so," she responded. Patting her body, checking for sore spots. "Are you okay, Hester?"

"Thanks to you I am," Hester grinned. She loaded tooth powder onto her toothbrush and started brushing.

Gerald stood to the side looking grim but grateful. "Thank you, Rachel," he said.

"No problem, Gerald," Rachel responded.

He seemed to deliberate for a moment before saying, "Call me 'Gerry'."

Rachel nodded to the ghost before her. She remembered when they'd first met—only a day and a half ago, though it felt much longer—he had said if they got along, she could call him 'Gerry'. Rachel still thought he was secretive and a know-it-all, but apparently they were friends now.

"Um, should we be worried that Horus is going to come back in here?" Liam asked, his mouth full of foam created by the tooth powder.

Everyone looked to the closed double doors. "Horus will go to the arena," answered Ra. "He will want to be there first so he can pick the side where the sun won't be in his eyes. He will not return."

Rachel joined the others at the sink. After pulling her hair band from her purse, she twirled her hair into her signature messy bun. Everything she did, she did on auto pilot. She brushed her teeth mechanically. She wasn't thinking about brushing, she was thinking about what they were practically willingly escorting Liam to—his death. After she finished brushing, she asked, "Couldn't we just run? Go hide in the forest or something?"

"You mean to avoid me facing Horus?" Liam inquired.

"Yeah."

Gerald and Hester looked sadly at each other, then at Liam and Rachel. Rachel could read everyone's faces. It was a "no."

"If we ran, Horus and that young looking god would search for us. And they live on this planet so they probably know all the hiding places," said Liam. "And the villagers would probably help hunt us down, too."

"He is right," said Ra. "Horus and Mafdet would hunt all of you down. Bast would most likely join them in the hunt. And when they found you, they would execute every one of you."

"See, Rachel, it's better we just go down to the arena," Liam said trying to sound encouraging. "No, I don't want to die. But, even if I die at least you guys won't die, too."

The clang of the bells put a stop to that conversation. "Those are the third bells. It is time to go to the arena," said Ra.

"Not before I tinkle," insisted Hester as she ran a comb through her white puff of hair.

After Hester (and everyone else) had *tinkled*, they followed Ra out of the bath chamber, down the hall, and out the front doors of the palace. Ra went left, so they all went left. This was the first time Rachel had seen the outside of the palace, besides the courtyard. And this was the first time any of them had seen the palace in this much light. The sun still hadn't broken the horizon, but the sky glowed with the light of almost morning. The world around them was dim but visible.

Rachel wasn't sure what she had expected, but it wasn't what she saw. The palace and its grounds looked beautiful and pristine. Everything was bright and clean, even in the low light. There were colorful flowering plants all along the sides of the palace, and trellises with hanging plants all over. From the window of Ra's bed chamber, Rachel had only seen the palace gates and the section of the village closest to the palace. What she saw now, walking along a stone path made of the same stone bricks Rachel recognized as being what formed the palace, was mesmerizing. The only thing the palace lacked to be paradise were song birds.

High green hedges interrupted the stone of the palace walls. "That must be the courtyard," she told herself. And though she didn't know, she walked past the opening in the hedge where her friends had entered the night before. If this weren't such a day filled with anxiety, she'd want to explore her surroundings. Everything was so beautiful!

Rachel was snapped out of her reverie by Liam. He was walking ten feet ahead of her, trying to keep up with Ra. He called back over his shoulder, "Come on, Rachel. Don't get left behind."

Hester and Gerald were even ahead of Rachel, so she jogged to catch up with everyone. Her purse bounced against her hip. Past the structure of the palace, they walked through an extensive garden with both vegetables and flowers. The path was no longer stone, just earth. The garden was closed in by hedges—like those of the courtyard—that acted as walls.

Rachel wondered if this was where the food they'd eaten in the palace came from, or if the food came from the villagers as tribute, the way it did in *The Mighty Arm that Built Egypt*.

Rachel kept a fast pace beside Liam and tried not to get distracted by the surroundings. They exited the garden and crossed a wide wooden bridge that covered a swiftly moving stream. "Or is it a river?" Rachel wondered. "Stream? Creek? I think it's a creek. Or maybe a creek that widens into a river downstream?" Between debating with herself the difference between a stream, a creek, and a river, she also pondered whether this creek might be the same one that traveled through the cavern where they'd made camp.

On the other side of the bridge, the street again was stone. It was wider and grander than the paths they'd been on previous, and looking up at the large structure in front of her, Rachel was certain they'd reached the palace arena. They passed under a massive archway with unfamiliar characters etched into the stone. Unlike the inscription on the face of the cave, this wasn't Greek. Rachel guessed the characters were the language of the villagers—Janusis.

The arena reminded Rachel of a football or soccer stadium, but with stone seats like an ancient coliseum. Two thirds of the seats were already filled with villagers. As Rachel and her friends got closer, they could see that Ra was right—Horus had laid claim the side of the arena where the sun would be behind him.

A section of the crowd was chanting something. Rachel tried to focus on their words, but realized they were speaking Janusis. For the first time Rachel wondered why Ra and the other gods did not speak Janusis amongst themselves. It would have been easy for them to exclude Rachel from conversation in the banquet hall had they spoken the unfamiliar tongue.

"I will escort Liam to the priests," Ra said turning to face them.

"Should we stay here?" Rachel asked. She didn't want to leave Liam alone. She didn't want him to feel abandoned.

Ra looked around as though he were searching for something or someone. He stopped his searching when he spotted a tall goddess standing over a woman carrying a child, and called, "Sekhmet!"

Sekhmet looked up, smiled, then approached the group. "Greetings, Ra. I was talking with a villager who believed the spirit," she said gesturing to Gerald, "had made her child ill. I assured her that was impossible, but performed a blessing over the child to ease her nerves."

"Foolishness," Ra mumbled before asking, "Will you stay with Rachel and her friends while I escort Liam for the ceremonial cleansing?"

"Yes. I will offer my protection," Sekhmet answered. Ra nodded in response as the fourth set of bells clanged. At the sound of the bells the people in the stands stood and chanted louder.

"Liam, follow me," said Ra.

Rachel, Hester, Gerald, and Sekhmet watched Liam follow Ra across the arena to a tent made of deep purple fabric. It was set away from the stands filled with villagers and had two guards with spears positioned before its entrance. The tent was large enough for Ra to enter, but small enough that he had to duck. Ra said something to the guards and they stepped out of the way, allowing Ra and Liam to disappear into the tent's purple folds. A moment later the group saw Horus cross to the tent and enter.

Rachel turned her attention again to the crowd. "What are they chanting, Sekhmet?" she asked.

"Shacook, shameck, shamee," Sekhmet answered, her voice sad. "The basic translation is 'let pain, let justice, let death'."

"Cheerful group," Hester chirped.

"I wonder if they'd shut up if I ran over and scared them a little," Gerald suggested. Even in his ghostly form Rachel noticed his eyes twinkle. Perhaps his eyes had been pretty like Liam's when he was living.

Sekhmet shook her head and took a step to stand between Gerald and his view of the villagers in the stands. "Please do not scare the villagers. They are a superstitious foolish lot. If you go near them and then something happens to one by chance, they will be calling for another challenge. And who will fight next?" she asked, gesturing to Hester and Rachel.

As if to taunt Gerald, the chanting in the stands grew louder. "Shacook, shameck, shamee!"

The stands were almost full. Most of their faces looked fiercely angry. In a section removed from the thick of the crowd Rachel spotted Kesi, Halima, and Mert. They did not chant. Rachel wondered what made these three so different from the other villagers. Ra's faithful servants sat quietly, not even speaking to one another. They only stared—their eyes focused on the purple tent.

"What are they doing in the tent?" Rachel asked, trying to distract herself and forget the villager's chants.

"They are meeting with the priests for the cleansing ritual. The ritual begins at the start of the fifth bell. The priests will bathe and anoint the feet and hands of the fighters, and say a prayer they will only be used in the pursuit of justice and righteousness," answered Sekhmet. "After the ritual is complete, it will not be long until the start of the fight."

The fifth bell rang out. The final bell seemed louder and longer than all the other bells. It reverberated in the ground and up into Rachel's bones. Her stomach did a flip and for a moment she feared she would lose what little she ate for breakfast. It was almost time, and they still didn't know how Liam would survive.

"What are we going to do? How do we save Liam?" Rachel's voice shook.

With her small delicate hand, Hester grab Rachel's stronger one. Looking up into Rachel's face, Hester said, "I don't know, dear. But Gerry says it's going to be okay, so I believe it."

Rachel looked down at the tiny optimistic woman. The wind played with her poof of white hair. Her round face was smiling and childlike, despite her age. But she was so small and so fragile. *How were they going to survive? How were they going to make it off this planet?*

"Bunny's right," Gerald said gruffly. "No sense in losing hope now."

Rachel eyed Gerald suspiciously. She couldn't shake the feeling that Gerald still hadn't told them everything he knew. How had he gotten off this planet?

The crowd changed their chant. "Mafdet! Mafdet! Mafdet!" they screamed.

Mafdet had entered the arena followed by Kuk. Mafdet was evidently a favorite among the villagers. "Mafdet! Mafdet! Mafdet!"

Sensing Rachel's question, Sekhmet answered, "The people love Mafdet because he brings justice. That is, they love him until justice is being served against them."

Mafdet approached the crowd and feigned disapproval of their chanting. The villagers only chanted louder, "Mafdet! Mafdet! Mafdet alhorah! Mafdet alhorah!"

"Mafdet live forever," Sekhmet translated.

Rachel remembered the unfamiliar characters on the stone archway. "Sekhmet, what does the inscription say above the archway for the arena?"

"The arena belongs to Mafdet, so the inscription is his motto," Sekhmet answered.

"What is his motto?" wondered Rachel.

Sekhmet smiled patiently, and said as though explaining to a child, "I have already answered this question. It is what the crowd chants. Shacook, shameck, shamee. Let pain, let justice, let death."

Kuk approached the group and stood among them as though this were the place he always stood. He didn't speak, he just stood.

"Greetings Kuk," said Sekhmet.

Kuk grunted a greeting, then looking around asked, "Where is Ra and the Earth man?"

"They're in the priest's tent conducting the ceremonial cleansing. They're surely almost finished, for the sun is almost rising," answered Sekhmet.

As the sun's rays teased over the horizon, the entrance to the tent was flung open and out walked Horus followed by Liam, Ra, and a group of five priests in gold trimmed scarlet robes. Horus joined Mafdet in front of the chanting villagers. He reminded Rachel of a professional wrestler, working up the crowd, enjoying their worship. As Liam and Ra crossed back across the green lawn of the arena to their group of friends, the rising sun shown off Ra's shaved head and turned Liam's brown beard to auburn. Liam was somehow still smiling.

"Are you okay?" Rachel asked.

"Uh-um, no, not exactly," Liam answered with his face in a permanent smile. "But I'm trying to be."

"Say what you need to say, Liam. It is nearly time for you to be in the center of the arena," Ra instructed.

Liam walked between the tall gods to Hester, who looked especially small in this group. "If it looks like I'm going to get badly hurt or worse, promise me you'll look away," he said to her, his brows furrowed, a look of protective concern on his face. Hester held back tears as she nodded her head. Liam pulled her to his chest and held her for a good long hug.

"You'll be okay," Gerald mumbled in a fatherly voice.

"I hope so," Liam replied.

Rachel's knees felt weak as the reality of the moment sank in. Liam approached her and hugged her without saying a word. He could feel her shaking in his arms and searched for something encouraging to say to her.

"Rachel," he whispered, causing a chill to run down her spine. She leaned heavy against him, not feeling able to support herself. "Rachel, it's okay to be scared. I'm scared. But, somehow I think it might be okay still. Every time Gerald says it's going to be okay I really feel it, deep down in my gut, that it is going to be okay." He paused, and it sounded like he also might start crying. Liam took a deep breath then added, "Whatever happens, stick close to Ra. I don't think he'd let anything happen to you or Hester."

"Okay," was the only response Rachel could manage.

"It is time," interrupted Ra.

Liam gave Rachel a tight squeeze then let her go. He turned to the group and said, "Okay, everyone, wish me luck." Without waiting for the chorus of their well wishes, he turned from the group to walk to the center of the arena.

Rachel wiped away the tears that streamed down her cheeks with the back of her hand and watched Liam walk away. The sun, peaking up over the horizon, was in her eyes which made her think about what Ra had said earlier about Horus. He was already standing in the center of the arena, his back to the horizon. Liam slowly marched toward him.

For the first time Rachel took a good look at the center of the arena where the match would start. It was stone. A large stone disk that appeared to be about 8 feet in diameter. The rest of the arena was grass. Rachel strained her eyes trying to get a better look. *Did her eyes deceive her? Was this wishful thinking?* She took a few steps forward to get a better look. "Hester! Gerald!" she called.

The elderly couple joined her the few paces before Ra and the other gods. "Does that look familiar to you?" Rachel asked.

"Huh? Does what look familiar?" asked Hester.

"That," Rachel said, pointing to the stone disk in the center of the arena.

"Sweetheart, I can't see that good. I'm not sure what you're pointing at," Hester confessed.

"The stone disk," Rachel said excitedly.

"It's like at the hotel," said Gerald.

Rachel was almost jumping out of her skin. The lack of excitement from either of her friends was bewildering and slightly annoying. "Yes, it's exactly like what was on the ceiling at the hotel ballroom. The thing we were under before we were transported here," she observed.

Liam was standing in the center of the arena just outside the stone disk when the sun completely broke the horizon. From somewhere in the stands a trumpet sounded—four long notes—the signal for the start of the match. Everyone in the stands were on their feet. Horus leaned forward as though to intimidate Liam with his hulking size. In answer to the threat, Liam took a step forward, onto the stone disk, and in the blink of an eye he disappeared.

CHAPTER 23

Rachel stood motionless, her mouth agape. Beside her, Hester kept asking, "What just happened? What happened? What just happened?"

The crowd screamed and yelled wildly. Alone in the center of the arena, Horus snarled and cursed. He walked around the stone disk, to where Liam had stood moments before, and stamped his feet.

Ra said to Sekhmet and Kuk, "We must calm the villagers," and the three departed to speak peace to the people in the stands.

Rachel with Hester and Gerald stood dumbly on the arena grass. *What just happened to Liam?*

Rachel's heart beat erratically, and she forced herself to mold her thoughts into a coherent sentence, "You guys, do you think Liam got back to Earth?"

"Mercy me, did he disappear? Is that what happened?" asked Hester. "I thought my eyes were playing tricks on me."

"Yeah, he stepped into the center, on the stone disk, and he vanished," Rachel said almost breathless.

"He's okay," Gerald answered.

"So you think he got back to Earth?" Rachel asked Gerald.

"Yes, I believe he did," answered Gerald.

Rachel looked back to the stone disk where Horus paced outside its boarder, then around at the chaos in the crowd. There were so many angry faces and they were sure to still demand justice. Either she or Hester would be challenged to fight next. They had to make their escape.

"Okay, you two, we need to get out of here," Rachel said. "It looks like Liam might have gotten out by stepping on the stone disk. We need to try it, too. Right now it looks like our only hope."

Hester and Gerald agreed, and the three began to cross the arena to the center. Horus had turned his back on them. He was walking away, toward the sun, to where he had stood when Liam disappeared. The muscles in his back tensed—the large falcon tattoo looked lifelike and menacing stretched from shoulder to shoulder—and Rachel was glad he was walking in the opposite direction of herself and her friends.

The crowd chanted again, "Shacook, shameck, shamee!" *Let pain, let justice, let death!*

To her right, Rachel heard Mafdet bargaining with the crowd. "Certainly you must know we had no knowledge that the invader was a trained magician. Had we known, we would have put him in enchanted fetters or instantly executed him. Allow me to offer my deepest apologies. I am quite certain we can come to some sort of arrangement to appease you all. What can I do to make this right?" he asked like a slick restaurant manager when a patron sends back a dish.

The villagers' chant continued. "Shacook, shameck, shamee!" Their angry voices echoed all around Rachel, Hester, and Gerald. As they made their way to the center of the arena, Rachel grabbed Hester's hand. Hester gripped Rachel's hand tightly, and Rachel wondered if Hester felt as afraid as she did. Rachel didn't want to ask though. If Hester and Gerald weren't thinking it, she didn't want to share her fears with them, that she was certain the crowd's chant meant only one thing—the impending death of Hester, herself, or both.

As they approached the stone disk, for the first time that day Rachel saw Bast. In her catlike manner, Bast slinked across the grass to where Horus stood about thirty feet from the disk with his back to Rachel and her friends. With a bored look of disdain Bast spoke to Horus, then gestured to Rachel and her friends. Rachel knew that couldn't be good. The last thing they needed was Horus' attention. They were only a few paces from the stone disk. They were almost there, but they were far enough away that Horus could stop them if they didn't move fast.

"We've got to run, Hester," Rachel said to her octogenarian friend.

Without waiting for a response, Rachel broke into a run, dragging Hester along with her.

Just as they were about to reach the stone disk, Horus turned. He looked straight into Rachel's eyes and his nostrils flared. In another instant he was charging at them like an angry bull.

Rachel pushed herself and Hester harder, and before Horus reached the stone disk, they were both already standing on its surface, Gerald along with them. But nothing happened. They didn't vanish the way Liam had. They were still on Janus.

Horus joined them on the stone disk. He panted and snarled. "You dare to meet me here? You feeble human women wish to challenge me?" he shouted at them. Horus' spit peppered Rachel's face.

The crowd's attention was drawn to the center of the arena. They saw their champion again facing a human foe and their chant changed. It became, "Horus alhorah! Shacook, shameck, shamee!"

Ra and the other gods looked to the center of the arena to see the cause for the crowd's change. After seeing Rachel,

Hester, and Gerald standing upon the stone disk in front of Horus, Mafdet turned back to the nearest section of villagers and cheerfully said, as though Rachel and her friends' push to the center had been planned, "See, we're taking care of it."

Ra was the furthest from the center of the arena, further than any of the other gods, and he was last to realize what was happening. When he saw that Rachel stood in the center of the arena with Horus, fear surged through his long body. He raced across the green lawn of the arena, trying to make it to Rachel before Horus had the chance to fulfill the desire of the bloodthirsty villagers.

"We don't want to challenge you," Rachel tried to explain to Horus. "We just want to go home. We thought..." She trailed off looking down at the stone disk upon which they stood. They hadn't disappeared. The only thing that had disappeared besides Liam was their hope in ever getting home.

"What did you think, foolish human?" Horus yelled.

"I thought if we stepped on this stone we would get transported back home—to Earth. But clearly I was wrong," she explained, defeated.

"Back to Earth?" Horus sneered. "Back to Earth?! There is no way I will allow you to go back to Earth—back to Earth to lead other Earth men here to destroy us!"

"I don't know why you think I would lead people here to destroy your planet. If I got back to Earth, I would just try to pretend like this never happened. I would just be thankful to be home," Rachel protested.

By her side, her breath a little labored from the short run, Hester nodded her head fiercely in agreement. On the other side of Hester stood Gerald dutifully. At that moment it occurred to Rachel that she had been selfish. She hadn't considered what would happen to Gerald if they were transported back to Earth. *Would he go back to being invisible? Would it mean he and Hester would no longer get to talk to each other? That Hester would no longer even get to enjoy his ghostly appearance?* Rachel's train of thought was interrupted by Horus taking one giant step forward. With Horus standing so close, it hurt Rachel's neck to look up at him.

"I don't believe one lying word you say, human," Horus sneered. "And I will finish this now."

In one lightning-fast motion Horus picked Rachel up with one hand, and Hester with the other. In the same instant, Ra reached the center of the arena.

Ra shouted, "Horus, no! Set them down. It doesn't have to be this way. They mean us no harm!"

Horus grinned menacingly. "Now this is a dilemma, Ra. Because you want me to put these humans down, but they—" he said jerking his head towards the villagers in the stands, "—they want justice. They want me to kill them."

Horus held Rachel and Hester firmly around their ribs. Rachel squirmed in his hand, and Horus only tightened his grip. She was sure if he held her much tighter he'd break her ribs. She looked across at Hester, held far from her in Horus' left hand, Rachel in his right. Hester looked like she was struggling to breathe. Rachel wondered if he was holding Hester as tightly, or if Hester might be having an asthma attack from the fright of the situation. Below, on the ground, Gerald stood below his wife, utterly terrified.

Sekhmet had soundlessly joined the group. She stood beside Ra, looking solemn. "Horus, harming these women will change nothing," she said in her soothing voice.

But, Horus would not be pacified. The terrible grin left his face and he bellowed, "Harming these women? Harming? They will destroy all of us and our planet, Sekhmet. I'm not going to harm them! I'm going to KILL them!"

Horus squeezed Rachel and Hester. Rachel screamed in pain and Hester gave a pathetic whimper. The crowd cheered. Rachel gasped, trying to breathe, the sharp pain radiating through her ribs made it difficult. The thought of broken ribs seemed minor compared to Horus' proclamation he would kill them.

Rachel looked across to Hester and tried to assess through her own pain if Horus had done the same damage to her friend. Hester hadn't screamed when Rachel had, so Rachel hadn't lost hope. Then Hester's head lolled on her shoulder and Rachel feared the worst.

Mafdet gleefully joined the group. "Are we having a new match? Both ladies against Horus?" he asked. "It doesn't seem quite fair—two against one—but I'm sure the people will love it."

"A match?" shouted Horus. "No, we will not have a match! We will only have an execution!"

On the word *execution*, Horus gave Rachel and Hester another terrible squeeze. Rachel grimaced. She wouldn't give Horus the satisfaction of another scream—though her already broken ribs screamed internally. Hester also didn't make a noise, but Rachel could see she was now alert. The breeze rumpled the tiny woman's white hair, and a determined look gleamed in her eyes. She leaned her small, white head forward and bit Horus as hard as she could.

Horus roared, and before Rachel knew what had happened, Hester lay crumpled on the stadium grass. From several feet up, in Horus' angry hand, Rachel looked down at her friend. Rachel's body felt numb. *What just happened?*

"That wasn't very sporting," Mafdet said under his breath.

Gerald hurried over to where Hester lay on the green turf.

Ra began to speak, "Horus—"

"St-st-stop!" Horus sputtered, holding Rachel up higher. He looked like a frightened, caged animal. His threat to throw Rachel was his only bargaining piece.

Everyone stood still and quiet. Even the crowd had stopped their chanting. The first sound to break the silence was the sound of crying. Through his tears, Gerald cried, "Bunny! Can you hear me? Hester? Bunny? Please! I can't help her, someone help her!"

Rachel watched the scene before her, utterly helpless. Surely Horus would kill her soon. There was nothing they could do. Then it dawned on her if all was lost, then she couldn't lose anything more.

"Horus," she rasped through the pain of her broken ribs, "please set me on the ground with my friends. Just let me check on my friends. I will face you if you let me do that."

Ra tried to interject, but Horus put up a warning hand and said, "I will honor what this human wishes."

Horus set her down on the stone disk on which he stood. The moment Rachel's feet hit the stone they were running to the grass to her friends. Hester's crumpled body was face down on the grass. "Gerald, I am so sorry," Rachel said to the ghostly old man. "Is she... gone?"

"I don't know. There's no way for me to check," he said while tears rolled down his transparent weathered cheeks.

"I'm going to try to roll her over," said Rachel. She started to roll the old woman over when she remembered how just the day before Sekhmet had healed the old woman. She looked over to the group of gods several paces away, and called, "Sekhmet, can you come help us over here?"

Sekhmet nodded and began to walk over. Rachel returned her attention to her friend lying on the ground. Rachel eased Hester onto her back and Rachel placed her ear against Hester's chest to listen for a heartbeat. She heard a gentle *bum-bump, bum-bump, bum-bump*. Then nothing.

"No," Rachel mouthed, unable to make a sound in that horrible moment. "No," she finally voiced as Sekhmet reached them and crouched beside her. "Her heart was beating, then it just stopped," Rachel explained, panic overflowing out her eyes in tears.

"I cannot bring back the dead," Sekhmet said softly, her eyes communicating the remorse and pity words could never communicate.

"CPR. C-CPR," Rachel stuttered. "I'll try CPR. I've never done it, but I can try."

Picturing every scene she'd ever seen in a movie where CPR was performed, Rachel assumed the position. She interlaced her fingers, placing them on Hester's chest. She hummed the tune to "Stayin' Alive," like she'd heard you should do, and pumped Hester's chest in rhythm. "Come on Hester, please don't be dead. Don't die. Please."

"Sweetheart, it's okay," Rachel heard Hester say. Rachel stopped pumping and looked down at Hester's still, pale face.

"Behind you, dear."

Rachel turned around to find Hester standing hand in hand with Gerald. Both were a beautiful blue-green and smiling ear to ear.

"Oh, Hester!" Rachel exclaimed, tears streaming down her face.

"It's all right. I'm all right. See?" she said putting her tiny ghostly arm around the translucent body of her deceased husband.

Tears still glistened on Gerald's cheeks when he said to Rachel, "We're okay."

"I... I don't know what to say," Rachel confessed.

"Don't worry about that, dear," Hester said, then dropped her voice. "You need to focus on getting out of here. We'll be okay. No one can hurt us now. You need to take care of yourself."

Rachel's eyes scanned the people in the stands of the arena. Seeing the second ghost materialize brought them out of their quiet stupor. They became a buzz of voices. A hive of angry bees, buzzing for justice they believed hadn't been fully served. The chant began again—"Shacook, shameck, shamee!"

"NOW WE FINISH THIS!" raged Horus from the center of the stone disk. He stamped his feet, and Rachel was again reminded of an angry bull.

Rachel stood and dusted off her clothes. She felt her ribs ache, but she ignored them. She calmly began the walk back towards the stone disk and Horus.

"Wait," Sekhmet called, in an uncharacteristically loud voice.

In a second she towered at Rachel's side. Sekhmet crouched so she was eye level with Rachel. She looked her deep in the eyes trying to convey some sort of message. Sekhmet spoke in a voice that reminded Rachel of bad actors in school plays. "Here, let me help you finish dusting yourself off," she said woodenly, before placing her large hand on Rachel's broken ribs. "Mended," she whispered.

The sensation Rachel felt was like water being poured into a glass. Like her entire being was pliable and bendable to anything Sekhmet wished. She felt her broken ribs fuse together. Rachel took a deep breath and no longer experienced shooting pain.

“Th-thank you,” she stammered.

Sekhmet nodded, rose, and walked away without a word.

“Enough, Horus!” Ra interjected, standing at the edge of the stone disk. “Killing another human will not sate the people’s hunger for justice. It will only produce another specter for the people to fear.”

“I have to agree with Ra,” added Mafdet. “Once we’re out of humans, then what?”

“Exactly,” Ra agreed.

“Fighting and subsequently killing is lunacy,” Mafdet continued. Ra nodded in agreement. Mafdet smiled broadly before adding, “Naturally, it makes much more sense to torture her.”

Rachel reached the stone disk and stood next to Ra. She watched his nodding stop so suddenly, she was surprised he didn’t get whiplash. “You barbarian!” Ra spit. “Torture?! I will not allow it!”

Ra looked from Rachel beside him to the blood thirsty crowd still chanting, “Shacook, shameck, shamee!” Before Rachel knew what had happened, Ra had snatched her up in his arms and was running across the arena in the direction they’d entered. He yelled to Gerald and Hester, “Distract the crowd!”

As Ra raced from the center of the arena with Rachel in his strong arms, Rachel saw Gerald and Hester split up—Gerald rushing toward the crowds on one side of the arena, Hester toward the crowds on the opposite side. The people shrieked and screamed in terror.

CHAPTER 24

Ra shifted Rachel in his arms so she was looking over his shoulder back at the chaos that erupted in the arena. "The crowd will be incensed by the spirits. Horus and Mafdet will be forced to stay to calm them. That should provide us at least a minute or two head start," said Ra, his words sounding only slightly jostled by the cadence of his quick stride.

Rachel gasped.

"What is it?" Ra demanded.

"Bast!"

Bast raced after them with the catlike speed one would expect of such a being. Her silky black hair streamed behind her. Her bare feet were soundless on the stone street. Ra pushed himself harder, his sandals slapping the ground. He dashed onto the bridge, and before Rachel knew what had happened, they were in the water. Ra had jumped off the bridge into the creek. Or stream. Or river. Rachel now guessed it might be considered a river, because it was deep enough that Ra wasn't walking in it, he was swimming.

"Hold on to my neck," he breathed as he swung her around onto his back. The current was moving with them, rapidly propelling them down stream.

Rachel was waiting for a splash behind them, or any sign that Bast still followed. As though he read her mind, Ra answered, "Bast will not follow us. She cannot swim, and the current is too quick for her to keep pace running next to the stream. And I have stopped time for a moment. She still stands just a few paces outside the entrance of the arena."

The world on either side of the river flashed by them, a blur of first buildings, then trees. Rachel took a deep breath and held tight to Ra. She was glad to be out of the arena—away from Horus, Mafdet, and the horrible crowd—but her heart still pounded in her chest and her stomach was still tight.

"If you could just stop time now, why didn't you stop time earlier when Horus had me and Hester?" Rachel asked.

"Horus isn't affected by my power," Ra answered. "And it's not as easy to do as you might think."

She had so many questions. They all seemed trapped on the tip of her tongue. Finally she asked, "Where are we going? What are we going to do?"

Ra did not answer. He continued swimming with the current. His powerful arms and legs propelling them forward faster than any human body could.

Rachel asked again, "Where are we—"

Her question was answered before she could finish asking it. Before them a mountain rose swiftly. It was the same mountain where she had first found herself transported with her friends. *Had it been a full two days now?* It felt so much longer, yet like no time at all.

In an instant they were inside the mountain. Rachel was right—this river was the same river that flowed through the mountain. Rachel felt Ra's muscles strain against the force of the stream as he swam to shore.

Ra gently removed Rachel from his back and placed her on solid ground. She looked around and observed that it looked like the cavern she had stayed in with her friends, but it wasn't quite it. She guessed that their campsite was further downstream. It was dark except for the light from the tunnel the river had carved out of the mountain side, and a small crack in the mountain far above their heads.

Rachel watched as Ra bent to pick up large stones from around the cavern. His lean bronze body glistened in the low light. He had the body of a swimmer. "That's what's different about his build from the others," thought Rachel. "Horus looks like a body builder, Kuk is stocky, but also more like a body builder. Ra is strong and lean like a swimmer." As an afterthought she mentally added, "And Mafdet is a skinny psychopath, apparently."

Ra carried the stones he gathered to the tunnel they had entered the mountain through. He dashed from one side of the cavern to the other, swimming back and forth across the stream to gather all the stones he could to fill the mouth of the tunnel. In just a few minutes he'd created a stone wall blocking out most of the light.

"That won't hold for long. But it might slow down anyone who attempts to follow us," Ra said as he picked Rachel up again and placed her once more on his back. He climbed into the water and swam. The rocks Ra used to cover the entrance changed the swift current into a softly moving stream. Without the force of the steam behind them, Ra and Rachel traveled at a more moderate pace down the stream.

As Ra swam, Rachel looked from right to left, to the scenery inside the mountain. It was mostly dark and hard to make out. The mountain was separated into chambers. The first chamber where Ra had gathered the rocks and plugged up the entrance was large and high ceilinged. The next chamber was smaller with a lower rocky roof. Rachel spotted clay pottery like the bowls and jugs they had found at their campsite. It was tough to be sure though. For a time they traveled down the river through a tunnel that boxed them in on all sides. It was so dark Rachel was sure Ra could not see what he swam towards. She couldn't see Ra's large head in front of her.

Rachel prayed for light. She felt claustrophobic and wondered if Egyptian gods ever felt claustrophobic, too. But how could they? Weren't they who had invented sarcophagi? Why make such a compact space if you hate confined places? Rachel was still contemplating the terror of being stuck in a sarcophagus when she became aware of light ahead. She also became aware of Ra's breathing. It had become labored. He puffed, "We will be at walking height soon."

"Huh?" Rachel answered, unsure what he meant. Ra issued no response but to continue swimming.

After five or more minutes of silence between them, the tunnel opened into a cavernous chamber. Without a warning, Ra stood in the stream and said, "I will walk now."

"Oh, walking height!" Rachel realized.

She looked around and recognized her surroundings as the cavern she and her friends had used as a campsite their first day on Janus. The cavern Kuk said belonged to him. The clay jugs and pots, the barrels, and the charred spot on the rocky floor where their fire had been, reminded her of a movie set. *Had it been such a short time ago she had been here with her friends?*

Her friends.

For the first time since their flight Rachel allowed her mind to wander to her friends. Hester was dead now, but she was most certainly happier. She could hold her husband again. They could hug and hold hands. They could be happy together here on Janus. They didn't need food and no one could hurt them. *But what about Liam? Where was he? Back in Austin? Someplace else? What if something happened to him? What if he was—*

"It will get dark again," Ra said, interrupting her morbid thoughts.

They passed out of the familiar chamber into another tunnel. The light stayed behind as they journeyed deeper into the mountain. Ra stayed standing and walked up the stream. When it again became too dark for Rachel to see she relied on her ears to tell her that the water had gotten shallow enough for Ra's steps to break the water's surface. The splashing sound was rhythmic and Rachel wondered if she wasn't so nervous about Horus, Mafdet, and the crowds of angry villagers if the sound of Ra's walk might put her to sleep. After a while of traveling in the dark to the steady splashing rhythm of Ra's feet, something felt different to Rachel.

"Are we going up?" she asked.

"Up the mountain?" Ra replied.

"Yeah."

"Yes, this stream climbs up the mountain half way, then curves down again. We will follow it until we reach the next chamber," Ra answered.

Light again filtered around them. Everything was gray in the dimness of the mountain tunnel.

"Is time still frozen?" Rachel asked, picturing Bast standing motionless mid run in front of the palace arena.

"No, Bast is no longer frozen," responded Ra.

"Um," was all Rachel managed to say. *Could he read her thoughts? Did he see the picture inside her head of Bast?*

He answered her unasked question, "I actually did not stop all time in that moment. Had I stopped all time then the river would have stopped flowing. We needed the river's speed. I stopped time around Bast so she could not follow us or perceive which direction we had traveled."

They reached the chamber and Ra stepped out of the stream and set Rachel on the ground. A small opening in the mountain wall lit the chamber, but just barely. This chamber didn't have clay pots or evident provisions, but it had torches like the campsite chamber, and like the walls of the palace. They were unlit. For a moment Rachel wished she were like Liam—carrying useful, emergency-type things like water proof matches. They would be handy right now. She didn't have matches, but if Ra wanted to read more of *The Mighty Arm that Built Egypt*, she would be happy to pull her water-logged copy from her purse. Before Rachel finished that thought, from somewhere on the ground beneath one of the torches Ra found what Rachel guessed to be a flint, since she was pretty sure there weren't lighters just lying around. He had the torch lit in seconds, and with its light bouncing off the rock walls and ceiling she could see the chamber they were in was just barely high enough for Ra to stand.

"We will rest a minute," Ra said, sitting on the ground beneath the torch he had lit.

"Okay," agreed Rachel. Her wet sneakers squelched as she crossed the small chamber to where Ra sat.

"You are soaked. I apologize for our mode of travel. It was the fastest way of escape," explained Ra.

"Oh, it's okay. You saved me from Horus and Mafdet torturing me. I'll take drenched over tortured any day," she said. "Though the contents of my purse didn't exactly enjoy the swim." Rachel pulled the soggy book from her purse and held it up for Ra to see.

"Perhaps it does less harm wet," Ra smirked.

"We can only hope," she said in return. Rachel put the book back in her purse and sat down by the giant. "Can I ask you a question?"

"Yes," he answered simply.

Rachel wasn't prepared for him to relent so easily. She had become accustomed to Ra avoiding answering questions directly or acting as though he might not answer at all. His quick agreement took her by surprise.

"Will you answer multiple questions?" she tried.

Ra laughed a throaty laugh, then again answered, "Yes."

She took a deep breath, then asked, "What is your real connection to Egypt?"

In the dim light of the stone chamber Ra's eyes were black. Rachel couldn't distinguish his pupils from his dark irises. He looked deep into her eyes, like he had so many times since she had met him. As he spoke, his words came alive before her.

"I was in Egypt before it was Egypt. I was in Egypt when it was all green and flowers and forest. I was there with my friends. We lived peaceful and joyous lives. But knowledge corrupts. We discovered we were powerful and we amazed ourselves. My friends and I built great stone monuments to celebrate our wonder," he said, pausing. His face was thoughtful and sad. "And then the world became less green. The humans we had only occasionally encountered became residents of our land. They worshiped us. We did not ask for it. We could not stop them. And we could not blame them either. We were magnificent and the closest thing to God they had seen with their own eyes."

Rachel pictured it all—the paradise they had lived in on Earth that was Egypt before it was Egypt. An Eden. She stated, "You built the foundations of Egypt."

"Yes," he said, then added with a wry smile, "I am the mighty arm that built Egypt."

Rachel guffawed. "Oh, yeah. I forgot," she said jokingly.

Ra smiled down at her. "You have more questions?" he asked.

"Why did you leave Egypt and come here?"

"It was no longer paradise; it was no longer home. The Earth is too large, and we were amassing too much power. We fought constantly amongst ourselves, and the pressure we experienced from the expectations of the humans was too great. Not all of us wished to leave. Horus and Mafdet wanted to remain on Earth. That would never work. We needed to all stay or all go. The rest of us desired the peace and tranquility we had experienced in our early days on Earth, so we took a vote and overruled Horus and Mafdet."

"So you came to Janus?" Rachel asked.

"Yes."

"But, how?"

"That's far more complicated a conversation than we have time for at present," he answered.

"Okay, but what about the villagers on this planet—are they humans?" she asked.

"Yes, we brought a small number with us. Humans are amusing and they give us purpose."

During the last couple days Rachel had experienced many moments where she wondered if she might be dreaming. It was all too crazy to be real. She had magically been transported out of the ballroom at the Sunrise Inn and Suites to a planet she had never heard of where she discovered Egyptian gods were real living beings. Now, she—Egyptologist, Dr. Rachel Conner—was basically interviewing Ra on the beginnings of Egypt. If she got back to Earth the textbooks she could write would be groundbreaking.

Ra stood, interrupting her reverie. "We should continue up the mountain. Do you need me to carry you, or do you think you can keep up with me?" he asked, grabbing the lit torch from the wall.

She guessed this meant the interview was over. Rachel got to her feet. "I should be okay," she said, seriously doubting herself but not wanting to seem like a wimp.

Ra held the torch in his left hand and pointed with his right towards a dark crevice in the chamber. "We're going that way," he said.

Rachel followed Ra into the crevice. It felt dark even with the torch, and uncomfortably snug. Rachel wondered at how Ra so quickly navigated the small space. It made her again feel claustrophobic, and if it weren't distracting herself thinking about the things Ra had just told her, and focusing on keeping up with him, Rachel was sure her panic would have bubbled over already.

They traveled like this for some time. Both wondering how close their pursuers were; both feeling exhaustion creeping up their legs. Rachel wondered if Ra had a plan. *Were they going somewhere Horus and the others wouldn't know? Was Ra planning on hiding Rachel and then going back to reason with the others? Would they be mismatched outlaws—the human and the god—on Janus for the rest of their lives? Could Ra even die? Why hadn't she asked any of these questions when they were resting in the chamber?*

The dull rhythmic slapping of Ra's wet sandals on the stone floor of the mountain tunnel slowed, then stopped. Rachel noticed just in time to avoid running straight into him. The tunnel they'd been in intersected with another. *Which way would they go? Right or left?* Rachel stood silently behind Ra, waiting for any indication of which way they'd turn.

Ra bent and with his right hand removed his sandals. "Too much noise," he muttered. The barefoot god kneeled on the cool ground before Rachel. "Climb on my back," he commanded. "If we are pursued, we need to move swift and silent."

Without a word of argument, Rachel obeyed. She wrapped her arms around Ra's neck. *Was she choking him in this position?* Her small human arms must not bother him. He hadn't complained yet, and she'd traveled in the same position most of the way up the stream.

Ra stood, turned left, and noiselessly continued his hike up the inside of the mountain. He moved quickly. Fast enough that the torch flickered and Rachel felt a slight breeze on her face.

The tunnel they traveled down curved, then opened into another tunnel. Rachel looked right and left. To her right she could just barely make out a dim light; to her left a dark tunnel. Ra turned left.

The torchlight bounced everywhere, disregarding all of nature's laws. Rachel knew where they were. "The other way... if we had gone right—would we have ended up on a mountain ledge? One where the mouth of the tunnel is an actual mouth? Like the face of a man carved into the mountain?" she asked.

"Yes," Ra whispered. "Please, no questions for now. We must remain quiet."

"You need to freeze time so that the torch doesn't extinguish," Rachel insisted. "The wind down this tunnel will cause it to go out."

Ra didn't say a word, but the flame before them froze. From far behind them Rachel heard a bird's shrill cry and what sounded like excessively large wings beating the air. Ra broke into a sprint.

"What was that?" Rachel asked, her heart in her throat, her stomach left somewhere behind.

"Hush! You must be quiet. We are being followed," Ra hissed.

The tunnel angled down, and with the downward momentum Ra ran faster. He held the torch far in front of them as he ran. The flame perfectly still. Were it not frozen in time it would be licking the back of his hand and wrist. He ran at a speed Rachel guessed might beat a greyhound or a cheetah. A car even. She tried to focus on how impressed she was with Ra's speed instead of focusing on what was behind them—what followed them. What followed them? Rachel hadn't seen or heard any sign of a single animal the entire time she'd been on Janus. *What was this animal that chased them? Why did it sound so impossibly large?*

Ra burst out of the tunnel and into a large circular chamber with roughly cut stone walls. Rachel instantly recognized it as the place she and her friends had first found themselves on Janus. The torch's flame again moved. Ra placed it in one of the empty wall mounts before pulling Rachel off his back and setting her in the center of the room. He took a defensive position in front of her.

CHAPTER 25

Rachel could hear her heart beating in her ears and the scraping *click, click, click, click* of whatever hurried down the tunnel after them. In the next moment, something huge erupted through the tunnel entrance into the chamber. All claws and feathers and shocking orange eyes. It was a giant bird—a falcon. The thing was as large as Ra until it spread its terrible wings and became twice his size.

"Oh, my god!" Rachel yelled.

The massive falcon screeched and lunged a Ra. Ra delivered a heavy blow against the side of the beast's head. The falcon staggered and slumped against one of the ragged walls.

"Leave this place!" shouted Ra at the creature.

The falcon stumbled to his feet and again squared off with Ra.

"What is that thing?" Rachel asked in a voice that sounded too loud to be her own.

"That thing is Horus," Ra answered. He turned to her and saw the sudden flash of horror and confusion cloud her face. He turned back to his adversary before saying over his shoulder, "There isn't time to explain. You need to clear away the dirt under your feet."

The falcon attacked again, this time with its awful claws. Rachel screamed in terror. *Was this thing going to kill Ra?* Anything that stood so fiercely against Ra could finish her in an instant. And then she remembered Horus' enormous falcon tattoo across his back. This was the same animal. The only animal she'd seen on Janus.

"Dig!" Ra commanded as he landed another strong blow to the animal. It again retreated.

Rachel dropped to her knees and dug at the ground with her hands. Her nails scooped up dirt. This is what she hated about archeological digs—dirt under her nails. She'd often opted to take notes in such circumstances, instead of get her hands dirty. That wasn't an option today. Ra told her to dig, there must be a reason for it. To her surprise the dirt easily yielded, and in no time her nails scraped against stone. She cleared more dirt away and found it was a large stone with many carvings.

"What is this?" she muttered, more to herself than to her companion. She already knew the answer.

Ra answered, "It is a transportation disk."

Rachel cleared away more dirt, no longer distracted by the dirt under her nails. It was a disk just like the one on the floor of the arena—just like the one on the ceiling at the Sunrise Inn and Suites. She saw the scarab in the center and the hieroglyphs for "Ra," "Ka," and "Shen." God, Spirit, Eternity.

"You brought me here to send me home," she said, climbing to her feet.

In front of her, Ra struggled with the falcon—with Horus. Rachel remembered earlier—in the bath chamber—how easily Ra had pinned Horus to the wall. But Horus was in his strongest form now. Handling the beast wasn't so easy. There were claws to contend with, and quick animal reflexes. Time and again Rachel watched as Horus flew at Ra, claws forward. She wanted to cover her eyes, to make the scene before her disappear.

Rachel half expected to faint. She'd fainted in far less frightening or overwhelming circumstances. *Why not now? Why did everything feel so clear?* When overwhelmed by fear in the past her vision would tunnel and the world around her would blur until it disappeared. She'd wake up a few minutes later feeling better than she did before she fainted. Rachel always pictured it like her brain was a computer that just needed to restart sometimes when too many programs were left running. But she didn't faint. Rachel hadn't fainted when Liam disappeared. She hadn't fainted when Horus broke her ribs in the arena. She hadn't even fainted when she watched her friend die in front of her. Rachel thought of the old saying, "Whatever doesn't kill you, makes you stronger." She'd always hated that saying. She thought of how bad experiences—like her first experience on a panel at a symposium—only filled her with more fear and reservations. In the past Rachel would have said most of the bad things that happened to her in her life had only made her feel weaker. But her experience on Janus was different. Rachel was now different. *Was she still afraid?* Yes. But she wasn't overwhelmed. Nothing would overwhelm Rachel again.

Ra had Horus in his mighty arms—the same arms that built Egypt. Horus flailed, yet Ra managed to get a chokehold on his downy neck. The giant bird struggled madly. Their shadows danced from wall to wall. Blood dripped down Ra's arms—the wounds inflicted by Horus' enormous claws—but he didn't slacken his grip on the bird. Slowly the falcon's thrashing became a weak struggle, until what Ra held in his arms was no longer fowl but man. Ra gently placed Horus' unconscious body on the ground. Rachel stared at the weary blood stained giant in front of her. He stared back.

"Is he dead?" Rachel asked.

"No. He is temporarily asleep. He will wake soon. You must leave before he wakes," said Ra.

"How?" Rachel asked.

Ra stood outside the boarders of the stone disk, gesturing to it.

"I see the stone disk. I get that it must be some sort of transportation thing... but I don't know how to use it."

Ra took the pendant from around his neck and held it out to Rachel. When she first met Ra, she had noticed the flat, gold disk he wore on a chain around his neck. But, until now she hadn't realized that what he wore facing forward was the back of the pendant. Rachel now saw that the pendant was a collection of three scarabs, just like the ones she and her friends had received at the awards banquet—just like the ones Liam had in his pocket when he disappeared from the arena.

"Take it," he said, from outside the stone disk. His voice was commanding and his dark eyes intense.

Rachel didn't move. She stood still in the center of the stone disk. "I don't understand any of this. I don't know if I should be mad at you, knowing you could have sent me home any time, or grateful that you saved my life. *The Mighty Arm that Built Egypt*! You acted like it was ridiculous that Malachi had sent Ra to his home planet with his magical pendant. And now you're sending me home with your pendant? I don't understand why you would or wouldn't do any of this. You're a complete mystery to me. You're unreal! If your necklace could send me home, why not send me home after Liam went, or after Hester was killed in the arena?!" she demanded.

"The same gateway can only open once within a twenty-four-hour period," he answered, ignoring her other accusations.

"Okay," she accepted. "But why not send us all home together? Why not send my friends and me home last night?"

Behind Ra, Horus opened his eyes, puffy from the many blows he had received. "Because you're going to kill us all!" Horus roared rising to his feet. "You're going to destroy our planet if he sends you home," he added leaping towards Rachel on the disk.

Ra tossed his pendant to Rachel. She instinctually caught it. Near her feet, parts of the stone disk glowed red. Looking up, the last thing she saw was Ra grabbing Horus before he took one step onto the stone disk.

CHAPTER 26

Rachel willed her eyes to focus and see her surroundings. Everything was black, just like when she'd been transported from the hotel ballroom in Austin to the inside of the mountain on Janus. This time it was taking longer for her eyes to readjust. *Or was she just impatient to know where she was? And perhaps more frightened this time because her experience taught her danger could be lurking in the darkness?* Before her was nothing but a black void. Everything around her was darkness until a dim green glow played at the edges of her peripheral vision. *What new and terrifying thing would she face next? Was she on another alien planet?* Only this time she wouldn't have the sympathetic Ra to assist her. She'd seen enough sci-fi movies to know green glows didn't typically spell safe harbors and happy endings.

Slowly Rachel turned her head to face the glowing green light. Every muscle in her body was tensed...

She exhaled the breath she didn't realize she'd been holding. Her exhale turned into a relieved laugh. The green light was an exit sign. It was an exit sign above the large doors of the ballroom at the Sunrise Inn and Suites in Austin. She was back on Earth.

♦ ♦ ♦

Rachel stretched her legs in her airline seat. She was on a plane headed back to Chicago. This time she didn't have a chattering white haired octogenarian beside her to keep her company. She did still have her book though. Rachel opened her battered copy of *The Mighty Arm that Built Egypt*. She smiled to herself thinking there couldn't be many books that could boast having been to an alien planet, or survived a waterlogged swim upstream on the back of an Egyptian god.

When Rachel had exited the ballroom under the light of the green exit sign, she was met by yellow police tape and two of Austin PD's finest. They were shocked to see her, asked her if she knew this was a crime scene, and required she fish her driver's license out of her damp purse. Upon determining that she was in fact one of the three people who had mysteriously disappeared, Rachel was detained to speak to police detectives, the FBI, then some suspicious men dressed in all black who didn't identify themselves, but she assumed were military. The faculty of the university, including Dr. Goldblum, and later the press also showed up to ask her the same questions the police and everyone else had asked—*What happened? Where did you go? Where is Hester Hilford Mays and Liam Hawthorne?*

How do you answer any of those questions without sounding deranged or worse, like you're lying? Hester was dead, but still around because she was a ghost on a planet unknown by any astronomers on Earth. Liam was... *where?*

Liam.

He hadn't made it back to Austin, she knew that much. The moment the police started questioning her about her friend's whereabouts she couldn't help but lose most of her hopes for Liam's safety. He could be anywhere. Another planet even. And that's assuming he was still alive.

Rachel sighed loudly in her seat on the airplane, forgetting for a moment she wasn't alone with her thoughts. The flight attendant who pushed the beverage cart up the aisle, stopped next to Rachel's seat.

"Would you like something to drink?" asked the kind face above the crisp uniform.

"No, I'm fine," Rachel answered.

The flight attendant offered beverages to the two people to Rachel's left—the person in the middle seat and the person with the window seat. Last time it had been Hester at the window, and Gerald in the middle seat. A smile found its way to Rachel's face. She had thought the old woman was crazy for buying a seat for her dead husband's ghost (or as Hester had guessed—wraith). So much can change in a week. A week ago there were no such things as ghosts. A week ago there was no Janus and Egyptian gods were myths, not living breathing, beings. Ra was a character in the book she was reading.

Rachel looked down at the book she held open. This book was Ra and yet it wasn't Ra. Ra was an enormous, frightening, powerful being. He had built the foundations of Egypt. But, he was also somehow her friend and the person who had saved her. In her mind she could still see the blood running down his arms after his fight with Horus. She hadn't had time to thank him, or ask him how Horus could turn himself into a giant falcon, for that matter. If he hadn't been trying to kill her and it if it weren't so terrifying, Rachel probably would have thought it was cool.

"I hope Ra's okay," Rachel thought to herself. "And Liam."

She was headed back to her regular life in Chicago, but it felt like she was traveling further away from home. *How could she go back to her life there and forget about her friends?*

She couldn't.

Another deep sigh escaped Rachel's mouth. *What could she do?*

She wiped a tear from her eye that threatened to drop onto her open book. She read the page she had opened to.

> *"I am not the being you think I am," bellowed Ra.*

"If that's not the truth, I don't know what is," agreed Rachel. She hadn't read this page before, but with all the chaos of the past few days she wasn't sure where she was in the book.

An idea struck her. She knew this book was based off things Gerald had told Hester. It also had lots of similarities to her own experience on Janus. *How does it end?*

Rachel flipped to the last page of the book.

> *Ra's brows were storm clouds; his eyes were melancholy. He sat on a gilded thrown in the glittering throne room of his palace on his home planet. Malachi had freed the people of Egypt from him and his fellow gods. He had banished Ra, and the other gods had followed.*
>
> *Thinking of the Egyptians, he mused, "I am humbled. I am filled with remorse. And though I did cruel things as their*

master, I loved the Egyptians. If I could change things..."

Ra stood, and as though addressing all the people of Egypt he said, "If I could change things—if I could live this life again... I would do it better. I will never come to you again unbidden, but if you desire my return, I will make it so. And if you wish to come to me—to travel to my home planet—you are welcome."

Ra sat back down on his throne and contemplated the life he had led on Earth, the Egypt he had built, and the future that no one could foresee.

Rachel closed her book. That was Ra.

She hugged her book to her chest. It was real. *It was all real.* There was an alien planet that Ra existed on, and if she visited there, he'd welcome her again.

She placed her book back in her purse, under the seat in front of her. Rachel relaxed into her seat. She closed her eyes and slipped her right hand into the pocket of her sweatshirt. Her fingers wrapped around the cool metal object inside, her thumb tracing the familiar outline of a scarab.

If she went there, he would welcome her.

Thanks for reading *Rachel and the Mighty Arm that Built Egypt*!

For more information on *Rachel and the Mighty Arm that Built Egypt*, M.E. Ellison, or her current and upcoming projects visit www.meellison.com.

Or follow M.E. Ellison on Twitter @The_ME_Ellison.

Made in the USA
San Bernardino, CA
28 February 2020